REDEMPTION'S
WRATH

REDEMPTION'S WRATH

D. W. Larsen

iUniverse®

Redemption's Wrath

This is a work of fiction. All of the characters, names, incidents, organizations, and dialogue in this novel are either the products of the author's imagination or are used fictitiously.

iUniverse books may be ordered through booksellers or by contacting:

iUniverse
1663 Liberty Drive
Bloomington, IN 47403
www.iuniverse.com
1-800-Authors (1-800-288-4677)

Because of the dynamic nature of the Internet, any web addresses or links contained in this book may have changed since publication and may no longer be valid. The views expressed in this work are solely those of the author and do not necessarily reflect the views of the publisher, and the publisher hereby disclaims any responsibility for them.

Any people depicted in stock imagery provided by Thinkstock are models, and such images are being used for illustrative purposes only. Certain stock imagery © Thinkstock.

ISBN: 978-1-4917-6562-3 (sc)
ISBN: 978-1-4917-6561-6 (e)

Library of Congress Control Number: 2015906020

Print information available on the last page.

iUniverse rev. date: 05/22/2015

DEDICATION

This is my first novel. It is dedicated to my dear Grandmother, Ida Laplante, (formerly Larsen, nee Riise), known to me since my birth as 'Nana', who passed away a few years back at a nice old age. I wanted to be a writer of stories since I was little but it was Nana that reminded me of that many years later. After her passing, my uncle, Norm Larsen, sent me a small box containing some of her possessions. It was full of simple things, a broach she liked, some earrings, and a few other things that people would call trinkets. But underneath all of these things I found a 20 page hand-written manuscript written by myself at age nine. Now you wouldn't think 20 pages was that big of a deal but try getting a nine-year old now to put that many pages together, using real ink!

So this was a big deal for me and was a strong reminder that even way back then I wanted to be a writer. Life seems to get in the way sometimes, and the years passed. So, thanks for the reminder Nana. Thanks to you I can now say that I have completed my first full length novel. I know you will be proud.
Don

CHAPTER ONE

(Private Care Facility, British Columbia, Canada)

WILLIAM Carterell opened his eyes for the first time in nearly three years. They were drawn immediately to a bright light coming from a short distance to the right of him, probably a window, or brightly lit area. He tried to focus in that direction but realized his eyes were not in focus, with what felt like a thick film covering them. He blinked several times, and without thinking he weakly raised his hand to his face to gently rub the film from his eyes. That done he was now able to slowly scan the room starting at the source of the light, which was indeed a window. Lying low on a bed of some sort, he was not able to actually see much out of the window other than some blue sky and cumulous clouds. There were brightly colored curtains pulled off to each side, and below the window sat a dresser, the top of which held a vase of fresh flowers and pictures that he could not recognize from this distance. There was a chair beside the dresser but little else on that wall. As his eyes wandered further, he sensed movement to his left.

Muriel Knight took great pride in her work. She knew it was not the norm for people to actually care about the jobs they did; however, it was not in her to just go through the motions.

Like this room for instance, where she had been visiting several times each workday, doing the same thing on each and every one of them. Making sure the curtains were open and perhaps popping the window open a hair, allowing in some much needed fresh air, changing the flowers when they started to wilt, and dusting where needed. Her job was to directly look after this patient, but after being here for so long she now acted as unofficial support staff to the rest of the facility, and they treated her like one of the regular staff. At nearly sixty years old, she left the professional care to those trained to do so, and always made sure her duties were fulfilled as best as she could. After all, that is what Mr. Bartlett had brought her here to do. And besides, she loved every minute of it.

Muriel was in the process of those duties and was just on her way to check the flowers, when she saw something she hadn't expected.

She froze, all duties forgotten, as she realized the patient actually had his eyes open, and appeared to be looking right at her. This patient was supposed to be comatose forever and was only being looked after because of a trust fund that continued to pay the bills. But, sure enough, the man in the bed was definitely looking right at her. When her heart rate returned to near normal she decided she had better get someone in here to see this.

William looked directly at the woman, who, the second she realized he was looking at her, seemed momentarily stunned. She starred back for a few seconds, as if trying to see if it was her imagination, or if the light from the windows was playing a trick on her. He tried to say something but before he could the woman had quickly left the room. He continued his visual tour of the room, turned up nothing of interest, then found himself drifting off after only a few seconds.

What could have been minutes, or hours later, for he had no sense of time, he felt more than heard a presence near him. Opening his eyes he was surprised to find the room dark, with only a faint light coming from a lamp beside his bed. Standing in his line of vision was a man in a white medical coat. Gray hair curled over his ears and almost to the collar. The man leaned over slightly towards William.

"Mr. Carter," he said, "It is with great pleasure that I welcome you back to the world of the living." The man placed a chair beside the bed and seated himself so that he was close to William and did not have to speak loudly to be heard.

William examined the man closely and could see kindly eyes and a large nose that dominated his face, over a thin white neatly trimmed beard. He watched as the man continued to look at him, almost as though he had some trouble believing what he was seeing. "You gave Muriel quite the shock, I must say," he said. "I think she will need a bit of time to calm herself down, that's certain. She has been looking after you for a very long time now, and I'm sure was convinced that your condition would never change, even though we tried to tell her that this could happen."

William tried to reply but when he opened his mouth to speak, no words would form. It was as if his tongue was stuck to the roof of his mouth.

"Here, let me give you some water before you try to speak," said the doctor. He moved a glass toward him. "You have been on feeding tubes for quite some time, so I suspect your throat will need some time to get used to drinking directly from a glass."

With the man's assistance William took a drink and found the water to be cold and wonderful. He wanted more, and the man allowed him to drink until the glass was empty. He could feel the water's soothing effect on his throat and tried once more to speak.

"Where am I, and who are you?" he managed to get out.

The man nodded and said. "We will have lots of time to answer your questions, but right now it is important that you rest. For now I will tell you that my name is Doctor Francis and you are in a special medical care facility, and in very good care, I must say. Once you are rested I will be happy to tell you more, but for now I must insist that you get some rest. It is very late, and I too must get some sleep. I will see you first thing in the morning, and we will have a chat. Good night Mr. Carter. It gives me great pleasure to be able to say that I will talk to you in the morning."

William realized that he had been holding his head up from the pillow since drinking, and now felt like someone was pushing him down from above. He allowed himself to settle back, and, closing his eyes, had one last thought before falling asleep. 'Why is he calling me Carter?'

William awoke to the sound of the curtains being opened, followed by rays of bright sunshine that flooded the room. He immediately noticed the same person that had run from the room when he had woken. This time she again noticed him looking at her, but made no move to leave the room. Instead she smiled slightly and continued with the task of securing the curtains on each side of the window. With that completed, she moved towards his bed. "Good morning, sir! It is nice to see you awake. My name is Muriel. I am so sorry for running from the room yesterday. It was just that you hardly ever move, and to see you actually awake, and looking at me, well, you scared the sh...., well, you scared me half to death. Anyway, it is good that you are back with us. I will tell the others that you are awake. You must be starving! The doctor is here already this morning, and will be excited to see you." She hurried from the room.

William didn't have long to wait, as after only a few minutes, he heard several voices approaching his room. Dr. Francis entered shortly afterward.

"Ah, Mr. Carter, Muriel tells me you are awake and hungry, so I have asked the kitchen staff to make up something light for you to start with. You haven't eaten a solid meal in a long time so we don't want to push it," he said, with a jovial tilt to his voice.

"How long *have* I been here?" William questioned.

"I think this might come as quite a shock to you, young man, but you have been with us for a very long time, ever since the accident. Nearly three years!"

"Jesus! Three years! What accident? I don't recall an accident!"

"I'm afraid I don't have the details, but suffice it to say that you were brought here quite some time ago with serious injuries. Our instructions were to give you the best care we could in the hopes that you would someday recover. And here you are!" he said happily.

William was even more baffled than when they began, and an anger started to grow inside him.

"I'm sorry doctor, I don't mean to be rude, but I don't know what the hell you are talking about. What is this place, and why am I here?"

The doctor looked at him, and sighed. "I'll make you a deal. Let me examine you thoroughly, and, once that is done, I will tell you all that I know, although I admit it is precious little. I can say, however, that I will be in contact with someone that will be most excited that you are awake, and I'll bet that he will be here almost immediately to answer all of your questions. How does that sound?"

For over an hour, the doctor pulled and pushed, probed and prodded, finding that the patient's moving parts all worked quite well, albeit very weakly. This was not a surprise, as the medical team had exercised him every single day since his arrival, but it was still nice to see him able to do a few things on his own.

For his part, William was able to quiet his impatience, and went along with the examination. He found that he was able to move his arms up and down to his face, and move his legs and feet well enough to slowly reposition himself in the bed. It took all of his effort, with the assistance of the doctor, to move on to his side. By the time the doctor was finished, he was exhausted, and lay back with his eyes closed, his arm lying across his face. He had so many questions to ask, but lacked the strength to form the words.

The doctor, sensing his frustration, pulled a chair up close to the side of the bed closest to William. "As I said before, I know very little about the circumstances that brought you here, but what I know I will share with you. I must leave it to others to explain everything else. Is that fair?"

William pulled his arm from his face, turned his head towards the other man. "I just need to know what happened, what is going on with me? Where am I and, most of all, where is my dad and sis?"

The doctor looked directly at William and began. "You are in a very private medical care facility in Canada, about two hours north of the USA border, near the city of Kelowna, British Columbia. You were brought to us by air ambulance with serious head trauma. We were told that you were in some sort of accident, although not too many details were given to us. Please know that by 'very private facility' I mean just that. Ours is a place where those who wish to be kept from the public eye can come to heal in privacy and peace. I have no details as to what your accident entailed, only that you were struck by a very hard object to the back of your head. I am certain that this blow, had it been directly to your skull, would have killed you, but instead, it must have hit you flush with the upper part of your neck. After a few surgeries to remove some blood clotting, we were confident that we had done all that we could, and that the rest was in the hands of someone with a lot more power than us. My staff diligently worked with you every day to keep your legs and arms moving, though I must be honest here, we often wondered if it was pointless, as you never showed a single sign of waking. As I said, we were quite certain after a while that your initial injury was healing, but were unsure if you would ever come out of the coma."

The doctor paused, stared out the window at a patient and nurse slowly edging their way along a concrete walkway, surrounded by small trees whose branches swayed gently in the breeze. When he looked back at William his facial expression was again serious.

"Look, Mr. Carter, and that really is who we know you as, I am not at liberty to say anything more, nor do I really know much more than I have already told you. Perhaps Mr. Bartlett will be able to explain things more clearly."

This confused William even more. "I don't know any Mr. Bartlett! Who is he, and what does he have to do with me and my accident? I have to admit that this is really starting to piss me off? Can't anybody tell me anything?"

"I can only tell you that Mr. Bartlett has always kept in contact with this facility to make sure your needs are looked after. You will have to get the rest from him."

"Okay, when do I get to meet him?"

"I have left a message with his office, and expect to hear from him quite quickly actually, as he has never made us wait in the past.

I will inform you immediately the moment I hear from him. In the meantime I suggest you get your rest." With that he turned and left the room, leaving William staring at an empty doorway.

For the next three days William was visited regularly by Muriel and a host of other nurses, none of whom could answer his many questions, nor provide further insight into what had happened to him. They started gradually sitting him up, supporting his back less and less as he got used to holding himself upright on his own. They worked his legs until he could, ever so slowly, move them up and down on his own. After each 'workout' he was left totally exhausted, but still completely baffled by where he was, and what had happened to him. He spent long hours watching the activities outside his window. He watched tall trees blowing in the wind, birds flitting past, people going about their outside duties, cutting lawns, raking leaves, and standing together in small groups, probably talking about family, pets, jobs etc. He grew frustrated that he could not see more, but was simply too weak to do anything about it. He had so many questions that no one could seem to answer. Who was he really? What had happened? Why was he here, and who was making sure he was taken care of? And mostly, where was his family, and why all the secrecy?

It was at the end of the third day. After a long session of motion exercises to help him raise and turn his head (which surprisingly showed no ill effects from his injury), sit up, bend his legs, and lift his arms; that William slipped into a deep, but normal, sleep.

And he dreamed. Or at least it felt like a dream. Visions formed in his mind of a pretty young girl, a football game, and a wisely old man. There was a group of men yelling, and a girl screaming. All of these thoughts flew at him randomly, making no sense. The girl again, calling out to him, reaching out with one arm, the other being pulled by a man he could barely see. He reached out for her, and cried out, "Chrissy"! His eyes flew open with the realization that he was sitting up in his bed, both arms stretched out before him. Sweat poured from his brow, his bedclothes also soaked through. Slowly he managed to calm down, and realized there was another presence in the room.

In the doorway stood a medium sized man, with thinning and slightly receding reddish hair. He sported a pair of dark-rimmed glasses on an unemotional face. The collar on his white shirt was crisp, and was accompanied by a neatly tied red bow tie. He wore a dark blazer, with the buttons done up, and dark grey trousers over tan loafers.

"Good day, sir. My name is Harold Bartlett." His voice was gravelly, but distinguished, like an actor. "It is so good to see you are back in the world with us. I have many things to discuss with you, and I'm sure you have a great many questions to ask of me."

CHAPTER TWO

(Village of Canming, China)

THE homemade whip snapped in the air mere inches from Zhuo Tan's ear! Instinct and habit caused her to duck out of the way at the last second, avoiding what could have been a serious blow. She was lucky because the whip holder was very experienced in handing out this type of punishment, often at the slightest of provocation. Sometimes none at all was needed, for it was her father that held the other end of the crude, yet effective, implement.

It was well known throughout the small village of Canming that Ho Tan was very disappointed when his wife gave birth to a female. He wanted to dispose of this child, but allowed his wife to convince him that there could be some benefit in the future to having a female child. When the second girl was born he was beside himself with rage, but his wife had had a very difficult childbirth and, once again, managed to persuade him to be patient. All of that patience wore thin over the years, and when his wife could no longer give him a chance at a male child, he started to take his frustrations out on his two girls.

The village of Canming was located in the Wuyi Mountains, deep in the valley, miles from the city of Sanming. The village produced 'Job's-Tears' rice, and lotus seed, for sale in the markets of Sanming, although Ho Tan did not produce those products. Instead, his land was luckily located on a small parcel of property with excellent soil, suitable for growing a wide variety of vegetables, which he sold to his neighbors. Having no male children to work the gardens, Zhuo, and her younger sister, Ling, found themselves toiling many hours of every day in the vegetable patches, overseen by an increasingly miserable and cruel father.

So it was that Zhuo's father lashed out at her, for apparently one of the carrot rows was not perfectly straight. She usually managed to ignore his cursing however today she sensed something else was causing his anger. She worked her way towards her sister and whispered.

"Stay away from poppa as much as you can, something is very wrong today."

"What do you think that is, my sister?" Ling whispered back to her.

"I do not know but be very careful and work very hard."

Their father heard their whispering. "Why do you talk all the time when there is much work to be done?" he yelled. "Any more talk today and I will surely whip you silly, and leave you out here for the birds!"

The two girls fell upon their work with renewed vigor, occasionally stealing sideways looks at him as he sat on an old stump and watched them.

In the distance the girls could hear a vehicle approaching. Ho Tan jumped up from his seat and walked rapidly towards their small three room house. As he approached the house a truck rounded the corner of the gravel road and, much to the girls' surprise, it stopped directly beside their father. He could be seen talking with the driver through the rolled down window. After a moment the driver's side door opened and a tall skinny man jumped down, causing a cloud of dust to rise about. Ho Tan and the man turned to walk towards the old house, but stopped before entering. At that moment Ho pointed towards the girls in the garden. He said something to the man, and they entered the house.

Once their father was out of sight the girls felt they could relax a tiny bit.

"What do you think that man is doing here?" asked Ling.

"I do not know, but I have a very bad feeling about this." Zhuo was relatively tall for her age, not yet twenty, with long black hair that fell nearly to her waist. Not that anyone could see the length, as she always had to tie it up and pin it behind her head with a small smooth stick she found, and made into a hairpin, for fear that her father would make her cut it off. Zhuo did not have the eyes of a normal Chinese girl, and her color was often described as tanned, but not dark. Zhuo's sister, Ling, was also quite tall. She lacked the long straight hair of her older sibling. No matter how much she tried to grow it the same as Zhuo, it would just end up a tangle of curls. Ling was quite pale and, in a different setting, could have been mistaken for being almost white. Both girls were strong, which came from many hours of toiling in the dirt between the rows of vegetables. Only in the winter months did they get some time away from those duties, but even then, they were expected to work with their mother, sewing garments for sale in the Sanming market. This was September, and the weather had been very mild for a long time. It was usually quite warm this time of year, however, the hot temperatures had never arrived. Today a light breeze blew in from the neighboring mountain valley, making it easier to work in the fields. A light scattering of clouds floated through the sky and the odd high flying hawk or eagle could be seen circling their prey. Zhou and Ling were working at opposite sides of a patch of green beans when they heard the door to their house open. The man from the truck, and their father, came through the doorway and, instead of walking towards the truck, they turned towards the gardens. Behind them came their mother, who was crying and holding her hands to her face. She screamed at her husband.

"Please do not do this! I will have nobody! You can not do this, who will help in the fields?" Ho Tan stopped in his tracks, spun around, and pointed at his wife. She froze in fear, lowered her head, and slowly turned around and re-entered the house. She pulled the door closed from within. The two men continued on their path towards the girls. Two other men, both carrying rifles, approached from behind the truck.

Ling looked at her older sister.

"What is happening? Who are those men with father? I'm scared!"

"I don't know Ling, but I too am afraid."

The men entered the garden area and the girls' father shouted to them. "Zhuo, Ling, you will come here at once!" The girls looked at each other again and walked over to the waiting men. To Zhuo they were revolting, with awful smells emanating from them. The taller of the men stared at her as she approached, his lips cracking into a sneer. Zhuo felt ill to her stomach, but nevertheless obeyed her father. When the girls were within reach their father shouted at them, spittle flying from his lips. "You are no use to me here! I needed boys and look what I got, two useless females who whine and complain about the hard work that needs to be done! I have had enough, and have made arrangements for both of you to go with these gentlemen."

Zhuo looked closely at the men, who were far from gentlemen, and before she could protest, one of them grabbed her arm roughly, and started to lead her towards the truck. "You cannot do this father! We are your daughters! Who will look after mother, and the crops, and making your meals?" Ling started to cry, as the third man manhandled her towards the truck.

"You will not speak to me this way and will go with these men. It is better this way!"

"But father, what will become of us. These men scare us, and we are afraid!"

"Enough! You will go with them and do as they say!"

Both girls were led to the back of the truck where they were told to crawl up into the musty covered box. Both did so and retreated to the very far area next to the cab, where there was a crude bench to sit on. The truck box had a dirty green canvas cover, but there were enough holes in the sides that Zhuo could still see her father standing in front of the house. He held something in his hands and it took a moment before Zhuo realized that he was holding a sum of money. Before she could shout out again one of the men jumped up into the truck box and sat near the tailgate, a rifle straddling his legs. He watched them closely for a while and then grinned, showing a mouthful of missing teeth, and those that remained were badly tobacco stained. He growled at them.

"You will now keep your mouths shut, and will do what I say! We have a long journey ahead of us." The truck lurched to a start amid a cloud of dust and dirt. The guard pulled the tailgate up with a slam, and the girls watched the only home they had ever known, disappear.

CHAPTER THREE

"*I* have been a friend of your grandfather's for a very long time, said Bartlett. "Sadly, I must inform you that he passed away about two years ago, and I have been entrusted with his affairs ever since."

It took William a few seconds to realize what this man had just said. "You mean my grandpa is dead? How did that happen?" Visions of his grandfather immediately came to mind. Always dressed properly, quite a lady's man too, he remembered.

Bartlett looked directly into William's eyes, and explained.

"Unfortunately your grandfather got very sick. He fought hard to be here for you, but it was just too long, and too tough a fight. With his last breath he asked me to look out for you."

"But where the hell am I, and what happened to me? Why is everyone calling me Carter?"

Once again Bartlett looked directly at him, sighed and then spoke.

"William, I have a fair amount of information for you about what happened, but you must be careful not to jump at things too fast. You have a long road of recovery in front of you, and you must take things slowly, even though the things I am going to tell you will make you want to do otherwise."

"What kind of things are you talking about?"

"Before your grandfather passed away he had certain people, friends of his, look into your 'accident'. They were not able to get all the information, however they did get a pretty good start. I am to share that information with you as soon as you are able to handle it."

William struggled to sit up. "I want to know right now. I can't just lay here and wonder who I am, and what is happening to me!"

"All in good time William, all in good time!" Bartlett said. "What is important right now is that you get as much rest as you can. The care here is second to none, and the doctor tells me that you should be able to be up and about in a few days, albeit with a little help. I need you to allow them to do what they do best. I promise you that I will return in a few days, and we can start the process of setting things right, as your grandfather would have wanted. In the meantime I will leave with you a letter he wrote to you. I have not read it, however, I will assume it will answer some of your questions." He placed an envelope on William's bed, nodded, and then turned and walked out of the room.

William stared at the brown manila envelope for a few moments. He was afraid to open it for what it might contain. His grandfather was dead, he had a different name, and this strange little man seemed to hold all of the secret answers. His thoughts screamed out of him! 'What kind of nightmare is this? None of this even seems real!'

He tentatively reached for the envelope, tore it open, unfolded several pages, and started to read.

CHAPTER FOUR

FOR the fourth time that day the truck came to a stop, the tailgate lowered, and two more girls pushed in to join those already there. Zhuo and Ling were now joined by six others, all equally scared and confused. They all had at least two things in common. All wore threadbare clothing, and were about the same age. Of the two latest arrivals one wasted little time in forcing her way onto what little room remained of the bench occupied by Zhuo and Ling. Others were forced to sit on the floor and try to hang on as best as they could. With every lurch the truck bed filled with more dust, making conversation impossible and breathing just about as difficult. It was only a matter of minutes before the newcomers were just as filthy as Zhuo and Ling.

Zhuo tried to shelter her sister as much as she could, and when the guard reluctantly passed a water cask around, she made sure Ling had some of her own share. Ling seemed to still be in shock as she did not speak, and only looked into Zhuo's eyes with bewilderment. Zhuo tried to calm her by brushing her hair, and holding her close. She tried hard to hide her own fear.

After what felt like many hours the truck finally stopped again, this time at what appeared to be a small camp by the side of the road. There were two tents set up, and a small fire pit. Once fully stopped, the guard opened the tailgate, and signaled the girls to jump down from the truck bed. He pointed to one of the tents and motioned them towards it. Zhuo took Ling's hand and led her as far into the tent as possible. Almost the entire floor of the tent was covered with stained old mats, and only the barest of blankets. They dropped on to a couple of mats in the far corner of the tent, and tried to make themselves as comfortable as possible. It wasn't long afterwards that the last arrival, and biggest of the girls, made her way towards where they lay.

"I want that corner," she said.

Zhuo looked up at the imposing figure. "There are plenty of spaces," she replied. "My sister and I will stay at this one. You are most welcome to take the one beside us."

"Your mat is thicker and you will give it to me now, or I will take it from you," said the woman.

Zhuo stared back at the woman and exclaimed. "I do not want trouble from you, so if you are so in need I will gladly give my mat to you, however we are staying in this corner, and no one is going to move us."

The woman looked at her for a moment, as if taking her measure, and then shrugged. "I am too tired to argue with you tonight," she said. "But you and I will talk again." The woman threw her mat towards Zhuo, who did likewise with hers, and they both settled down to their respective spots. She did not show it, but Zhuo was trembling inside. She did not know what she would have done had the bigger girl attacked her.

Shortly after getting settled a guard entered the tent, and in a guttural Chinese dialect, barked an order for all to exit the tent. Once again the fear was almost overwhelming, however, when they exited the tent, they found a long table with food on it. They also found that they had been joined by another group of young girls who were waiting patiently beside the table. The guard explained, more with motions than language, that the girls were to take a plate from the end of the table, and their food would be dished out to them. Zhuo led Ling to the stack of cracked and stained plates and lined up with the others. They moved slowly along the table, and when it was their turn, received a small ration of rice, with some type of meat in it, and bread. The bread was surprisingly fresh and the girls quickly consumed it before someone could take it away. The larger girl that had confronted Zhuo in the tent was immediately behind her in the line, and when the guards were not looking, she whispered, "take extra bread in case there is no more," and she took a slice and quickly slid it into her top. None of the guards noticed, so Zhuo did the same. She was about to take a second for Ling, when one of the guards came up from behind her and gave her a shove.

"What are you doing, little bitch? You think we don't see what you are doing? There will be no talking!" Zhuo let out her breath as she was sure the guard had seen the bread. The girl beside her looked at her and winked.

After their brief meal, they were led back to the tent, where they once again tried to make themselves comfortable.

"Where are they taking us?" asked a frightened Ling.

"I do not know. All I know is that we must be quiet when the guards are around, and not make trouble. Do not worry little sister, we will get away when we get a chance."

"I don't think so," said the girl on the mat beside them. "I have heard of these trucks before. I have heard that they ship girls to far away places to act as workers for the round eyes."

"But why would................"

"Shut up in there! I said no talking! The next person talking will be beaten!" yelled the guard with no teeth.

Zhuo hugged Ling close to her, and whispered in her ear.

"I will take care of you Ling, please try not to worry."

Before closing her eyes Zhuo heard another whisper. It came from the mat beside her.

"My name is Jing-Wei. I can see that you are strong. We must help each other. Let us talk in the morning."

As night fell over the camp, the wind picked up and helped ease the temperature inside the crowded tent. None of the girls could sleep, and murmured conversations could be heard throughout. They feared what the morning would bring.

CHAPTER FIVE

Dear William,

    If you are reading this letter now it is a sign of, both good news, and also not so good news. The good news, shall I say GREAT news is that, if indeed you are reading this, then you have awoken from your deep sleep, and are on your way to recovery. At least that is what I hope in my heart. The bad news is that I am no longer around to share it with you.

    There are so many things I wish I had talked to you about but it always felt like the wrong time. We had a lifetime ahead, and there would be ample opportunities to sit down and talk. Funny how things work out eh? Anyway, the only chance I have now is to write this letter to you, and hope it will all make sense.

    First of all, the reason I have left this letter, and am not there in person is that it seems like I have developed a bit of Cancer. They say it is pretty well spread throughout my body, and I have limited time left on this planet. Interestingly enough, I feel pretty good. They say I will eventually lose my hair, and a lot of weight, but I want you to know that as of this writing, I am not doing too badly.

    Where to start!

When your mom passed away you were just children, and your dad tried his best for a while. He took the loss very badly but eventually decided to take a job out of the country. Your grandmother and I thought he was really running away from reality, leaving you and your sister in our care. I guess we knew then that he would never return, although we talked about it often and always hoped that he would. You and Chrissy where never that close when you were little, but when your dad left, it seemed that a steel bond formed between you. Very seldom would one of you do anything without involving the other.

I also guess that it would be normal for grandkids to form attachments to their grandparents, and that is what happened. You became inseparable from your grandma, and little Chrissy became the apple of my eye. When your grandmother became ill, and soon after left us (God bless her heart), it seemed that you went into a bit of a shell. Chrissy and I remained very close, but I just couldn't seem to reach you. I know you still loved your dear old Grampa but there was a gap there that I could never fill. Chrissy, on the other hand, became like a part of me. I am so sorry if, over the years, I seemed to favor her over you, as I am sure you must have thought,, but I did not mean that to happen.

A large part of me died the day your Grandmother passed, and the rest of me followed the night you and your sister were taken in that alley. Part of this letter is to say how sorry I am that some things between you and I were strained, but the other part, and maybe more important, is to tell you what I know about that night. I say this because I am not sure if you will remember much of what happened, and if telling you helps in some small way then it will have been worth writing. I hope your memory will be okay and you will be able to fill in the many blanks in my story.

That tragic and horrible night, you and Chrissy were downtown at your favorite bar, Dragon's. You were on your way to your car, when a group of guys you knew from somewhere, approached. They might have been drunk, and started giving you and Chrissy a hard time. It seems things got out of hand, and it developed into some pushing and shoving, with lots of yelling. At least that is what a witness told the police. This is where it gets unclear to me. Apparently you and Chrissy managed to break it off with these guys and headed to your car. The next thing is, you are found in an alley unconscious, and my poor Chrissy was nowhere near.

They found her body the next day about a mile away. She had been beaten, sexually assaulted, and then strangled and left to die, like some animal. Until I got sick, I never stopped trying to find out who could have done this to you, and I have managed to come up with a bit of information. I have attached everything I found out in an envelope accompanying this letter.

William, I have been very lucky over the years in that I have invested wisely, and I must say, luckily, in some ventures that have done extremely well. It has allowed me ample time and resources to look into that night. Unfortunately my illness will not let me go to the lengths that I would like, so I am passing along the information to you in case someday you will want to look into it yourself. I would be a liar if I said I hoped you would not. Call me a bitter dying old man, but I want those bastards hunted down, and made to pay for what they did to you and your sister!

You are presently in a special, and private, care facility. I have set up a trust that was to look after your care until such time as you recover. I have always been optimistic that you would. It is my wish that you will eventually be able to leave that place under your own power, and will find your way back home.

Mr. Bartlett has been a business partner, advisor and best friend to me for most of my life. Since I knew I would not be around I have entrusted him with everything, including delivering this letter and information to you. He will also explain to you some very important things that you need to know, and do, once you are able to leave the facility. The people that took Chrissy, and left you for dead, are very bad people. And since that night, they have become even worse. If you are to stay safe, they must not know that you have returned. I have gone to great lengths to have them think that you did not make it that night, thus I ask that you please listen to all that Mr. Bartlett tells you.

I am very saddened that I will not be there for you when needed, and can only say that I loved you kids like you were my own and hope you will carry that thought with you forever. I am not a very religious man, but if there is any way I can watch over you from above I will do my best. You have all my love.

Please remember that Revenge is mighty, but it cannot be taken upon by those who are unprepared!

Gramps.

William reread the letter and then laid his head back on the pillow and let the tears come. How could all of this have happened while he lay here sleeping? His memories of his grandfather, and especially his sister, came flooding back to him. He cried out to no one, and to everyone! The memory of that night in the alley also came back to him. They had gone for a simple drink as brothers and sisters often do. When approached by those guys, why didn't he just leave? He remembered wanting to get Chrissy away from there, but there was something about the guys that made it more than just a random meeting. He remembered something about the way they talked to Chrissy. Did she know them? A memory deep within told him that one of the guys was familiar. Was he a friend of Chrissy's that he had seen around? God! Why didn't they just leave? Why did he have to turn around and try to be the hero by defending his sister. The shouting, swearing, pushing, more shouting, he could picture it all now as the flood of bad memories overtook him. He remembered movement from behind, and then a stinging pain in the back of his head. He went down, and while falling, could see two or three other men grabbing at Chrissy and hear her screaming. Then all had gone blank. Until now!

His tears continued to flow as he realized that he had not been able to protect his sister, and had just laid there while they dragged her away, and brutalized her. Why couldn't he protect her? The memories proved too much of a strain on him, and mercifully, he collapsed back on to his pillow.

It wasn't until the next morning that William awoke fully, and his first thought was to once again read his grandfather's letter. After doing so a few times, he reached for his call button.

Muriel entered the room to find her patient already trying to sit up, his face flushed with the exertion. "My, my, Mr. Carter, what are you trying to do to yourself?" she said good-naturedly. "You need to take your time, and do things slowly, if you are not to hurt yourself."

"I need to get back on my feet, and I need to do it as quickly as possible" replied William, although the effort to just sit up told him that getting to his feet would take some time.

"Well now, that is what we will do, but you have to be patient and take things one step at a time."

"I think I realize that, but it is important that I do so quickly, and could somebody call that lawyer that was here yesterday, Mr. Bartlett? I need to see him right away!"

CHAPTER SIX

THEY awoke from a fitful sleep to the sound of a guard yelling through the tent flap. The young women were told to rise immediately, and bring whatever blankets they had with them. It was still dark, and the air was chilly. The threadbare blankets were used to hold in what warmth they could. The food table from the night before was gone, and all that remained were baskets of left- over bread. They were told to take as much bread as they could carry, and to once again board the back of the truck.

Zhuo and Ling stuffed as much bread as they could in their blankets and clothing, and then shuffled over to the truck. The guard looked Ling over longer than normal, and Zhuo stepped in between them. His breath was almost overpowering and he pushed Zhuo to the side, grabbed Ling's arm, and pulled her closer to him. He ran his hand through her hair, and was about to do more, when Zhuo again stepped between them, glaring at the guard, daring him to try something with her. He must have seen her fury and thought better of doing anything else, because he grunted loudly, and pushed both girls towards the truck.

The eight women, including Jing-Wei, who also carried a blanket stuffed with loaves of bread, boarded the truck and took the same spots they had sat in the day before, thus avoiding any argument over who sat where. Much to their surprise though, they were joined by the eight other women they had seen at their meal the night before. This made the back of the truck even more crowded, and they all had to move closer to make room. Even before the truck started up, Jing-Wei leaned over to Zhuo and whispered, "I can see that you are strong willed. We must help each other if we are to survive."

Zhuo looked back at the woman, "I agree, but we will not be cruel to the other girls, as you have been."

"I am only that way to protect myself. They will take everything if they think we are weak. We must show that we are stronger than them even if it is not as we feel inside."

Zhuo glanced again at the other woman, this time looking into her eyes, and was surprised at what she saw. There was more to Jing-Wei than she first thought. She decided, for the time being at least, that there was safety in numbers.

"Let us help each other, and see if we cannot find out what they are going to do with us." She said.

"Oh, I think I already know what they have planned for us. I have heard of this before and only hoped that it would not happen to me. I have heard that they buy girls from poor villages, and send them over the great sea to other lands, where we will be used as slaves."

"Let us hope that we will find a way out of this before that happens," said Zhuo.

Both women settled back and tried to get comfortable. The truck started up, and with a billowing cloud of dust, started its way down the trail, for it could not be realistically described as a road. Deep ruts on each side made it a slow journey, with the women inside being constantly thrown from side to side, many times having to hold on to each other to avoid tumbling across the truck bed.

It seemed like they had traveled all day, and the sun was indeed low in the western sky when the truck finally pulled to the side, and the women were allowed out of the back, and onto the hillside to relieve themselves, and just stretch their weary muscles. The stop was dismally short, and soon all were again loaded into the back of the truck, which lurched to a crawl on what seemed like a never ending trek.

It was only a few hours later, for the sun was still visible at the horizon, that Zhuo started to notice a change in the air. She had never been allowed to leave her little hillside village so had no idea that there were different climates to experience. Ling seemed to be able to sleep almost anywhere, and was doing so now, so Zhuo nudged Jing-Wei who, amazingly, was also fast asleep. Zhuo's contact startled her, and she jumped in her seat, startling several of the other girls.

"What is it you want? You nearly scared me to death!"

Zhou was excited, "Can you not smell that? What is in the air?"

Ling also came awake with the motion and spoke, "I too smell something. It is almost sweet!"

Jing-Wei looked around at the other girls, who all were noticing the same change in the air, and whispered to Zhou and Ling, "we are nearing the sea. That is the air off the salt water of the sea that you smell."

Even the miserable guard, with the ever present rifle on his lap, was now sitting up and paying more attention to the land slowly passing by.

Jing-Wei nodded her head several times. "Yes, I am sure of it. That is the smell of the sea. I fear that what I said before is true. That we are to be sent across the sea to strange new lives."

Zhou then spoke, "I have heard my father speak of the sea before. He always said it is a magical and wonderful place. We used to send our products there with all of the other merchants from our village, but I do not know of anyone that had actually been to see it. Is it really as big as they say?"

Jing-Wei smiled. "I have heard that it is even bigger than we can imagine. That it stretches farther than the eye can see. It is full of salt and many strange creatures. It is the salt in the air that you smell."

As the truck followed the crude road, the ocean's aroma grew stronger, and they could hear squawking and squealing of many birds. It was growing dark, but the holes in the canvas still allowed quick glimpses of large white birds circling and flying everywhere. Soon they entered a thick fog which encompassed the truck like a glove, allowing no further view through the canvas, although the noises continued.

Suddenly a tremendously loud sound rang out, like a mighty beast, startling all in the truck, including the guard. It lasted several seconds before dying out, leaving only its echo to fade out behind it.

"That was a ship's horn," said Jing-Wei. "They sound them often when the fog hangs near the water. It is the way the mighty ships keep from hitting each other."

As if to make a point, the loud roar came at them again, this time seemingly much louder and closer than before.

A short time later the truck made a sharp turn and entered a new roadway, this one much smoother than the other. The fog was still too thick to allow them to see where they were going. Zhou watched as the beaten old trail they had been on was left behind and their jostling came to an end. The air was thick now with the scent of the ocean and each of the girls huddled together in frightened anticipation of what unknowns lay before them. Even the guard now seemed on edge, and was busy dusting off his clothing and hat, as though making ready for something.

That something came soon after, as the truck took a sharp turn off the paved roadway, and stopped suddenly. Through holes in the canvas, Zhou saw one of the men get down from the cab, and walk towards the front of the truck. The truck then moved slowly forward, and she could see that the first man had held open a gate, through which the truck now drove. Once the gate had been closed behind them, the man jumped up on the tailgate, and the truck proceeded forward again.

This trip was short lived as it was only a few minutes before the truck came to a stop alongside a large building. Both guards dropped the tailgate, and the girls were ordered to jump down, bringing with them their blankets, and any food that they still carried, although that was in short supply, as their hunger had forced them to eat a good part of it.

The girls were lined up and ushered into the large dirty yellow building, which must have been a warehouse at one time. When they entered through a small side door they could see that the building was mostly empty, except for several very large box-like containers.

Jing-Wei leaned over to Zhuo and explained. "That is how products are shipped across the sea, in those giant containers."

Zhuo did not reply, but simply stared at the enormousness of the building. The ceiling had to be at least fifty feet high, and the structure itself ran easily two hundred feet long, and one hundred feet across. There were six containers in the middle of the building, all of which could be seen to be empty, as the doors were all wide open. Zhuo's feeling of trepidation increased when she saw that inside each container there were benches along both sides. She had no doubt of what those benches were for, and as her panic increased, she started to look for a place to run. She had no sooner turned her head around to search for possible escape routes when another small door, similar to the one they had entered through, opened on the other side of the building. This time, instead of only sixteen girls, which was the total of Zhuo's group, what must have been nearly one hundred girls, all of similar age, entered the building, followed again by guards with rifles in hand. Zhuo's heart dropped as she saw no possible means of escape.

All of the girls were herded into the middle of the building and, strangely, the guards backed far away from them. They were still present and dangerous, but seemed to want to put some distance between themselves, and the group of ragtag girls. Before they could even speak to each other, yet another small door opened before them.

A solitary man entered. He was very different from the guards they had spent the last two terrifying days with. This man was several inches taller than any of the guards, and he was completely bald, so much so that his scalp shone under the hanging lights of the warehouse. He wore a dark colored jacket over a pale blue shirt, and matching dark trousers. The girls had never seen a man dressed as nicely and cleanly, and they were speechless as he approached. He walked calmly past the group of girls, looking them over individually, often pausing here and there for a longer inspection. He did not say a word.

What made him even stranger to the girls wasn't the clothing he wore, nor was it the way he casually walked amongst them. It was the fact that this man was not Chinese. This man was white!

CHAPTER SEVEN

IT was three long days before Bartlett re-appeared at William's door, and in that time William had eaten as much as he could, and had progressed from barely sitting, with assistance, to now getting himself up and going for slow, albeit shaky, walks around his room, the ever present Muriel Knight, or another nurse, by his side.

On one of his treks, for that is how he looked at them, he decided that simply walking around in his room wasn't enough. He wanted to explore a little, to break the monotony. With Muriel by his side he took a few tentative steps towards the door to his room. He was feeling pretty good, and full of confidence, so he did not hesitate to step through the doorway and found himself in a sort of sitting room. The room was nicely furnished with a couple of couches, tables with lamps, and even a deep brown leather recliner. All showed very little if any use or wear and tear. There was a big screen TV on the wall over a faux fireplace, either gas or electric. The windows in this room were also much bigger with a wide view of the lawns and gardens surrounding the complex. What caught William's eye though was not the scenery, nor the comforts of the room, but rather a large full-sized mirror hanging on the wall behind one of the entrance doors. He caught a glimpse of himself from a distance, and immediately hobbled over.

Once standing directly in front of the mirror, he was shocked at what he saw. Of course he still had his six foot height, but that was all he seemed to have retained from his previous life. He no longer had shoulder length curly hair, but instead now sported a short cropped style that was almost like the old-style crew cut worn by the military. He knew that he no longer had his beard, but was still surprised to see his face without it. He had small ears and a pointed nose, all of which seemed to stand out now that the facial hair was gone. His eyes were a deep-set hazel with thick dark eyebrows above. His jaw was square and his cheeks were sunken, showing the amount of time he had been laid up. He had never been a fitness buff, and was always on the pudgy side, so was even more surprised by what he saw. Now his arms appeared skinny and his waist was non-existent, proven by the fact that his pajamas had to be tied securely to keep them from falling. All in all he knew he was lucky to be alive and vowed to get back to his normal health as quickly as he could. For the sake of his *new identity* he would forgo the long hair and beard. He had to admit to not minding the new look.

He was standing on his own beside his bed when Bartlett at last made his appearance.

"I was wondering where the hell you've been?" said William. "I have been asking for you for days now!"

Bartlett grinned, "It has only been three days sir, and I have been very busy on your behalf. I congratulate you on your progress."

"Yeah, well, I can't get out of here soon enough!" Realizing that Muriel had also appeared at his door he added, "Nothing to do with you Muriel, or this facility. It has all been first rate. I just need to get on with my life. I'm sorry if I offended you."

"No offence taken, Mr. Carter, we all understand completely and want to get rid of you as fast as possible too!" She said, with a slight twinkle in her eye.

He looked back at the lawyer, "So, Mr. Bartlett, what have you been up too, on my behalf, as you say?"

"Well sir, I think now would be a good time to sit down because I have several things to tell you, most of which you won't want to be standing for."

Muriel helped William to a small round oak table in the corner of the room, where she made sure he was seated comfortably in one of two matching chairs. Bartlett seated himself in the chair facing him while Muriel placed a picture of water and two glasses on the table in front of them and then left the room, closing the door behind her.

"She really is great. I don't know if I could do this without her and I wonder if she ever leaves this place."

Bartlett looked at the closed door and said, "Yes, she is exceptional and was told that you were to be a priority for her."

"I wondered how she always seemed to be available whenever I called. I hope she will be taken care of once I am able to leave this place."

"Yes, she will," said Bartlett.

"Thank you for that," said William. "And now, let's get to that giant stack of paperwork you have with you."

Bartlett had placed a leather satchel on his lap and had pulled out a small pile of papers and folders, which he placed in a neat stack on the table in front of him. He put the satchel on the floor under his chair and then placed his hands together on the table.

Looking at William, he said, "Firstly, let me again say how pleased I am that you seem to be making a speedy recovery. Your grandpa would be very happy."

"Thank you Mr. Bartlett," said William.

"Please call me Harold!"

"Okay, Harold, I apologize for being so rude when you arrived, it's just that I am having trouble understanding what the hell is going on and what I am to do from here on. My grampa's letter only tells me so much and there are so many holes to fill."

Bartlett stared at William for a full minute before speaking, "Let us start from the top, and hopefully when I am done you will know what it is you want to do. "The first thing I will explain is why you have a new name."

William's head shot up immediately.

"That was going to be my first question! It is driving me nuts, Mr. Carter this, and Mr. Friggin' Carter that! I can't seem to get through to them that they have it wrong. And now you are going to tell me that *I* have it wrong?"

Bartlett let out, what for him was as close to an actual laugh, as he would ever let out. "Well, sir, that is correct. They are going on the information used when you were moved to this place. To them you are Jonas Carter and let me tell you why. You see, the tragic event that took place in the alley that night, where we lost Christine and nearly lost you, involved some local thugs, one of which you may have known. I will get into that later. Anyway, we believe there were four men involved. We also think they were known to police even back then. Apparently nothing could be proven against them, so they went unpunished for their deeds. During the time of your stay here it is believed that these men have become even worse, and in fact, are now leaders in their professions, those being drugs, booze, prostitution and human smuggling."

"Your Grampa, being an ex-policeman, with a lot of contacts, got some information from the investigating officer that at least one of these guys knew who you were, and the word out there was that you may be the only link to the attack. A lot of strings were pulled and definitely some money spent, to have you 'pass away from your injuries.' You apparently never came out of your coma. You were secretly transferred out of the country to this lovely place in Canada, where many people have gone to 'disappear' for a while.

A new identity has been created for you. That is why these folks have been calling you Mr. Carter. You see, you are no longer William Carterell, but are now Jonas Carter."

"Jesus Christ!" William exclaimed. "That at least explains why these folks have been looking at me strangely every time I mention my name."

"Yes, they know they work in a very private place, and that Carter was probably not your real name, but they are paid well to not ask questions."

"So I'm Jonas Carter now?"

"Yes, I'm afraid you are."

"How far does this go?"

"I have very authentic identification, including passport, Driver's License, and credit cards, all in your new name. A great deal of expense has been incurred to make these acceptable wherever you go. Your Grampa wanted you to be able to return home safely, and without notice. It will also help that your appearance has changed considerably," Bartlett said while looking 'Jonas' up and down.

Jonas smiled for the first time. "I had quite the shock when I first looked in the mirror. Even I wouldn't have recognized me."

"Yes, there are many things you will need to get used to besides being a new person.

Bartlett continued, "Your Grampa was very shrewd, or as he would say, quite lucky, with his investments and he did very well. Very well indeed! He left instructions for me that, in the hopeful event that you would recover, I was to set up accommodations, and the like, for you back in Seattle. That is what kept me away these last few days. I have arranged quite suitable living quarters in a very nice townhouse complex in a nicely secluded neighborhood. I assumed you would want to remain 'under the radar' when you return. I will leave furnishings and all else to you. I have several papers and books of records that you will have to go through, and signatures that are needed." He handed Jonas several file folders, each crammed with papers.

"Holy shit, Harold, is this correct?" Jonas passed a folder to Bartlett. In it was a bank record.

"Well yes, it is Jonas. As I said, your dear old Grampa did well for himself."

"Christ, I'll say! What do I do with it?"

"I think that will all come to you in time, my friend. As I said before, you will need to furnish your new place, find a mode of transport, and that sort of thing."

"This will do a lot more than that Harold, a lot more!"

"I'm sure you will put it to good use. In the meantime all is taken care of, and you just have to get yourself back to good health."

Jonas was shaking his head, still amazed at what was left to him.

"I can hardly wait to do just that. I've laid awake these last nights re-living that horrible night in the alley. I miss Chrissy so much it hurts all the time. If only I hadn't taken her with me that night, none of it would have happened, and she would still be fine now, we both would be."

Jonas wiped a tear from his eye and asked Bartlett. "You say I might have known one of the guys? In my dreams, or thoughts, whatever they are, I keep seeing this guy. He is looking directly at me, and I feel like I know him, or he knows me somehow. But then everything goes dark. It's so bloody frustrating! I will find this guy!"

Bartlett looked over some notes in one of the folders. "Does the name Dieter Sanderson ring any bells for you?"

"You know, it does, though I don't know where from. Maybe my brain is still screwed up."

Bartlett continued to study his notes. "That could be, but this Sanderson fellow also might have known Chrissy. I'm guessing that she might have gone out with him or one of his friends. Do you know anything about that?"

"I didn't hang out with her when she was with her friends but maybe that is why the name stands out a bit. Maybe she mentioned him to me once. But Harold, why are you thinking this Sanderson guy had anything to do with Chrissy's death?"

"It seems that you had a bit of a shoving match outside a nightclub, Dragon's I believe it is called, and a girl who was there said that she thought it started between your sister and Sanderson, and that you stepped in."

"Did the police follow up with her?"

"They did, but Sanderson claims that he was nowhere near the club the night in question, and apparently has witnesses to back that up. He also claims that he did not know either you or Christine."

"Who was the witness? Maybe when I am out I can talk to her. At least it will be a place to start."

"Unfortunately, the young lady was in a car accident a few months afterwards and did not survive."

"Shit! Well that just sucks, now doesn't it? I don't imagine the 'accident' was suspicious, was it?" A thought was forming in Jonas's head.

"Bartlett looked up from his papers. "It was a hit and run. It was investigated, but there was no link found to your case."

"Maybe I can talk to the police when I get back. Do you think they will answer my questions, even if I am now Jonas Carter?"

Bartlett shook his head.

"I believe the file might still be open, but it has certainly grown cold, especially since the lead investigator, a Mr. Brent Jameson, had to retire. He has been in a wheelchair for the last year and was forced to take early retirement, although I don't know the cause. He knew your Grampa, so I'm sure he'll talk to you."

The older man could see that all of this information was taking a toll on Jonas, because, all of a sudden, he gathered up his remaining papers, putting them back in his satchel.

"Jonas," he said, "this has been tough on you and a lot to absorb. We can finish this paperwork at another time. I know you will give this a lot of thought, but please do not do so at the cost of your recovery. You will undoubtedly have many things that you will wish to do however none will be possible unless you are well."

Jonas recalled the line of his Grampa's letter. 'Revenge is mighty, but it cannot be taken upon by those who are unprepared!' He would heed that advice.

"Thanks so much Harold! I really do appreciate all that you have done for my Grampa, and now for me. I will make two promises to you, but mostly to myself. One: I will do all I have to do to recover and get my health to where it needs to be to get home, and Two: I will get those responsible for taking Chrissy from us.

"That is a promise!"

CHAPTER EIGHT

THE white man stopped pacing, and just stood in one spot, staring at the ragged line of girls. He was immediately joined by a very short Chinese man, also dressed in a suit and crisp shirt.

The man spoke in a language not known to the girls, however after a few words he would pause, and the short man would speak, obviously interpreting.

"My name is Lamar. I have made arrangements for you to have a new life. You should look at this as a very good thing, a very lucky thing, for not everyone gets to leave their pitiful little village, and start a new life in an exciting new country. In a little while you will begin your journey, to a new and exciting land called America. The journey will not be easy, but it must be done. In America you will work for me and my partners until the cost of this transport is repaid. You will then be allowed to go and do whatever you wish and to make your new life." The man stopped talking long enough to take a cloth from his pocket, and rub it over his bald head, where beads of sweat had started to form, and threatened to run down on to his face.

This allowed his interpreter time to catch up, "You must remember this. Always do as you are told and do not make trouble. We do not tolerate trouble makers, and if you become a problem to us you will not be allowed to complete your journey. If you follow the rules you will be fine. If you do not, well, very bad things can happen. You will reach the first stop on your journey in a few days, and I will speak to you again then." He abruptly turned on his heels and walked away, leaving the building through the same door through which he had entered.

A great murmuring swept through the girls. Everything from tears of misery for missed loved ones, to even some who seemed genuinely excited to have a chance to start a new, and hopefully, better life.

Ling stayed as close to her older sister as she could, and asked, "What does all that mean? Where are they sending us?"

Zhuo held her sister to her and replied, "I just do not know little bell, but we have to try to be strong and not make trouble. He might say we will be free, but he has the look of someone who has cruelty in his heart."

Jing-Wei moved closer to the two sisters, "I have heard of men like him before, and have never heard anything good. We must be very careful around him, and the men that work for him."

For the next two hours the girls occupied themselves with walking around the inside of the big building. As there really wasn't a place to escape too, the guards allowed them to walk freely around the inside of the building. The three girls stuck together and used the time to closely examine the large container units lined up in the middle of the building. There were four of the units, each about sixteen feet wide by about forty feet long. Each had been modified to add a small toilet enclosure at the far end, and wide benches along both sides. There was also a large pile of blankets in the middle of the floor of each unit. The girls were surprised to see that each of the units was built on a frame which was attached to large truck wheels. The exterior of the units was all metal, however there were evenly spaced 'holes' along the sides about five feet from the floor. Jing-Wei noticed that one of the units had larger 'holes' along the sides and some were about one foot square.

She spoke, "I think we are to be loaded into these units which will then be loaded on to a ship. I think we should stay near this one as it appears to be the best of the four. See the larger holes in the sides? Some of them even have little doors that can be locked from inside. This is the one we should be on, do you agree?"

Zhuo quickly and quietly answered her new friend, "Yes, I see what you mean by the larger windows. I think they are for fresh air. Let us be on this one if we can."

Shortly thereafter a group of men entered the building, each carrying large baskets. The baskets, about twenty of them, were placed in a line on the floor and one of the men stepped toward the girls.

"This is food for your journey. It is not much, but will have to do. Each girl will take an equal amount. You will be given water once a day as well, so I would advise you to be careful how much, and when, you eat and drink."

He motioned for the girls to line up and to move along the line to receive their 'ration' of food. The baskets contained mostly bread products but there was a small quantity of dried fruit, cheeses and rice cakes for each girl. They hurriedly bundled their new treasure as best they could, and moved away from the line. Zhuo, Ling and Jing-Wei each filled a small basket and made their way back to their chosen container unit.

They no sooner arrived back at the unit when one of the guards started yelling instructions to the group to make their way towards the parked units.

"You must find a place immediately." he said, "There is room for twenty-four to each unit, no more than that!"

A guard placed a small set of steps at the entrance of each unit, and the girls were instructed to climb up and into each.

As they were already close to their chosen unit Zhuo, Ling and Jing-Wei were the first to climb aboard. Taking their baskets of food with them, they looked despairingly at the benches that would be their home for the foreseeable future.

Zhuo immediately grabbed Ling and Jing-Wei and pointed to the bench near the middle of the one wall. "We must take a spot near the middle. I do not want to be too close to the doors for fear that it might be cold, and also not too close to the toiled area in the back. Also the hole in the side in the middle is bigger, so might let in more air."

The three girls quickly sat down on the bench near the middle and spread their blankets out for them to sit on, placing their food baskets under the bench below their feet. Moments later the unit was full to capacity with confused and frightened girls. No one spoke and, after finding a place on the bench, most stared blankly at the floor not knowing what to do, or whether or not there was anything they could do. Zhuo could feel the despair in the little room.

It wasn't long afterwards when three men approached the back of Zhuo's unit, carrying what appeared to be a large barrel. They grunted with effort, but managed to set it up on the floor level of the container. One of the men motioned to the side of the barrel where a small spout of some type was located. He tossed several small cups to the floor.

"This is drinking water only," he growled. "Do not use it for anything else or you will run out. It has to last all of you for several days!" He then backed away, and the remaining two men started to pull on heavy chains at each side of the entrance. This lowered a steel panel into place, and when it slammed into its resting place, the unit became dreadfully dark. More than one girl screamed when the door crashed into place, and several more started to cry.

The sudden darkness struck Zhou and the rest of the girls, and it took some time before their eyes became accustomed to it. With the help of limited light coming through the air vents, they were soon able to at least make out those closest to them. Still no one spoke. There was nothing to say. They were locked in to this prison of hopelessness.

Zhuo was directly below one of the larger vents with Ling on one side and Jing-Wei on the other. With her head in her hands Zhou spoke softly. "Why was this happening to them? How could her father do this? Had they not worked hard every day?" But she knew her questions would go unanswered. She remembered many times, when, as a young child, she would hear her mother and father arguing over the simplest of things. There were other girls her age in the village and most of them seemed to get along fine with their fathers, but Zhuo's father was of the old ways. He wanted only boys to help him work the gardens and, no matter how hard Zhuo worked to make him appreciate her, even if she was a girl, it was never good enough. Her mother did not stand a chance against her husband, and always ended up crying alone in their parent's room. Things got worse when Ling was born. Their father wanted to immediately get rid of the new baby, and Zhuo did not want to know how he would do that. She had heard of some families that had baby girls "mysteriously' disappear shortly after birth. No one questioned where they had gone! Surely her father would not do that! And would her mother stand by and let it happen?

As the years passed and the girls grew up, all the while working very hard to please their father, it seemed that maybe things would work out and they would live a reasonably happy life. But then something happened in the market place. People that had always purchased regular quantities of their products stopped buying so much, or any at all. More and more often their father would return from the market with almost as much as he had taken early that morning. Zhuo heard her father telling her mother that it was the same everywhere. Something was happening a long way away that was affecting the whole world, and people in the surrounding villages simply did not have money to purchase goods as they once did. Their father's mood grew even worse as the weeks went along.

Zhuo, although now slightly past her teens, was still considered a young girl, and still, in most ways, acted that way. She still had dreams of one day leaving their little village, and perhaps living in one of the small cities that were not too far out of the hills. Once, when she was about ten, her whole family made the long journey to the great city of Nanping. They were in the back of a large truck with several other families, each with their own products, and were to set up in a small market just outside the city limits. Peeking between the older people's outstretched arms and legs Zhuo, was able to see many wondrous things. In the distance she could see very tall buildings although they never got close enough to see what they were, and the streets were paved so smooth they felt nary a bump. They shared the roadway with many automobiles, some of which were so shiny and sleek they were hard to look at for long. No matter, because they all passed the old truck as if it were standing still. Of course, Ling was with them, and Zhuo was in charge of her for the whole time they travelled, so she was not allowed to move through the crush of people and goods to get a better view. Unfortunately the weather that day turned very bad, and the sky opened up, soaking them all within minutes. Luckily they were able to sell their produce to a man who purchased it all, albeit at a steep discount, so they did not stay near the city for long. Zhuo remembered daydreaming all the way back about the big city that had been so close. She took those dreams to bed with her every night. Those dreams were completely and horribly shattered the day the men in the trucks came, and her father finally got his wish by ridding himself of his daughters. Here they were, two frightened girls locked in a strange prison, surrounded by strangers, neither of them knowing what the future held, or if they even had one.

Her fear multiplied again when she heard what she thought was the sound of trucks entering the building, the roar of their engines proceeding to the front of their unit. They were immediately assaulted by fumes from these vehicles that made their eyes water. Their small prison was suddenly rocked when one of the trucks backed up to it, causing the girls to fall violently to the side, crashing in to each other, causing heads to collide, and more screams. Before they could straighten up, the truck lurched forward, causing them to be thrown again, this time in the opposite direction. Their container seemed to be moving and Zhou, peering through the vent could see that they had moved outside, into the fog and even more darkness. The only familiar sound being the squawking of the gulls, which seemed to increase as the trucks moved along.

After only a few minutes they came to an abrupt stop, once again causing the girls to stumble around in the darkness. Much clanging and crashing of metal came from all sides, and then suddenly, as if by magic, all sounds ceased. Even the terrified girls honored the moment as not one seemed to move, each one dealing with their own internal fears. And then, as if by a giant hand they felt the entire unit rise into the air, freezing the girls with terror, as they continued to rise higher and higher. Although the fog was still too thick for them to be able to see much through the vents, they could feel in their stomach's the continuous raising of the unit that trapped them all. The unit now started to sway from side to side, with the arch seeming to get wider as they went higher.

The rising motion stopped all of a sudden, and the swaying slowed until the unit was again still. Once it was so, it began to lower, causing a nauseous sensation in everyone's stomach. It kept going down, seemingly forever, until, with only the slightest of bumps, did it stop, and the unit rested.

"I think we have now been loaded on to a ship" said Jing-Wei to no one in particular.

A voice across from her replied, "How do you know of such things?"

"I do not know for sure but have heard this is how goods are shipped across the sea."

Zhuo joined the conversation, "So we are 'goods' now, to be shipped and sold?"

Jing-Wei looked sidewise at her new friend, whom she could make out in the darkness, "I am fearful that this is true."

A different voice said, "What are we to do?"

As no reply was forthcoming from Jing-Wei, Zhuo spoke up, "We must all try to survive this together. We all have some food, and they have given us water, so we must share and make it all last, for we do not know how long we are to be kept here."

And so they sat, on their uncomfortable benches, each thinking their own thoughts, leaning on each other in the dark.

Zhuo comforted Ling as best she could and was glad Jing-Wei was by her side. "You are correct Jing-Wei. We must find a way to take care of each other until we know what they are going to do with us."

Jing-Wei did not answer, as she too, was lost in her own thoughts.

The darkness did not subside, and the gulls had started up again, when a mighty blast from the ship's horn rang out, scaring the girls even more. As the horn's echo slowly faded away, the unit vibrated, and they could sense more movement.

"Can you feel it?" One of the girls yelled out. "We are moving!"

"Yes, the ship is moving!" said another.

CHAPTER NINE

OVER the next three weeks Jonas's condition improved dramatically. He progressed from needing assistance to sit up and stand, to being able to do so without help, and to take walks up and down the hallways. He became a familiar sight to the few other patients and staff as he sauntered up and down the hall at all hours of the day and night. It was no surprise then, that this became not enough for him, and he started taking to the outdoor sidewalks for his strolls. It was almost magical for him. He noticed everything. The different species of birds flittering around, flowers, trees swaying gently in the breeze. It was if the blow to his head opened up some area of his brain that was now filling itself with everything his senses could record. During these outdoor walks it wasn't only nature that his brain occupied itself with, but also the details of how he came to be here. Everyday more and more information was becoming 'uncovered' in his head, and he spent a great deal of his solitary time thinking about what he was to do once he was well enough to leave. That time was fast approaching.

Bartlett continued to visit every few days, and they spent a great deal of time just walking around the grounds and talking, discussing everything, including news and events that happened while Jonas was in his coma. Jonas was becoming increasingly impatient and was eager to leave the facility. He needed to begin the healing process, and that could not start before he had all the answers, and those responsible for his sister's murder had been dealt with. It was his primary focus, his only focus, his addiction.

Bartlett took the brunt of Jonas's frustrations, and acted as the 'voice of reason' whenever he talked about revenging his sister's death.

"Jonas, my friend, you are not yet well enough to leave. You must be patient a little while longer. Once you are fit then you can do what you have to do."

"Harold, Chrissy wouldn't have been there if it wasn't for me. It is my fault what happened to her. I must make it right. It is killing me that those animals are out there still living full lives without a care about what happened."

Tears formed in Jonas's eyes, "I just have to make it right, Harold. I just have to!"

"Give it one more week, Jonas. Next Monday I will personally pick you up, and drive you back to Seattle. I will get you settled in to your new place, and then introduce you to a few people that may be able to assist you. How does that sound?"

"Alright, Harold," he sighed, "one more week!"

That week did not pass quickly enough for Jonas, and when Monday finally arrived he was more than ready. During the week he had taken to walking, not just around the grounds, but down the road a ways. There was a winery not too far off, and he took to walking there and back at least twice a day. He felt like he was finally getting back into some semblance of shape.

When Bartlett appeared at his door he was already dressed, packed, and ready to leave.

Bartlett chuckled, "We can't just go storming out of here, you know. There are tests you have to have, and a whole raft of paperwork to be signed."

"Well, let's get to it Harold, I need to get on the road!"

After an hour of various tests, it was determined that he was healthy enough to leave. Paperwork was signed, and all that was left was to say his goodbyes. He was walking down the hall towards his room to say goodbye to Muriel, when he came upon both her, and Harold, sharing a laugh in the middle of the hall. Jonas approached Muriel with his arms wide but instead of the anticipated hug, Harold spoke. "Jonas, my boy, I think I have a bit of a surprise for you! It seems that we have been just a wee bit dishonest with you all this time."

Jonas looked from Harold to Muriel and back again. Both had big grins on their faces. "What are you two up to?"

"Well, you see, Muriel actually doesn't work for this facility."

Jonas was confused. "What do you mean?"

"Our good friend Muriel actually works for you. She was hired quite some time ago, by the trust, to supply exclusive care to you while you were ill. Now that you are well enough to leave, I hope you don't mind but, I have taken the liberty of asking Muriel if she would be kind enough to continue her employ in your new residence."

Jonas was thrilled. "That would be wonderful." He looked at Muriel. "Is that what you want? We'll have to find a place for you to live as soon as we get down there. Harold, you say I have a place in a quiet neighborhood. Could we find somewhere close?"

"Not to worry, Jonas. Your new place has living accommodations for staff. I made sure of it when I purchased it on your behalf."

"You sly old coot, you had this planned all along, didn't you?"

"I must admit that Muriel and I have had some discussions." He said while looking at Muriel.

Jonas thought he saw a bit of a twinkle in the old lawyer's eye. Could it be, Harold and Muriel? Well, he certainly hoped so!

"That's' terrific! Let's get the hell out of here then!" he said.

"Jonas, you and I will ride in my car. Muriel has some things to take care of up here, so won't be joining us for a few days."

Jonas finally got the anticipated hug from Muriel, and with a promise to see each other in a few days, said their goodbyes.

Jonas watched Harold as they walked towards the parking lot. In the last month he had learned a lot about Mr. Bartlett, as he liked to be called. Despite his finicky and proper behavior, he was certainly a good man to have on his side, and a fine lawyer. He obviously had been very fond of Jonas's grandfather and was determined to look after Jonas in his place. So it was a great surprise when, after entering the parking lot, Harold approached an incredibly beautiful 1966 Mustang, keys in his hands.

"You've got to be shittin' me!" Jonas said, while laughing out loud.

Bartlett's eyes lit up like a kid's.

"I got this baby brand new in '66 and haven't had a single problem with it in all these years. Haven't changed a thing on her either, still has the original 289 engine and the seats have never been touched. I think you are the first passenger in years."

"Incredible. I would have put you in a Volvo station wagon or something," Jonas was still laughing. The mint condition mustang was yellow with a black hardtop. It looked like it just came off the factory line. "Will wonders ever cease?"

"Shall we go?" replied Harold, who threw his satchel in the back seat and hopped in behind the wheel. Jonas took the passenger seat, closed the door with a satisfying thunk, and off they went.

Jonas remembered how he had felt when, as a young boy, his Grampa would get them ready for a 'road trip', which could have been anything from a three day drive into the country, to a trip downtown to a Mariner's game. It didn't matter. That was the feeling coursing through Jonas now although it wasn't joyous excitement, but rather eager anticipation of doing what he had to do.

They left the vineyards of the Okanagan area of British Columbia, and drove the Coquihalla freeway through massive forested valleys, and past fast flowing rivers, until they reached the relative flatness of the lower mainland. They encountered no problems with Jonas's new identification at the Sumas border crossing, and soon were winding their way through the vast northern Washington farmland. It wasn't long before they reached the I-5 freeway and were able to open the Mustang up, making good time towards Seattle.

Two short hours later they began to pass the many Outlet Malls along the highway, and then they would catch an occasional glimpse of the high-rises scrapping the sky in downtown Seattle. Although Seattle has more cloudy days than clear, today was one of the clear ones, and even Mt. Rainier's snow covered crest could be seen in the distant south. If one looked hard enough you could even catch a quick glimpse of the Space Needle, built over fifty years ago and still looking like something out of science fiction.

They did not make it as far as those majestic buildings though as Harold took a left turn at the 520 junction that leads to Foster Island. From there he took a right at Lake Washington Blvd until turning left again on to Madison Street.

"Welcome to Madison Park, Jonas, your new home!" he proclaimed.

They slowed and turned off of Madison onto 38th Ave, drove down a couple of blocks, past what looked like an elementary school, until they reached East Chaplin Street, where Harold turned sharply and immediately faced an imposing gate. A sign beside the gate said "CHAPLIN ESTATES". Harold produced a plastic card, and pulled up to a machine at the side of the driveway, swiped the card, and drove forward as the gate slid smoothly open.

"Jesus, Harold, this is a nice place!" exclaimed Jonas as he viewed the complex. What he saw were very large townhouses built two to a unit. The exterior was finished with hardy plank in beige with dark brown trim around the windows and doors. As they pulled up to one on the units they could see that each "double" unit shared an entrance set of steps up to very nicely finished double doors. Harold pulled the Mustang into one of the vacant parking spots in front of the building. They got out of the car.

Harold tossed a set of keys to Jonas.

"There's underground parking for two vehicles, but you can look at that later," he said. "Let's go on inside. I think you will be impressed."

Jonas walked up the front steps ahead of Bartlett, and was about to open one of the doors, when it opened outward suddenly, causing him to quickly pull back his hand before the door crashed into it.

"Oh, excuse me, I'm so sorry. I didn't hear you coming up the steps," cried out a very pretty blonde woman, as she came through the door.

"You must be my new neighbor," she said.

Jonas stood there for a second, trying to find his voice, for this woman was truly very pretty. She stood almost as tall as Jonas, was quite slender, and had blonde hair just over her shoulder in a style some now would call almost Farrah-like, which suited her perfectly. When she smiled, she revealed a set of perfect pearl white teeth. And what a smile it was, thought Jonas. He couldn't remember seeing anything like it. She wore a white knit top and matching skirt to her knees, and a plain pair of pumps on her feet.

She looked at Jonas with amusement, and thrust out her hand. "I'm Tracy Wallace. I guess we share this entranceway so you'll probably be seeing me a lot"

Jonas quickly recovered, "My name is Will-----Jonas Carter, I look forward to running into you out here often, but I'll be a bit more careful around the doors."

"And I'm Harold Bartlett," as Bartlett stepped forward and shook Tracy's hand. "You will probably see me around a bit too, as well as a lady by the name of Muriel, who will be residing in the house-keepers quarters. She should arrive in a few days."

"Oh, you have a house-keeper! Maybe I can make use of her too, as I work a lot, and never seem to get time to keep up. Can we talk about that later, when she is here?"

"That would be great! I guess we'll see you later." Jonas and Bartlett made their way through the doors and watched Tracy continue to the parking lot.

"I told you this would be an interesting place to live," said a smiling Bartlett.

"Yes you did, Harold, yes you did," Jonas said. He took one last look at his neighbor walking away. Very interesting indeed!

To describe the inside of the townhouse as being large would be a bit of an understatement, for it was huge. The two men walked through the entrance foyer, where they had met the neighbor, and proceeded through a large solid oak door, into the suite itself. The main floor consisted of a very large, and chef friendly, kitchen, complete with all stainless steel appliances. Off to the side was a breakfast nook that could seat six in a semi-circle of cushioned bench seating. Immediately outside the kitchen was a large formal dining area, which separated the kitchen from a living room that spanned the entire width of the unit, roughly thirty feet. A full sized washroom flanked that and another entrance to the house-keeper's quarters was beside that. A quick look inside, what was to become Muriel's area, showed a sizable one bedroom suite with its own kitchen, full sized bathroom and large bedroom. Through a French door in the bedroom there was a nice deck overlooking the golf course that ran horizontally behind the building

The men continued their tour by going upstairs where they found two incredibly full sized suites, each containing a large bedroom, with its own deck overlooking the golf course, a full bathroom with walk-in shower, double sinks, and Jacuzzi tub. Both of these suites were on the golf course side, so they shared a deck with only a small divider between. The other half of the upstairs footage contained two 'guest' bedrooms which shared a full sized bathroom in between.

"This is quite the place, Harold! I have no clue what I'll do with all of this room," Jonas said, while looking around and shaking his head.

Bartlett replied, "I thought it better to have something with more than you need rather than something that would turn out too small. I also thought you would turn one of these large rooms upstairs into a gym of some sort."

"That's a pretty good idea and I just might do that," added Jonas.

Bartlett spoke again, "I actually picked this unit because it is in a very quiet area. Most of the folks here have high end jobs and keep to themselves. Even the elementary school that we passed is for private enrollment only, so I think you can remain quite anonymous here." Bartlett again chuckled, "or at least I hope so, but am not too sure now that I have seen your next door neighbor."

"Ha, Harold, you are a card! Don't worry about the neighbor. I have things to do, and won't be having much time for any of that."

Bartlett nodded, "Well, how say we go for a bite to eat. All that driving has made me quite famished. I think I saw a few restaurants down the road a ways back, and I know there is a car rental place around there too. You need to get a vehicle for a few days so I can get back to work."

After a hearty dinner at a nearby Red Lobster, Bartlett dropped Jonas off at a car rental agency, gave him all the phone numbers he would need, and said his goodbyes with a promise to be in touch in a few days. Jonas picked out a new model Chevy and made out a list of things that needed his immediate attention.

Two days later he checked out of the small motel he had stayed in while shopping for furniture and stocking up his new townhouse. Today his purchases were to be delivered, and true to the company's word, when he arrived at his new place, the truck was already backed up to the front door.

A few hours, and yes, a few beers for the guys, later, his new home was starting to take shape. The kitchen cupboards were full of dishes, although he hadn't gone out for groceries yet, the dining room now sported a nice oak table with six chairs around it. In the living room he has placed a tan suede couch with a leather recliner on each side, all facing the fifty-five inch flat panel TV, of course complete with PVR, and a Bose surround sound system. Jonas wasn't sure when he would get to use this system, but at least it was there if needed. The same could be said for the upstairs rooms. He furnished both suites almost identically, with king sized beds, night tables on each side, dresser and armoire. Thankfully, as Muriel would come to say, he had the foresight to have different wood in each room, his being dark oak, and the second being a much lighter grain.

Speaking of Muriel, she timed her arrival perfectly as Jonas was pretty well set up when she walked in the door. She was very pleased with her accommodation as well. Jonas had also picked out the furniture for that area, and apparently had done a good job of it.

"You've done a wonderful job setting this up, Jonas. Now please let me do the rest. I'll get unpacked and then go shopping. I need to get you stocked up. I hope you don't mind?"

"Not at all, Muriel, I was hoping you would say that! I need to call Harold anyway, so you do what you want to do, and I'll get the hell out of your way."

Bartlett agreed to come over the very next morning to help Jonas with his plans. In the meantime Jonas went in search of a vehicle. He had passed a BMW dealership the day before and one of the display cars had caught his eye. He thought to himself 'hey, Grampa left me a shit-load of money. I might as well use it!'

Three hours later he had returned the rental car and was now driving a sparkling white BMW 3 Series Coupe 335i, loaded with 300 horses ready at the slightest touch, leather heated seats, and a look that turned heads as he drove down the street. 'Not the smartest car to be driving when he wanted to stay under the radar. I'll have to get something else a bit more 'basic', he thought.

He pulled into the underground parking, ran up the stairs, and was surprised to find Muriel busy unpacking bag after bag of grocery items.

"Now you go on, and put your feet up young man, and leave this to me. I enjoy doing this stuff, and certainly don't want a man gettin' in my way," she said with a laugh.

Jonas was suddenly too tired to put up an argument and made his way to his bedroom, where he threw off his shoes, and fell on to the bed, instantly nodding off. He awoke to the ringing of his newly acquired cell phone, and to Bartlett's voice. "I've just spoken with Brent Jameson, the investigator I told you about. He is very much looking forward to meeting with you tomorrow at nine. I will pick you up around 8:00. Have a good sleep. Oh, I just spoke with Muriel too and she says you are all set up now. You have intercoms throughout the townhouse that you can call her from, and here is her direct phone number." He rattled off the number. "She says you are to call her anytime. She really is a peach. We are lucky to have her!"

"Thanks Harold, I will make sure I look after her well."

"Good night then!"

No sooner had Bartlett hung up when the phone rang again. This time it was Muriel. "Oh, Jonas, this place is wonderful! I love it here already. Are you hungry? I can cook you up something in a jiffy. We are fully stocked now."

"Thanks Muriel, but I'm bushed. I think I'll just have a shower and turn in for the night. I'll see you in the morning. Mr. Bartlett will be here to pick me up at 8:00."

"Oh, well, I'll have something ready for both of you in the morning then. Good Lord knows that Harold doesn't eat properly, you know!"

Jonas looked at the phone after she had disconnected.

"What was that all about? Harold doesn't eat properly? How would she know that? I wonder..................Nah!" Jonas had a quick shower, and a few minutes later was again sleeping soundly.

Bartlett arrived at precisely 8:00 AM the next morning and was ushered into the kitchen by Muriel, who had enough food prepared for a small army. When Jonas sauntered downstairs he found bacon, eggs, hash browns, sliced tomatoes, several types of fruit cut up, and of course, coffee. He also found Bartlett and Muriel engaged in a friendly banter that only ceased when he entered the area.

"I see that Muriel has everything under control" said Jonas. He took in the hearty meal presentation, and took a seat at the table with the two of them. It turned out to be the best breakfast he could remember ever having.

"Let's take my car," said Jonas as the two men, now fully fed, prepared to leave. "No point putting on extra miles on that old beauty of yours."

Following Harold's detailed instructions they soon found themselves back on the I-5 heading north, Jonas enjoying the feel of his new BMW and its smooth 300 horses. It wasn't long before they past the Alderwood Mall in Lynnwood.

"Take the next turn off the freeway," said Harold, pointing to the traffic signs ahead. The turn led them off of the freeway, and on to a two lane paved road that headed east.

"It's about fifteen minutes down here and then we'll have to make another turn to your left."

True to his word, fifteen minutes later Harold pointed ahead, "See the end of that fence? Turn left there."

Jonas did so and they found themselves on an unpaved driveway of sorts that seemed to run as far as the eye could see into dense forest.

"You sure this is the place? It seems like more of a logging trail then anything!"

"You'll see. He really has a nice set up here. Not too many people know of this place, and that is the way he likes it."

Jonas turned his head towards Harold. "You haven't told me much about this guy. I'm not even sure why you want me to see him."

"Patience, my good man, and you will learn everything you need to know in a very short while."

They continued down the road, which looked as if it hadn't seen any significant work done on it for quite some time, but was nevertheless passable. Jonas's fears for his new car were quieted when he saw that the road wasn't too bad. After a mile of more Jonas spotted a clearing ahead.

"That's the cabin." said Harold.

Approaching the clearing, Jonas could make out a log cabin set back toward the far side. It wasn't huge, but it also wasn't your ordinary hunting cabin. It was made of huge logs that all fit snuggly together. There were two large windows facing the front and Jonas could see a couple of small ones on the side facing them. He assumed there were more around back. The front of the cabin was wrapped with a porch, plus a railing right out of an old western movie. If he had a horse Jonas was sure he could just ride up, sling reins around the post, and dismount. Adding to this picture was the figure sitting in an old fashioned rocking chair beside the front door. He made no move to greet them, but merely gave a short wave.

Jonas followed Harold from their vehicle and walked up a few steps to the porch, where Harold turned towards him and said.

"Jonas, I would like you to meet Brent Jameson. He and I have become quite good friends over the last couple of years and I think you and him will have lots to talk about."

The man rose from his rocking chair, albeit very slowly and with some difficulty. He had neatly cut salt and pepper colored hair, and a slight growth of beard on his chin. He wore a black t-shirt with no logo, and well-worn jeans.

"Jonas. It's good to meet you, and please call me Brent" he said, offering his hand. "There was a time when none of us would have bet on you returning, let alone looking as fit as you do standing here now."

"I think the pleasure is mine, Brent. I would like to say that Harold has told me all about you but that really isn't the case. In fact, he has told me pretty well nothing."

Jameson laughed, "Then he was doing what I asked. You and I will get to know each other soon enough, but for now can I get you fellas some coffee or a beer?"

"It's a bit early for a beer but I'll certainly take that coffee," replied Harold.

Jameson slowly turned and reached out for the only item on the porch that did not fit the decor, a wheelchair. He was not an overly big man, and you could see that he was used to getting in and out of the chair, which he did quickly and easily. He wheeled himself towards the front door, nudged it with his foot, and entered the cabin, followed by Jonas and Harold.

Inside was just like most houses, a living room off to the left, dining and kitchen to the right, and a hallway entrance between the two. Jonas assumed that led to two or three bedrooms and a bathroom.

"This is home!" said Jameson, as he wheeled himself into the middle of the kitchen area. "Please grab a chair and I'll pour the coffee."

Jameson had altered the cabinetry so that he could easily reach everything from his wheelchair, so preparing the coffee only took a few moments. Once served, he pulled himself up to the table.

"You'll get used to me wheeling around, but don't be surprised if you see me standing once in a while. I haven't lost the full use of my legs but I can only use them for very short periods of time. I try to space those times out. You never know when I'll really need them," he chuckled.

"This is a really nice place you have here. Did you build it yourself?" asked Jonas.

"I would love to say I did all the work myself, but I'm afraid I can't do that. In fact, I didn't build any of it. I was a pretty good cop but a lousy carpenter. No, I had this built for me with some adjustments for the future when I won't be able to get out of this crappy chair."

"You were a cop?" asked Jonas.

"Yep, I was, twenty seven years and now retired due to injury. In fact, my being a cop is exactly why my good buddy Harold here, brought you up to see me."

Jonas looked from Harold back to Jameson, "I take it you were involved in my sister's investigation?"

Jameson looked into his coffee cup for a moment. "Yes I was son, and, maybe now that you are here, I am involved again."

Before Jonas could say anything Jameson continued, "Let me tell you everything I know."

It took all of two hours for Jameson to tell Jonas about being assigned as the investigative officer of the attack on Jonas and Christine. He told him of finding Jonas unconscious in the alley and evidence of the struggle that Christine put up, only to be dragged away. He explained how, other than some articles of clothing left in the alley, he had no other leads, and that he ran into dead ends every way he turned.

"It was almost like whoever did it just disappeared." said Jameson, recalling his frustration. "Then I got a break. I got a call from a young woman who recognized Christine's picture in the paper. She said she had seen her with another man get into an argument with a group of men outside Dragon's bar."

"That's where we always used to go and I know we were there that night. I remember it!" cried Jonas. "I need to talk to her!"

"Well son, I met with that young lady, and she told me what she saw. She even recognized one of the guys you were arguing with, and verified it when I showed her a picture of the guy."

Jonas interrupted, "Even more reason for me to talk with her. I need to know who the guy was. He must have had something to do with it!"

"I'm afraid all of that is a bit tricky. The young lady was involved in a hit and run shortly after talking with me. Unfortunately she died of her injuries, another dead end!"

"What about the guy? You had a picture. You obviously know who he is. Let's start with him!"

Jameson paused, looking directly at Jonas. "Look, Jonas, first tell me everything you remember. Then maybe I can fill in the blanks and we'll see where we can go from here, if anywhere.

Jonas began. "I've spent most of the last weeks thinking about that night. I've gone over and over it in my head and although some of it is still sketchy, I think I've been able to recall most of it. Chrissy and I were at Dragon's. We used to go there a lot and meet up with friends of mine. She and her friends didn't go there much but she seemed to like hanging out with my buddies. Anyway, we had had a few drinks, not many though, and were leaving when a couple of guys, out on the sidewalk, starting making rude comments to Chrissy. You know the type, had too much to drink and thought they were John Travolta or something. I told them to get lost, and one of them started badmouthing me. I'm not sure, but I think Chrissy knew who he was because I seem to remember her telling him to back off, and calling him by his name, but I can't remember it now. So we continued to walk down the sidewalk, and we thought the guys had taken off, but when we got to this alleyway one of them appeared right in front of us. There was another guy just behind him and I was pretty sure there was at least one more guy in the shadows. I told the guys to back off again but this time they weren't listening. The guy in front came at me, and we threw a couple of punches, nothing landing though, and I heard Chrissy scream. I turned towards her, and saw that two guys had come out of the alley, and were trying to pull her back into the dark. I think I dropped the guy I was fighting with and ran towards my sister. I remember her reaching her hand out to me and I tried to grab it. Before I could, something hit me from behind and I remember falling. The whole alleyway seemed to dance, spinning around and around, and I couldn't stop it. I saw Chrissy being dragged back into the alley, and I remember her screams. Then everything went black."

Jameson nodded, "Okay, that fits pretty well with everything we were able to piece together. Unfortunately there were no witnesses to what happened in the alley, and the only person who saw the earlier skirmish is no longer with us. The only thing we have, and keep in mind this is between us, and very unofficial, is that our witness, before her unfortunate accident, identified a man by the name of Sanderson, first name Dieter. Does that ring any bells for you?"

Jonas gave it some thought but nothing came to him, so he simply shrugged.

Jameson continued, "At the time, Sanderson was a small time thug who ran with the wrong crowd. He was involved in several things back then but nothing that could be pinned on him."

"Was he ever picked up or charged?"

Jameson shook his head, "That's where this again gets very interesting! You see, by the time we got a positive ID on him several weeks had gone by and Sanderson had already started his move up the ranks, so to speak. He must have made some very influential friends, because all of a sudden, he was untouchable. I was told, in no uncertain terms, to back off on the file."

"Who the hell could make that happen?

"I didn't know for sure, but had my suspicions. I think the other guys involved that night were even further up the food chain, and had some very powerful connections."

"This is unbelievable!" Jonas banged his hand on the table.

"Yep, these guys not only had the power to make the investigation go away, but were also able to make the one and only witness disappear forever. Her 'accident' was in broad daylight, no witnesses, and no tire tracks. Nothing at all."

"I need to know who these assholes are Brent," said Jonas. "I have to do something! Chrissy was with me that night because I wanted her to be. She was there because of me. I know I'll never get her back, but I have to do something. They have to pay for what they did!"

"Jonas, since you were away, these men became even more powerful. I believe this group is heavily involved in the drug trade, prostitution, and human smuggling. Not just here, but all up and down the coast. Even in LA! They are not to be fooled with."

"I have to do something," said Jonas.

Jameson smiled, "I think I know how you feel. Even now I keep thinking about this case. It stinks like a run-over skunk and I cannot just walk away again, pardon the pun. But every time I stuck my nose into it I got it clipped. You know, no witness, no evidence, nothin'. Just let go, and get on to something else, they said. Well I can't do that!"

"Look, Brent, I really do appreciate everything you did, and tried to do, and can imagine how frustrating it must have been. I have only two questions for you, and then I'll be on my way," said Jonas.

Jameson responded. "I want to help in any way I can. This cannot continue to be buried."

"Firstly, can you give me all the information you have, and secondly......," he paused. "Look, I know that once a cop, always a cop. Even though you are now retired, you are still a cop, but this all happened a long time ago and I'm sure has been buried by your old department. You seem to have a pretty good setup out here, and please forgive me if this is insensitive, but your handicap must restrict you somewhat, so I have to ask. Why you would bother? The case is gone. You have been told to back off! Why help me?"

Jameson hesitated then looked at Jonas as though studying him. He moved his wheelchair away from the table, put his hands on his knees, and spoke. "I'll tell you why Jonas, because our witness's hit and run wasn't the only one. The guys that did that, and the guys that took your sister from you, also did this to me!"

CHAPTER TEN

The Liberian registered freighter 'Dubaskia' was not a big ship, carrying only a few hundred containers. These were stacked neatly, three high, throughout the entire top deck except for a smaller area at the stern. This was reserved for some special containers, and would not be cared for in the normal manner by the crew. All aboard knew that these containers were the sole property of the freighter's owners, and not to be tampered with, or discussed at all. Thus, they were virtually ignored.

The six 'special' containers were not stacked, but rather placed side by side with only a minimal space allowed between. This space, although there to provide room for the cables necessary to fasten the container to the ship's deck, also served another purpose. This was to allow much needed airflow between each unit. On each side of the containers there were two 'windows' each about one foot square. They could be opened from the inside, thus allowing the 'cargo' to receive fresh air.

The days and nights became inter-changeable with only the amount of light seen through the air vents telling those inside that it was daylight, or the occasional glimpse of stars showing them the night.

Zhuo would often allow herself to sit perfectly still, her mind travelling far from the ship that was their prison. She travelled back to her early childhood where things never seemed so bad, the struggle not so evident. Although her father was never a loving man, he kept his distance, and it was clear that he was not happy to have daughters instead of sons. Their mother made up for his lack of feeling by always being gentle and caring, often taking the girls aside, where their father could not see or hear them, and telling them funny stories that she made up. She taught them to cook, sew, and how to heal a variety of wounds and illnesses, using only the plants that could be found nearby. For the longest time her love made up for what their father never gave. As the girls grew older he became agitated at the smallest of things, often threatening them with, and sometimes using, his homemade whip. It was these times that their mother stepped between them and their enraged father, often suffering abuse in the girls' place.

The sisters became very close, and Zhuo, being the eldest, made sure young Ling was always by her side. They went everywhere together, always sharing what they had, including their meals and meager belongings. Zhuo also became a buffer between Ling and her father, often taking the blame for something Ling had done. Ling, being very quiet, had trouble grasping some of the simpler duties assigned to them. She would, more often than not, make a mess of things, causing Zhuo to step in to repair the damage done, before their father caught on, or taking the blame when it was too late to do that.

As unhappy with them as he was, and as miserable he made their days, Zhuo could not imagine him actually giving them away, or worse, selling them to these men. But that is what he did, and here they were, locked into a cramped overcrowded container on a strange vessel, heading to a world they could not envision.

Zhuo looked around the container and in the limited light she could make out most of the other girls. They were all in the same age range, from mid-teens to early twenties, varied in sizes too, although most seemed fairly fit when they first started this journey. Jing-Wei was by far the biggest, and assumed the role as leader, while Ling was the smallest.

Zhuo watched her little sister as she slept beside her. Her even breathing suggested a calm that was not there, for looking around at the others, she sensed overwhelming confusion and fear in all of them. She wondered how many of them would survive. Could she survive? Not only survive, but could she protect little Ling, who was all she had left in the world?

They sailed for several days during which the girls tried their best to help each other. They rationed the water, with Jing-Wei in charge, and although they were not allowed outside their unit, they were allowed to open up their side vents any time they chose. These vents were about one foot square. Too small for someone to crawl through, but large enough to allow much needed fresh air into the unit, but most importantly, allowed each of them a turn to see a small glimmer of the outside world. Because Zhuo sat immediately beneath one of the vents, she was put in charge of organizing who would be next to take their turn looking through the little area, thus getting a small dose of precious fresh air. These short moments became sacred to the girls, because the smell from the toilet area was becoming overpowering, and several of them were becoming sick, one of which was constantly vomiting, making the smell even worse. They moved the girl as close to the toilet area as they could, but it helped little.

When it was time for Zhuo's time at the vent she would share it with Ling. They would sometimes make a game of what they could hear or see. They took turns sticking their heads through the vent and trying to rotate so that they could look up. Sometimes they could see a few stars, or even the moon. Often they would bring their head back soaked in rain, but neither complained. It was these few moments that gave each girl a moment of comfort, and allowed them to go on until their next turn.

One night, Zhuo thought it was the fifth or sixth, a loud banging was heard outside their container. Could they be at their destination? They had felt no change in the motion of the vessel, with the gentle rocking never ceasing, and they could still hear the sound of the water as the ship cut its way through the waves. So, no, they could not have stopped or she would have noticed it. Before she had time to think further, the loading door at the end began to rise. Half-way up it revealed a man, one of the guards from before, who motioned to Jing-Wei to come forward. Reluctantly, she did so, casting a worried glance at Zhuo, who touched her hand as she went past. The man spoke to Jing-Wei for a few minutes then pointed to the rest of the girls, making a motion for Jing-Wei to speak.

"We are being given a special treat, but we must be very careful not to misbehave. If we promise to obey this man he will allow us to step outside for a few minutes. They will also refill our water supply and empty out the toilet" Jing-Wei explained.

There was cautious murmuring throughout and the girls all indicated they understood.

Jing-Wei again, "I have told them that we will all behave. Remember, if we do not, we will not get fresh water and will have to put up with the smell for longer."

With that, the girls were allowed to jump down from the container, onto the deck. Some struggled as it was a long drop, and their weakened state made it even more difficult, but all made it without injury.

They were in a small area at the very front of the ship that was blocked off from the rest of the cargo. They could see very little of the ship, and assumed that no one could see them either. They could see no other girls yet and Zhuo hoped the rest of them would also be allowed to get out, at least for a little while.

Zhuo, with Ling in tow, and Jing-Wei, walked the short distance to the ship's rail where they could see nothing but water in front of them, and the crashing waves below. It felt good to stretch out and to take in as much of the fresh sea air as they could. It was a cloudy night, with only the occasional peak at a star, but there was no rain and the temperature was quite comfortable, especially in comparison to the crowded container.

"Where do you think we are going?" Zhuo asked Jing-Wei.

"Jing-Wei just shook her head, "I do not know but the air feels warmer than home so I think we may be travelling southward."

"I feel that too, but it tells us nothing. I want to know where we are going, yet I am also afraid that I might not want to know."

Ling looked up at her sister, "Do you think we will ever see home again, or mother?"

"I do not know Ling. We are already a long way away from home. I fear that we will never see home again, so we must try to be strong and make the best of what happens."

"I am glad we will not return home! I hated it there. But I will miss mother so much."

Zhuo turned her head from her sister back to the water, "I too will miss mother, very much."

Their time in the fresh air was ended by the guard ordering them to return to their container. This time there was a short ladder that they used to climb, and when entering they found the water barrel had been replenished, and the toilet no longer gave off the pungent odor of human waste. The guard made sure all of the girls were accounted for, and in their places, and then, once again slammed the door into place.

The days continued to pass, and no one knew which day it was when things started to change. The first evidence that something was different was the returning sound of birds squawking around the ship. The air changed as well, and the girls could now smell what seemed like slight fragrances, almost like there were petals of many flowers in the air. But the biggest change was in the ship's engines' cadence. The gentle rolling of the vessel, which had remained constant thanks to calm waters, now slowed, and eventually stopped altogether.

Jing-Wei was the first to speak. "We have stopped. I think we have reached our destination."

Zhuo was at one of the vents, but could see nothing. "The sky is so blue. I wish I could see further. The air is almost sweet. Maybe it will not be so bad."

A voice from across the container, "Even if we are in paradise we are still prisoners. Maybe it will just be a prettier place to die!"

Zhuo looked over at the girl who had spoken, "You may be correct but we must try hard to survive so one day we can get away somehow."

"Shush now girls!" cried Jing-Wei. "I think they are coming!"

Zhuo could hear heavy footsteps approaching the container and within a few seconds they came to a stop immediately outside. Seconds later the door opened revealing four guards, each carrying a rifle held tightly in their hands. The girls were once again herded out of the unit, and as Zhuo and Ling helped each other climb down, they could see tall buildings in the distance, and many other vessels of many sizes. She could even see palm trees lining what appeared to be a sandy shore a distance away. She was also surprised that the many birds they thought were gulls turned out to be pigeons. There was not a gull in sight! What a strange land!

The light of day was fading fast, and before it disappeared for the night, Zhuo caught a glimpse of the sun being swallowed by the sea, its orange glow slowly sinking into the water. Darkness soon followed as they were escorted from their unit, where they joined the girls from the other containers, all of them in the same sad shape, if not worse.

Zhuo was also surprised to find that they were actually no longer at sea, but instead tethered beside a very long dock, which led to the shore where several trucks, and men, seemed to be waiting. The trucks were similar to the one that transported them from their village with the exception of being in a much better state of repair. There were other vessels attached to the dock as well, however there seemed to be no one else around at this time of night.

The girls were told to form several long lines near a set of steps that ran down the side of the ship to the dock. Zhuo and Ling huddled together, not knowing what was to happen next.

They heard the booming voice first, although the language was strange.

"Welcome to Hawaii Ladies!" was followed almost instantly by the interpreter echoing the words and trying, but failing, to put the same enthusiasm into the shout. None of the girls felt welcome and the appearance of the bald white man on the ship's deck did not make them feel any more so.

He casually strolled towards the girls, and continued through his interpreter. "You might remember me from last week. For those that have forgotten, my name is Lamar. Some of you will be chosen to remain on this island where you will work for me and my associates until your transit costs have been covered. If I do not pick you today you will be continuing on your journey to work for another of my partners. If you act wisely you will have the opportunity to pay off your debt and then prosper like everyone else in America." His voice rose in volume. "But, you must follow all the rules. If you do not you will lose this opportunity, and you will be punished. Do not ever doubt me!"

Ling squeezed Zhuo's hand tightly and looked up at her sister whose own face mirrored her fear. For a moment Zhuo did not realize what was happening. This strange man's booming voice, echoed immediately by his little interpreter, cast a surreal image of the events spiraling so out of control all around her.

Lamar and his shadow pranced up and down the line of frightened girls, looking over each girl as he came face to face with them. At every second or third girl he would motion to his men and that girl was pulled from the line, and made to stand in a different group, nearer to the stairway to the dock below. He was fast approaching Zhuo and Ling, but reached Jing-Wei before them and paused. He looked into Jing-Wei's eyes and said something to the man closest to him. Both men laughed at whatever was said while Lamar continued to look over Jing-Wei from head to toe. He touched her hair, almost gently, and ran his hand down the length of her arm. Then, as Jing-Wei seemed ready to pounce, he chuckled to himself, and moved to the next girl in the line, Ling.

Horror instantly gripped Zhuo, as she saw what was about to happen.

"No!" she cried out, "she is my little sister. She must stay with me! Please, I am begging you!"

She desperately held on to Ling's hand. Ling was now crying uncontrollably as the man looked directly at Zhuo. He allowed himself a moment so his eyes could travel the length of Zhuo's body and back again to her eyes. She saw pure evil looking back at her, but would not break the contact. She tried to smile at this man so he would show her some compassion, but before she could even do that, he signaled his men to separate Ling from the line. Both girls screamed and grasped for the other, but it was no use. Two men easily pulled Ling from Zhuo's grasp while two others restrained a hysterical Zhuo who, despite her size disadvantage, tried to fight off the much stronger men. Eventually she was pinned in place and could not move. She watched Ling being led away and once again tried to beg the man to change his mind, or at least to send her with her sister, but it was to no avail as the man had already moved further down the line. Zhuo watched, stunned into silence as the man finished his choices, and as he walked back down the line, Zhuo watched his every step and when he approached her she stared at him so intensely that he stopped in front of her, said something she did not understand, and walked away. Seconds later he disappeared from where he came, down the steps towards the dock. The girls he had picked were forced to follow him.

Zhuo called out to Ling again who turned to her sister but appeared too dazed to say a word. "I will find you little bell. No matter what happens, or how long, I will find you!"
She barely got those words out when she was again herded back towards her container. As she rounded the corner she took one last desperate look back and saw, through her tears, her sister just as she disappeared down the first step, and she said to herself.
"I will find you little one, no matter what it takes, I will find you!"

CHAPTER ELEVEN

JONAS couldn't help looking down at Jameson's legs and asked, "How do you know they were responsible for your accident?"

"It was no accident. When you've been a cop as long as I was you get an extra sense that regular people don't seem to have. My 'hit and run' was no more an accident than Harold here was the President of the United States."

Harold, who up to now, had stayed away from the two men while they talked, looked up from the magazine he was pretending to read, and said, "I could have been you know, if only I hadn't screwed up my taxes that year."

Jameson chuckled at Harold, and returned his gaze to Jonas, "Just before I was hit, I had a feeling that something wasn't quite right. I managed to look at the approaching vehicle just as it deliberately swerved into me, and I am sure to this day that I recognized the driver. I'm not sure where from, probably a mug shot or something like that, but I know that I knew him from somewhere, and he certainly knew me. Unfortunately he caught me perfectly and screwed up both of my legs right at the knees. They tell me that I flew back quite a ways, and I managed to hit my head on the side of a cement parking abutment. I was out immediately, and didn't see anything else until I awoke later in the hospital. I'm told that I will never be able to rehabilitate my legs, and if I can use them once in a while, that will be a bonus. I guess I should be thankful that I can get out of the chair for some things."

Jonas spoke up, "Was there an investigation?"

"Not much of one, that's for sure. They had some paint samples to follow up on but that didn't lead anywhere. There had to be some damage to the vehicle, but that's easy to get rid of quickly too. So, it was just another investigation that went nowhere. Luckily, I was working at the time, so managed to squeak out a decent pension. I still stay in contact with a few of my buddies on the force but as far as getting anywhere on the case, it is a complete dead end. I guess that's why I'm eager to assist you in any way I can. Harold here can attest for me, that I am a man of my word."

Harold peeked up from his magazine and shook his head, but with a slight smile on his face, but then said, "You could have worse fellows on your side Jonas, that I can say. If Brent here says he is going to do something, count on it being done."

"Okay, where do we start?"

"Well, first you need to familiarize yourself with the kind of people you are up against," Jameson said. "This Sanderson and his bunch are not the type that you can just walk up to and accuse of a crime. They'd only laugh at you, and worse, catch up with you later. No, the way to get to these types of guys is to play by their rules, which basically means there are no rules. Are you prepared to do that Jonas, to take the law into your own hands?"

Jonas got up from his chair and walked away from the table over to the fireplace, which sat dormant. He had spent a good part of the last several weeks thinking of nothing other than finding those responsible for Chrissy's murder, but now the time had finally come where he must decide what he was going to do, what he was prepared to do. Was he prepared to hunt these men down, and what was he going to do when he found them? He thought of his sister's smile, her laugh, and how he had always tried to look after her, even though it was usually her looking after him. He thought again, for the millionth time, about how she wouldn't have been in that alley if it weren't for him. Her scream still bounced around in his brain, and he knew that it would never leave unless he somehow made them pay for what they had done. He realized that he had no choice. If he was to live with himself in the future, then his path had been set. He looked back at the two men who were staring back at him. "Where do I start?"

"Okay Jonas, the main guy you are up against here in Seattle is this Sanderson guy I was telling you about. His close friends call him Deets, which is short for Dieter, which is his first name. Look, this guy could be a movie star. He's over six feet, handsome as hell and when he puts on a tux and smiles the women melt. Hell, even I think he's cute, but don't let the exterior fool ya. Under it all lays a beast, a nasty one at that. Rumple up his clothes a little, mess his hair, take away his smile, and this guy is a pure all out shit-storm. He's been known to charm even his worst enemies and then, once he's gained their trust, will use them until he feels they are no longer needed, and then bang! He eliminates them! And this guy knew your sister from somewhere. I don't know if it was school or through friends but I think he knew her. One of the fellows that helped me with the investigation, whom you will meet later, knew of him and figures there was some connection. He thought they may even have dated once or twice in the past. I think that had something to do with the original run-in you two had with them on the sidewalk. Anyway, that's not the real scary thing here because Sanderson, as bad as he is, and I mean he is real bad, isn't the worst of the bunch. He is part of a group that is all the same, and he is still climbing the ladder. I think he was the low guy on the pole that night, and if we can get to him, we'll find out who else was there that night."

Jonas hadn't uttered a word until Jameson was finished, then said, "I need to get near this guy. No, what I really need to do is get him alone!"

"That is true," agreed Jameson, "But there is a lot to learn before you would have a chance against him. They will have firepower and you will need not only the guts, but also the tools to go against them. I want those bastards to pay as much as anyone, so here's what I suggest. For the next two weeks I want you to come out here every day and I will teach you as much as I can. I have a nice little assortment of weapons, and have access to more fun things that you will need to know how to use if you hope to have a chance. I also have some folks you need to meet that will be on your side and could be a tremendous help. What do you say?"

"I'm ready to get started right now," said Jonas.

"Well, the first thing I need you to do when you leave here is get another car. That Beamer of yours will be way too obvious once you start digging around, especially if they get wind of you. I suggest you get an old retired yellow cab. There are about a million yellow cabs around, and if someone is following you, and believe me, once this thing gets started, they will be, you will need to blend in as much as possible. You also can't take it home with you. There are too many neighbors around that would notice and remember. Find a private parking garage where you can pull in, preferably underground, and leave by another exit, and walk a couple of blocks where you can pick up your car. I think that's enough for today. Being Friday, why don't you use this weekend to find the car and parking, get yourself some rugged boots and clothing, and we'll get started first thing Monday morning. Are you okay with all that?"

"The sooner this starts the better, but I know you're right. I have to be prepared." said Jonas.

Jameson looked at him, "Are you sure you are up to this? These guys play for keeps. If they catch on to us before we're ready it will not be good for us. We are either in this full hog, or we should back away right now."

"Brent, I can't say how much I appreciate what you are willing to do for me. I have thought of nothing else but what these guys did, and I am more than ready."

"Okay, Monday morning it is. You have a busy weekend ahead of you. Better get at it." He stood and extended his right hand, which Jonas grasped solidly in his.

Harold, who had mysteriously and quietly disappeared while the two men talked, stood waiting beside Jonas's car. He took note of the expression on Jonas's face. "I gather by that expression that you are going to proceed and there would be no point in trying to talk you out of it?" he said.

"No," said Jonas, "there wouldn't, but I appreciate all you have done for me, and likewise, for my grampa before me, and will be forever in your debt."

Before getting into the car Harold looked across the roof at Jonas. "That sounds an awful lot like goodbye and I will tell you right now that I'm in this too. Your dear old grampa meant a lot to me, and I promised him I would look after you, and that is exactly what I intend to do. Besides, the more I'm around you, the more I am close to Muriel's cooking!"

For the first time in a long while Jonas smiled, and said, "Are you sure it's just Muriel's cooking you want to get close to?" Harold simply smiled, jumped into the car, and pulled the door shut behind him.

CHAPTER TWELVE

ONCE again locked into her container/prison, the devastation to Zhuo's spirit was total. Only with Jing-Wei's help was she able to make it to her place in what was now a half empty container. She just couldn't believe that her little Ling was one of the many left behind. Jing-Wei watched as Zhuo settled heavily on to the narrow bench, not uttering a sound, hardly even moving. That didn't mean her mind was idle though. She could not believe what had happened over the last few days of her life. First, her parents abandoned her and Ling to these evil men, and then, the worst, Ling being taken from her. Was this just a terrible dream, a nightmare? Over and over again her mind replayed the look on Ling's face when she last saw it. Would she ever see her little sister again? She had failed to protect her and keep her safe. She closed everything else out while inwardly prayed that she would one day be able to make things right.

The Dubaskia left the Honolulu harbor in the middle of the same night, and despite the obvious sounds and changes in motion to all inside the container, Zhuo was unaware. She had barely moved, and had not spoken since re-entering the container. The other girls, with the exception of Jing-Wei, stayed away from the grieving girl. Jing-Wei tried her best to get a response, but Zhuo was in a different place. Her eyes, while open, were not seeing, and after a long while even Jing-Wei decided it was best to leave her alone.

The old ship sailed through uneventful waters for several days. Each day saw their container door open to allow the girls a short, but precious time on the ship's deck, and in the fresh sea air. Jing-Wei made sure Zhuo made it outside each day although she remained unresponsive to all attempts at conversation. During the long days and nights of sailing Zhuo sat upright in her seat but made very little eye contact. She took her regular turns at the air vents during the day, but at night, when the other girls were sleeping, she spent much more time there. She would stare at the stars, if they were visible, or allowed the frequent rain to soak her upturned face.

During the day she ate her meager allotment of food and drank her water, and when on the ship's deck she walked by herself to the nearest railing, and focused on where the ship had been, silently sending her prayers and thoughts to her sister.

Several days had passed when the sound of gulls could be heard. Even Zhuo seemed to show a response, and when one curious gull landed on the ship, close to their air vent, Zhuo surprised all by standing up, looking at the bird through the vent, and then saying out loud "We are again nearing land! We should be ready for more horrors!" With that she took her place on the bench. Jing-Wei made eye contact with her, and for the first time saw that her look was being returned.

"We will get through this Zhuo, we will." she said.

Zhuo turned her head towards her only friend and replied, "Yes, we will, and a price will be paid for our misery."
For a moment both girls held their friends' eyes, and both nodded their heads slowly.

CHAPTER THIRTEEN

It was a very busy weekend for Jonas. He was able to track down a vacant apartment about a forty minute walk from his own condo, if he cut through the Japanese Garden, and the Broadmoor Golf Club. It was an older building that had undergone some renovations recently, making it clean but still modestly priced. He felt it would be a good place to "hide out" should he need to disappear for a day or two. A quick call to Harold took care of some furnishings, also modest, and emergency supplies he may require. The best part of the building was the underground parking, where each unit had one space reserved. Jonas was also able to find an older yellow Buick that, although had never been used as a cab, could easily be mistaken for one. A few stops ensured it was tuned up, insured properly, and deposited in its new underground stall.

The weekend turned interesting while Jonas was in the South Centre Mall one afternoon, laden with packages containing work shirts, heavy sport socks, two or three ski masks, some extra pairs of jeans, a couple of dark sweaters, a pair of heavy duty Timberland Pro work boots, and a pricy pair of walking runners. Lugging all of the bags around made him hungry, and it was while he snacked on some surprisingly good food-court Chinese food, that he looked up to see a woman standing beside his table.

"I thought that was you, but wasn't sure. You haven't been around much since moving in, so I wasn't completely sure, but thought, what the hell, I'll take a chance."

It was his new neighbor, who he remembered as Tracy Wallace who, he had to admit, looked stunning. She was wearing a hugging white skirt and sleek top to match. Her hair had the windblown look, with her long blonde curls spreading wildly over her shoulders. Her eyes lit up with a smile when she realized he recognized her.

"Hi Tracy, I didn't expect to run into you here. You'll have to pardon the cliché, but do you come here often?"

Tracy's smile widened, "Funny you should ask that because, to be honest with you, I almost never come here. I was working close by, and needed a few things, and thought I'd pop in here and maybe grab a quick bite to eat at the same time. That looks really good too!"

Jonas looked down at his plate. "It actually is pretty good. The sweet and sour is excellent. Can I get you a plate? I'd love for you to join me."

"I would love to, but stay put, I'll be right back." She wandered away towards the many food kiosks surrounding the crowded food court. Jonas found himself following her with his eyes. He couldn't help noticing her hair as it bounced musically with her step, and his eyes were drawn to the sway of a perfect set of hips, which danced across the floor. His eyes weren't the only ones following her, as many a head turned as she passed by.

A few moments later she was back, placing a tray of food on the table before lowering herself into the seat facing Jonas. She glanced down at Jonas's packages, and said, "I thought it was only women who went to the malls and loaded up, but obviously I was wrong. That is quite the haul you have there!"

Jonas couldn't help it. He loved listening to her talk but he finally said. "I have been away for quite some time and I guess I need a lot of things, so I thought I'd just get them all at the same time and have it over with." Why did he feel like a nervous teenager?

She continued to smile. "I guess that's what the mall is good for. You say you've been away. Have you been travelling?"

Jonas looked down for a minute, as if preparing a response, and finally said, "I was in a serious accident and was in a rehab hospital up north for a while. It seems like I have a different body now and nothing fit when I got back, so here I am."

Tracy looked concerned. "It must have been a pretty bad accident for that to happen. I hope it's all okay now."

"Yeah, I'm doing alright. It was a long road, but I'm back now and looking forward to beginning my life again. One day maybe I'll tell you all about it."

"I'm just glad that you seem to be alright, and I think it will be nice to have you as a neighbor."

"I couldn't agree more. I'm not sure what I am going to do for a while, so don't know how much I'll be around the condo but I'll look forward to running into you now and then. In the meantime, I think you've met my housekeeper, Muriel, who I am sure will talk your ear off sometime."

Tracy laughed out loud, sending an electric sensation through Jonas. "I'll make sure to find out all about you from her."

The small talk continued for much longer than either of them had planned. While Jonas was guarded about his past, he did talk briefly about his football days, and his childhood. Tracy, for her part, told Jonas about her past. She had been married to her childhood sweetheart, who turned out to be no "sweetheart" at all. Divorced with no children (luckily), she ran a small marketing firm which managed to keep busy, even in a slow market, throughout the city area. That was why she was in the mall on a Sunday afternoon.

Tracy all of a sudden sat up. "Speaking of working all over the city, I'm almost late for an appointment. I hope you don't mind if I rush off. It was really great to see you."

Jonas looked up at her as she rose from her chair. "Not at all, it was great to see you too. I hope we can run into each other again sometime."

"I think that would be really nice."

"Until next time then," he said, sounding more formal than intended.

They shook hands briefly, and off she went, leaving Jonas with a feeling he hadn't felt in a long, long time. What the hell had just happened?

Starting Monday morning, the following ten days were straight out of Army boot camp. Although Jameson could not get out of his wheelchair but for short periods of time, he seemed to make up for it by pushing Jonas even harder. The days were spent doing all types of exercises, both physical and mental. The standard physical routines of push-ups, sit-ups, squats, pulls and pushes of all types was followed by mental stresses of fast-fire questions about his childhood, his parents, and even his sister. Many a times Jonas would look up at Jameson, wondering what all of this had to do with his mission.

"Jonas, listen to me. These guys are brutal, but most of them are not the sharpest knives in the drawer. Not only do you have to be as tough, or tougher, than them, you have to think faster too. It won't be too hard to out-think the first layer, but once you get near the big guys, it will get a lot harder. Those guys didn't climb the ladder just because they were the toughest. They also had some smarts. I just want you to be both physically and mentally prepared. Now, let's get into some other things that I think you will find a lot more interesting, and then there are some guys I want you to meet."

Behind Jameson's home was a work shed, although once entered Jonas could see that it was obviously no ordinary work shed. The walls were laden with the usual work fare, rakes, shovels, power tools and pretty well all the other things needed for the upkeep of a large property. Parked neatly was also a heavy duty riding lawnmower with several attachments lined up in close proximity, and a large quad, the mud encrusted on its tired showing recent use.

"Hard to believe that this close to the city there are a lot of places nearby that you can take that baby out, and lose yourself up in the hills," said Jameson.

Jonas looked the machine over. "I would love to take it out one day".

"That would be great, and we'll do that. I have a buddy that would lend us his machine so we can take them out together." replied Jameson.

"Perfect. Now what did you want to show me?"

Jameson smiled and walked to the back of the shed, where a long workbench had been constructed. Several locked doors could be seen below the top work surface. He unlocked one, and pulled out what appeared to be an old army surplus trunk. It too was locked.

"I never get company out here so this is actually pretty safe. I only keep it locked in case some wandering kids somehow get in here and snoop around, and I wouldn't want them to hurt themselves," he said with a twinkle in his eye.

After unlocking the trunk and removing a cloth cover Jonas saw several handguns laying within a plastic mold, each shaped exactly to hold a particular gun. "These are from my past and I have a very strong feeling that they will become useful again."

"I can't use your guns! Aren't they traceable?" asked Jonas. "I might have to use them for self-defense, or something."

Jameson again chuckled. "Now don't you go worrying about that, you won't be using these particular guns. I'll use these to teach you, and then you can decide which one you like the best. I can then get you a different one of the same model, but one that is not traceable."

"Jesus Brent, I don't know much about handguns. I doubt if I could actually hit anything with one.

"Jonas, if you were looking down the barrel of one of these goon's guns I think you would know what your choices would be. Shoot or be shot! When the time is right you'll know what you have to do and I think you'll do it."

Jonas, although very uncomfortable with the conversation, nodded his head in agreement, and watched as Jameson placed each gun on the work table in the middle of the shed.

Jameson, obviously quite proud of his display, started no different than a high school teacher would start a math class. "What we have here are several different types of guns, or pistols, as some people like to call them. Pistols! Ha! What a pussy name! Pistols are for duels and old movie pirates. These are fucking guns and they are the real thing. These things will kill you dead, so treat them kindly and with a lot of attention."

Before Jonas could say anything Jameson picked up one of the guns and continued, "This is a Beretta M9. It is very close to the Berretta 92F, which is essentially a military weapon, and has been used a lot in Iraq and Afghanistan." He handed it to Jonas who gripped it in his right hand, feeling more than a little bit uncomfortable.

"Don't worry Jonas, you'll get used to the feel and will come to love these little babies!"

"If you say so Brent," said a dubious Jonas.

"I'm not sure the Beretta is right for you anyway, but I wanted you to get the feel for a few different types of hand-held."

Jameson handed him another weapon, this one a bit smaller and considerably lighter than the Beretta.

"That's the HK45 Compact. It has an older brother, the HK45 which I don't have right now, but probably wouldn't suit you anyway. This one's nice and light but with pretty good stopping power as long as you get in close. The nice thing about this little baby is that you can also attach a sound suppressor to the barrel if needed. We'll keep this one in mind. I've been savin' the best one for last. I don't want to pick your weapons for you, but if you were to ask for my recommendation this one would be on the short list."

He handed Jonas a sleek black handgun.

"That one there is a Glock. I'm sure you heard the name before. I think James Bond made it famous in one of his movies. Anyway, it is hugely popular with law enforcement staff, fairly light, has short recoil, which would be good for you as a rookie, and takes a variety of cartridges."

Jonas held the weapon, liking its feel right away. "This one feels a little different than the others. It fits in my hand better."

"I guess that is why a lot of cops like it so much. They say the same thing," replied Jameson. "Let's take them out in the bush and try them out."

Three hours later Jameson and Jonas arrived back at the house, having spent the time deep in the woods, firing each weapon many times, and practicing loading and changing clips. Jonas was surprised to find that he quickly became comfortable with the feel of the weapon in his hand, and was able to gain confidence with his shooting as the afternoon wore on, to the point where he confirmed Jameson's recommendation of the Glock as the best of the lot.

"Now, that was a lot of fun," said Jameson, as they entered his home. "I haven't done that in a long while. I guess I'll have to do it more often from now on. You catch on pretty quickly, I might add."

"Thanks Brent, but I think it had to do more with the teacher than the student, but I thank you just the same."

"Okay Jonas, it'll take me about a week to round up another gun and ammo for you. I think it's time to meet some guys you'll find very interesting and helpful. Let me make a couple of calls and we'll get going."

It was already getting dark when Jameson and Jonas, riding in Jameson's old Ford pickup, arrived at an older building across from the Lynnwood Mall. The building itself was similar in size to those surrounding it with one big difference. While the surrounding buildings looked to be used for storage or warehouses, this particular building looked exactly like an old western saloon, complete with hitching rail in front.

"Are we meeting John Wayne here?" Jonas asked with a smile.

Jameson also wore a smile, "Actually we are meeting many hundreds of people. Well sort of. I was undercover a lot during my last few years of duty and this fellow worked with me many times. This is actually his storage warehouse for a costume store he owns downtown. He could dress you up as any one of many, many, people. C'mon, let's go inside."

They went up three wooden steps and entered a faux saloon-type door to a large room filled with hanging racks of clothing of all colors and types. Jonas could see long coats of many different shades and huge comical hats, as well as racks of costume jewelry that glistened and shone, even in the low light of the room. A voice called out from somewhere behind the racks of costumes.

"We're back here, c'mon back!"

Shifting through and around rack after rack of outlandish looking clothing, Jonas and Jameson finally entered an area that was free of costumes and contained a few chairs, a long table, and was bordered on one side by a counter, which contained a small under-cabinet fridge, and a counter-top microwave. There were two men sitting at the table, and both looked up when Jonas and Jameson finally broke free of the costume area.

Jameson spoke first. "Hi guys. I'd forgotten how really weird this place is." Turning to Jonas he continued, "Jonas, I'd like you to meet two guys that have absolutely nothing in common with me but have somehow been indispensable to me over the years."

Both men stood up and Jameson continued, pointing to a tall wiry man. "This is Arthur Chapman. Not Art though, but

Arthur, or, as I've come to know him, AC." Chapman took a step towards Jonas, reaching out with this right hand, which Jonas shook. For a thin man he had a very firm handshake. He was slightly taller than Jonas. He guessed about 6.3', with a lightly colored mustache and thin rimmed glasses. When he spoke, it was with a surprisingly deep voice.

"Glad to meet you Jonas. Brent has kept us up to speed on what is going on, but we'll leave it to you to really fill us in before we will know if we can help."

Before he could reply, Jameson introduced the second man who approached. "This is Brad Howes, only the best make-up man there is. As I said outside, he owns this warehouse and a costume house downtown. He has come in handy many times when I didn't want to look as handsome as I do every day."

Howes shook his head and laughed, "If that is handsome you are in some kind of trouble for sure. Nice to meet you Jonas, please just call me Brad, or Bradley if you like. I don't use letters like AC here," said Howes, with a friendly tone.

"Brad here has done the make-up in several movies and has rubbed elbows with some pretty big stars, so you will have to forgive his air of superiority," said Chapman.

Jonas liked both men immediately, and was starting to like the feeling that he might have a team, and might not have to get through this by himself.

All four men settled into chairs around the table, Chapman and Howes on one side, facing Jameson and Jonas on the other.

Jameson started, "Gentlemen, let me get right to the point here. Jonas, I've brought these fellows up to date with pretty well everything that has happened up to this point. They know about your sister, and they know about what happened to me. They also know who I think is behind all of this, and now I want you to be the one to tell them what you want to do about it. Gentlemen, once Jonas has said his piece there will be absolutely no hard feelings if you choose to not take part in what we aim to do. All we ask is that you keep it to yourself, and forget we ever had this little meeting."

Both men nodded.

"I'm not sure why you guys would even want to help me out in this, or even how you could do so," said Jonas, "but I agree with Brent in that I am thankful for this meeting, and know that what I intend to do will not succeed if I don't have help along the way. Brent has already been a huge help and I can't thank him enough. But, in saying that, he has a common bond with me in that some very bad people have hurt us both. You guys don't share that, so I can't ask you to step into the middle of something that isn't your fight."

Chapman interrupted, "Jonas, let me break in here for just a second. First of all, if we do help you out here, we won't be stepping into the middle of something that we don't know anything about." He looked from Jonas to Jameson with a chuckle and a bit of a twinkly in his eye. "And as to that common bond that you have with our handsome, but very old, ex-cop friend here, we too have a very strong bond with him." Looking towards Howes, he continued. "Let me put it this way. Brent here has used his influence on a couple of occasions that have made life easier for both Bradley here, and me. We owe him big time, and want to be there for him like he was for us. In my book that means helping out his friends too."

Jameson leaned forward, "Guys, you know you don't owe me a thing. I was lucky enough to be in the right place at the right time to help you guys out, that's all, so don't feel you have a debt to me."

Chapman ignored Jameson and continued, "To sum it up, Jonas, we were both pretty well fucked until Brent showed up and pulled us out of the fire, we both want to help here."

"I thank you guys, but this is serious shit and there could be some bad times for anyone attached to me," said Jonas.

Howes sat back in his chair and said, "We think we know what your intentions are in this, and both AC and I have talked about it at length. We just need to hear it directly from you as to what you aim to do."

Jonas paused a moment and then in a clear voice, "Guys, I need to track these fuckers down. I don't know who all of them are yet and will need help finding them."

Chapman then asked. "And what will you do when you find them?"

"I guess the simple answer is that I will track them down, one at a time, and when the time is right, there is no doubt what I will do.

I will make them pay for what they did to my sister!"

CHAPTER FOURTEEN

THE small window-vent above Zhuo in the container revealed only fog and blowing rain, however, the growing squawking of gulls, and the gradual slowing of the vessel, told her that they had reached their destination.

She remained at the vent when the ship's movements came to a complete stop. "I can see nothing, but I think we are beside another structure of some kind, maybe another ship." She said.

She sensed that all those in the dingy container hoped that the journey was finally over no matter what awaited them. All had lost weight and were suffering illnesses of some magnitude, so had clung to the hope that their suffering would somehow ease once the ship reached its destination.

The ship's movements had not been stopped for long when the container's doors were opened. This time she knew it would be different. What she would see would be her new home. Although frightened beyond words she was hopeful that this would be better than the last many days stuck inside the dark confines of the container.

They were told to exit the container and could see that they were indeed moored beside another ship, between which ran a long wooden dock.

Zhuo and Jing-Wei were able to see through the fog, past the end of the dock, where many large buildings rose in what was obviously a very large and modern city. They could also see many other ships, most being larger than the Dubaskia, with monster-like cranes along the sides, moving side to side taking containers off, or loading them on to the vessels. They were only able to get a quick momentary glance at this strange new sight before men were yelling at them, and motioning them into a straight line on the deck in front of the containers. Zhuo noticed that there were now fewer girls than had entered the containers. Not long after forming a line did she notice a small group of men approaching from the ship's loading area. In that group two of the men stood out as the obvious leaders. They were both dressed in suits, with crisp shirts and ties, and polished shoes.

One man stepped forward and approached the line of frightened girls. He was the younger of the two men and when he spoke his voice was nervous at first, as if he was afraid of the older man behind him. Zhuo noticed that he quickly overcame his nervousness, and soon appeared confident, his voice loud and clear, even though in a language Zhuo could not understand. When he spoke, he almost smiled, and his black wavy hair moved in the wind, often falling over his eyes causing him to quickly shake his head so that the hair would move back to its rightful place.

Although Zhuo could not understand his words it became apparent that he was in charge and only once the interpreter started speaking could she determine just how bad their situation was.

The younger well-dressed man was almost yelling, causing the interpreter to also raise his voice, so that now the girls had to listen to two men trying to out yell each other.

"My name is Sanderson and this gentleman is Gant. We are in charge here. You work for us and will do as we say in all things. That must be understood! Look around you. This city is called Seattle. You are now in the United States of America, the greatest country in the world, and it is now your home. You will be fed and given a bed to sleep in. In return for your passage on this ship, and food and shelter, you will work for us until all is repaid plus interest. Some of you will work temporarily in sewing factories until you are needed elsewhere, and others will work immediately in the city. You do not have a choice as we will pick who works where and we will not tolerate any argument or discontent! Is that understood?"

Again all of the girls except Zhuo nodded their heads. She continued to stare at the man.

Once the interpreter had finished his translation, the girls had but a second to process this information, and nodded their heads in understanding. Only Zhuo stood motionless.

Sanderson continued, "We will now separate you into two groups, one for the factories, and one for the city. Again, you do not have a choice in this matter and you will be dealt with quickly if you do not comply!"

With this, the older man, known as Gant, and Sanderson, approached the lineup of girls from the left of Zhuo. They examined each girl in turn, and occasionally Gant would motion to the other man, and the girl they were looking at was removed from the line, and told to stand near the gangplank to the dock. Zhuo watched as the one group of girls was quickly becoming two and they were getting closer to Zhuo. Only Jing-Wei and two others stood between her and the two men. When they passed by the two girls and approached Jing-Wei, Zhuo could sense their threat. She was afraid but determined that she would do everything to not crumble under their stare.

Gant approached Jing-Wei, and looked directly into her eyes. Jing-Wei's stare did not waver. She was almost as tall as the man so their eyes were level.

Gant said, "What is your name?"

Through the interpreter she answered, Jing-Wei, which means Small Bird."

Gant looked at the interpreter and Sanderson, and said, "Small Bird? Are you shittin' me? This girl's as tall as I am for Christ's sake!" He laughed out loud and continued, "From now on her name is just Jing. She is going to the city." She was led away from the line to the other group of girls.

Zhuo wanted to reach out to her but could see that it would do no good. Instead she continued to stare at the men, who now approached her.

"What is your name?" he asked.

Zhuo did not look at the interpreter when she answered but instead continued to stare into the eyes of the man named Sanderson. "Zhuo" she said.

"Jew?" he said to the interpreter. "What the hell kind of name is that? She's no Jew!"

The interpreter spoke again, "In English the name sounds like 'Jew' but is actually spelled differently."

"I don't give a rat's ass how it's spelled. We can't call her Jew for Christ's sake! We'll call her Su! No 'e'. That's close enough. From now on your name is Su."

The interpreter was able to explain the name change to Zhuo, who finally understood that her English name was Su, and that is what she would be called from now on. She did nothing to indicate that she cared, and held the man's stare.

He seemed to grow uneasy with her and turned to Sanderson. "She's giving me the creeps Deets, you can have her." He left the newly named Su standing in the line, and approached the next girl.

As the men moved down the line, they selected two more girls to join Jing-Wei. Then they escorted their victims down the gangplank, and off the ship. Su realized her friend was leaving, and wanted to shout out to her, but instead remained steadfast in the line, refusing to look anywhere but straight ahead. Moments later their guards herded them towards the rail of the ship. Looking over Su could see the first group of girls already seated in the back of a truck as it crawled away down the pier. It wasn't long that they too were led down the walkway and loaded into their own truck. Su sat among the other girls, the rain starting to fall heavier now, and the fog prevented them from seeing too far from the pier. The truck started up and lurched forward, headed away from the pier, and onto a paved roadway. Su was startled at the number of vehicles using the road. Never had she seen so many vehicles at one time.

The truck drove only for a short time and slowed to turn, through a gateway, into a large fenced area. There were two-storey buildings on three sides of the area, The truck pulled up to a building situated in the middle of them. All of the buildings showed signs of many years of rain beating down upon them, with rusted gutters only partially keeping the running water from soaking the ground surrounding the building. The middle building that they parked near was the only one with lights on in what appeared to be a second story. The back hatch was lowered and the girls jumped down to the puddled ground.

"Welcome to your new home ladies! This is where you will live and work, for now at least. You will see downstairs is the sewing factory and upstairs is your accommodation. I suggest you make the best of this," said the guard. He motioned them towards a set of weathered double doors.

Before taking her turn to enter the building, Su was able to glance at her surroundings, and could see, faintly through the rain and thinning fog, many buildings on a hill overlooking the area that held this building. She wondered if anyone could see her down here, and if they could, would they really care. They should, she thought, because she knew she would not be a permanent resident of this place. She entered the building.

Su followed the other girls through a pair of large wooden doors which swung inwards on rusting, squeaky hinges. The first thing Su saw was row upon row of tables, each with some sort of machine on top. Seated at the tables, and facing each machine was a woman, some were young like Su, but most were older. Su wasn't sure if they were actually older, or merely worn out by their efforts. The ceilings were high with a hanging fan swirling slowly above each table. The noise level grew louder as they approached the work areas, with each machine adding a dull hum to the sound of the others, creating a uniform dull roar throughout the cavernous building.

As Su's group was led around the rows of tables she could see that the women tending the machines were fully engrossed in their work, shuffling material into one end, adjusting it, and helping it feed out the other. She did not look up at the new group as they passed. Only when they reached the far end of the tables did Su notice one of the workers watching her intently. The woman's table was the last one on the outside row, and as Su passed her table, the woman followed her with her eyes, showing no emotion. Su felt her own eyes lock with the woman's, and a chill ran down her spine, somehow knowing that she was not welcome here, and she would have to be careful.

Sanderson was again speaking to the group, the ever-present interpreter's voice echoing his. "Ladies, this is where you will work until you are moved elsewhere. An instructor will also be assigned to you in order for you to learn your duties. You will be shown your living quarters, which are upstairs. I remind you that you are here to work and to pay off your debt. Until your debt is paid you will work here six days a week, whatever shifts you are assigned, and you will do so with no complaints. The people here are under my instructions to not tolerate any problems. If you cause trouble your life here will be difficult, and you will be dealt with seriously and quickly. I am a very serious man and will act immediately and harshly should one of you cause trouble for me. I hope that is understood! Now, I will turn you over to Mrs. Chow who will assign you your sleeping quarters and explain how everything works here. I warn you now that challenges to her authority will be treated the same as if you challenged me."

He turned to an older, husky Oriental woman who spoke in a dialect close enough for Su to understand most of what she was saying.

"You will call me Mrs. Chow! I will be your boss until your debt is paid and you can leave. I will assign you to a teacher who will show you what your job here on the floor will be. You will start first thing tomorrow, which is Thursday, and will work six days and have the seventh day off to rest. As Mr. Sanderson said, you are here to repay your debt. You will be paid a salary of two dollars per hour, and will work twelve hours each day. From your daily salary will be subtracted the cost of your food and lodging upstairs, or about fifteen dollars a day. The remaining amount, less a little for you to keep as spending money, for your essentials, will be deducted from the debt you owe plus interest. It was expensive to bring you here, so you will have to work long and hard to pay this off. If you work hard you may be rewarded by moving into the city and working in one of the owner's houses."

Su wondered what it meant to work in the owner's house, but for now was determined to not cause problems that would draw attention to her. She also promised herself that she would not stay here long but realized that, for the time being at least, she should blend in, learn her role, and not make trouble.

She again listened to Mrs. Chow who, softening her tone, continued, "Girls, I know you are frightened and confused. This is a foreign land and you have been brought here against your wishes. There is nothing you or I can do about that. This place is not that bad. You will work long and hard but you will also have food to eat and a warm place to sleep. In many cases this will be better than you had before. All I ask is that you follow the rules and do as I say. If you do, all will be good and one day your debt will be paid, and you will be free to go wherever you want."

Then her tone drew dark again, "But if you do not follow the rules. If you do not do as I say. You will be penalized, and it will take you even longer to gain your freedom. You must remember that at all times! Now, we will go upstairs where you will meet your instructors, and be assigned your sleeping quarters."

She turned and started up steep wooden stairs towards the second level of the warehouse. Upon reaching the top of the stairs Su saw four neat rows of beds, all small singles, cots really, with a tiny two-drawer night table beside each. On top of each was an old looking lamp, its shade made of cheap paper which was spotted in places and torn in others. The bed covers were worn and of many different colors.

Each girl was taken towards the beds and told to stand at the end of a vacant one. There were only eighteen girls and twenty vacant beds, Su took the third one in from the end and the rest of the girls left those two vacant in order to move further down the line away from the stairs. Su stood dutifully at the end of the bed waiting for whatever was to come next.

Mrs. Chow spoke again, "You will sit on your bed and wait for your instructor, who will have a group of you to train, so you will wait your turn. She will explain what you are to do next."

She then turned and walked down the stairs, her shoes clunking on the wood, the sound fading as she reached the bottom.

Su sat patiently on her bed, which she found surprisingly soft, quite a bit softer than the small bed she had shared at home with her sister. She again thought of little Ling and hoped and prayed that wherever she was, she was okay. Su's determination to get to her sister only grew stronger with each day and her mind was already taking in her surroundings and wondering how she could turn them to her advantage so that she could escape the nightmare she was in.

After waiting for a long while Su heard someone approaching from the stairs. The footfalls were not as heavy as those of Mrs. Chow, and soon appeared a small oriental girl of about Su's age. She stopped at the end of Su's bed.

"My name is Lucy," she said. "I will be your instructor. I will show you what to do downstairs at your work station, and also explain how things work up here when you are not working. For now make your bed as comfortable as you can and tomorrow morning we will start.

Su watched as Lucy visited five other girls then dropped herself on the bed directly opposite her.

"This is not so bad a place if you behave. I will try to help you all I can, but if you get into trouble I too will be in trouble. Please try as hard as you can. It will be meal time soon and then you must rest."

Su examined the tread-bare blankets on her bed and finally lay down, having to double over her pillow to make it softer. She stared at the roof which, thankfully, seemed to be keeping the heat in and the rain out. She started to drift off to sleep when a loud horn sounded, startling all of the girls out of their short lived slumber.

Lucy jumped up from her bed and called for 'her girls' to follow her. They were led down the stairs and past the rows of tables to another large room, where that day's workers were already lined up at long tables, on top of which stood various large containers of food that was being scooped onto plates. The girls were told to join the line.

The food line moved quickly and Su was handed a plate and knife and fork, all plastic. Having used chopsticks or her fingers all her life, these instruments felt strange in her hands. As the line moved forward her plate was eventually heaped with a sort of stew and two pieces of bread. She followed Lucy to a table, and after watching the others use their utensils and dip their unbuttered bread in their stew, she did the same and managed to eat her dinner, surprised at how hungry she was. The food was strange tasting to her but not at all unpleasant, especially compared to her meals of the last many days while locked away on the ship. As with the others, she found herself using the last remnants of her bread to mop up every morsel of the remaining stew on her plate.

Lucy turned to her, "What is your name?"

"My name is Zhuo" she answered, "But here they tell me it cannot be said like that and they have changed it to Su, so that is the name I will use."

Lucy continued to look at her, "Then Su it will be. I am glad you have eaten all of your food. You will need your strength to get through the long days, but I will help you. I think I can see strength in you that can be a good thing, but it can also make trouble for you. Be careful who you talk to here and always obey the rules, and Mrs. Chow. I think you should also learn English so that you will better understand how it is here. I will teach you as much as I can."

Su returned Lucy's stare and, not sure what to say, replied, "thank you Lucy, I will want to get out of here as soon as possible to find my sister so I will try not to cause trouble for you."

Lucy turned to the other girls, "let us go back upstairs and get some sleep. Tomorrow we must be up at five AM to eat, and be at our work stations at six sharp. We must not be late!"

The girls followed Lucy from the dining area, through the work room, which was once again filling up with workers now that the meal break was mostly over. Then up the stairs to their beds. Su could see that many had already crawled under the covers and were fast asleep. Su, and the recent arrivals, had been on a long and frightening journey and needed rest more than anything. For most it was the first night's sleep in a bed, albeit not a comfortable one, in what felt like forever, and most soon fell into a deep sleep.

Su fixed her blankets as best she could and lay her head on her pillow, but it was a long time before sleep overtook her. Her last thoughts were of her pretty little sister. She pictured the thousands of times the two girls had been left alone, and how they somehow were able to get their work done, and occupy themselves with some games and laughter. Su's heart ached with longing for those times again. She prayed that Ling would be able to survive long enough until her sister could get free and come to her.

CHAPTER FIFTEEN

DIETER (Deets) Sanderson left the warehouse in a sour mood. There was something about this batch of girls, and one in particular, that bothered him, although he'd be damned if he could figure it out. He made a mental note to keep an eye out for trouble from that *one*. Why didn't Gant just save him the pain in the ass and take her too? Then he wouldn't have this nagging feeling in the back of his mind. He found her stare oddly intimidating and had the distinct feeling he would have to be careful with her. Jesus man, he thought to himself, you must be getting soft! Who gives a shit about some little bitch from the backwoods in China anyway? She'd probably end up dead soon enough and this little problem would be taken care of.

Approaching the huge SUV, he had to duck in order to not hit his head on the door frame, and flopped into the back seat, the door slammed shut behind him. Sanderson could almost hear the springs of the vehicle moan when his two bodyguards jumped into the front seat, as the more than six hundred pounds settled in.

As the big vehicle pulled out of the warehouse lot Sanderson looked back at the old rust-lined building and thought about the workers inside. This had turned out to be a sweet deal for him and his partners. Cheap products put together by even cheaper labor meant huge profits, rivaling even those from the drug side of the business. And once they sorted out the good-looking ones it would increase the bottom line. Add in the other hookers they had throughout the north-west and their little enterprise was turning out well. Of course, there were bumps in the road along the way but he had always found a way around them. His charming good looks, reputation from college football days, and a presence when entering a room, had all served him well.

Ironically, his parents had made their fortune also in the business of manufacturing clothing products. Upon their passing, their loving, only son, Dieter, had used his inheritance not only to continue his privileged way of life, but to make significant changes to his parents' business ventures, dismantling parts of the business, mostly those labor driven, and secretly resurrecting those same parts but with the use of cheap (don't call it slave) labor. His partners were thrilled and invited him into their other enterprises.

This warehouse, now only visible through the vehicle's rear window, was one of four that they jointly held. Sanderson was still amazed that a small monthly payment to a few well-placed dock executives, some higher ranking police officials and, of course, the always reliable stable of politicians, was enough to keep the building, and its inhabitants, completely off the radar. Of course their ownership was buried in mounds of false official paperwork and ownership documents, so that tracing it to 'The Group' would be nearly impossible. Only when he, and Gant, had to 'inspect' the new workers and their progress was there any risk as this was the only time that they could actually be found on the property and thus connected to it. This was probably why he felt so uneasy. Forget the new workers, for him the place was just a bit creepy and he was always glad to be away from it.

He leaned forward to speak to one of his bodyguards. The driver was named Lou, a ruthless, bald, very bad man. Sanderson wasn't exactly sure where he was from and didn't care as long as he did his job, and did it well. The other man up front was called Cam, a gentle name for brute of a man who liked to inflict pain on his victims. These two thugs had been with Sanderson for about two years now, and a very good paycheck guaranteed their loyalty.

"So what's the story on Riggs? I thought it was all under control, especially after the last time."

Lou responded, "He's back at it Deets! He's been short the last two times. You told us to tell you if it happened again and now it has, so we're tellin' ya."

"Fuck man. Is this guy stupid or what? Did he think we wouldn't know? What a fuckin' moron! Let's get this over with. Is everything arranged?"

Cam turned from the passenger seat, "It is boss. You just have to talk to him, and the rest is taken care of like you asked."

"Alright, the sooner this is done the better. I've got a dinner to get to."

Without comment Lou and Cam stared out the front window of the vehicle as it went up Mercer Street, turning just past some construction, and left into a parking lot surrounded by two story buildings containing mostly small businesses. They parked in front of an old brick building with a worn sign reading 'Pacific Parts' over a seldom used double garage door. There was a separate single door beside it, and this is where Sanderson and his two shadows entered the building. They walked past what had been a sales counter at one time, but was now reduced to a dust covered divider between some old desks and a narrow hallway that led to the back of the shop. The men entered the shop area and walked directly to what was once used for painting, and was mostly isolated from the rest of the shop. Sanderson pushed in the heavy old door and saw, to his disgust, a small man sitting on an old wooden chair in the middle of the room. Though the room was chilled the man was sweating profusely, with beads of moisture running from his temples, soaking the tops of his shirt collar.

"What's goin' on Mikey?" asked Sanderson, as he approached the middle of the room.

"Hey, Deets! Man I don't know what the fuck's the matter with me, but I fucked up again."

"Mikey, you did more than fuck up this time!"

"But Deets------"

"Don't you fucking call me Deets!" Sanderson shouted. "When you are part of my team, and working hard like the rest of the guys, then you can call me Deets! But you aren't working hard for the team, are you Mikey?"

"I'm sorry Mr. Sanderson. I know I fucked up again but I can make it up to you." He cried. "I know I can make it good."

"Mikey! What the hell's wrong with you? How can you make it up to me when you continue to rip me off? You know, when you rip me off you are ripping these guys off too?" He waved at the two men standing off to the side of the room. Mikey shuddered when he looked at them, and quickly looked away.

"I was just desperate Dee----, I mean Mr. Sanderson. I didn't know what else to do! I fucked up."

"You did more than fuck up Mikey, you've lost my trust. What can I do with a guy I can't trust?"

"Honest to God Mr. Sanderson, I didn't know what to do. I only needed a few bucks."

"For a hit Mikey, you screwed our whole team up for a fucking hit! How many times do I have to say it? You can sell the stuff but you can't use. If you do you can't work for me, period! So now I've got a user working for me. I can't have that. What would the rest of the guys think? How long do you think it would be before they thought it was okay, and the next thing you know my whole fucking team is wired, or high. I can't have that Mikey."

Sanderson paced the floor in front of the cowering man.

"Jesus fucking Christ Mikey, now we have a big problem and I have to do something about it."

"Please boss, what can I do to make this right?" he cried, tears flowing uncontrollably down his face.

"Well, there really is one thing you can do."

"What is it boss? I'll do anything, just name it."

Sanderson pulled a gun from his pocket.

"No boss, you don't need to do that. I told you, I'll make it right, really I will. It won't ever happen again. There has to be something I can do."

Sanderson stopped pacing and looked at Mikey, who looked back hoping there was still a chance he could get out of this.

"You know what Mikey? I think there is a way you can set an example for the rest of the guys."

"Just name it Mr. Sanderson. What can I do?"

"You can die!" Sanderson raised the weapon and fired one clean shot that entered Mikey's forehead just above his left eye, and exited with a mess on the floor behind him.

Sanderson turned to the two men, who had not moved during the whole conversation.

"Cam, please clean this up. You know what to do. Lou, get me out of here. I'm gonna be late for my dinner."

Forty-five minutes later Sanderson's black SUV pulled up in front of a trendy restaurant located as close to the middle of downtown as you could get. Sanderson exited the vehicle wearing his usual custom tailored suit with the ever-present bowtie (tied himself every time), and apart from his always perfect dress code, his hair stood out as his only flaw, with wild strands at the front always cascading over his forehead, causing the habit of either running his hands through his hair, or more often than not, simply jerking his head sideways, throwing the wayward hair back into place. This sometimes made people around him think that he had a nervous twitch. People that knew him also knew that nervousness was definitely not one of his weaknesses, far from it.

As usual, it was foggy and had been raining in Seattle, so when Sanderson stepped out of the vehicle he had to be careful to keep from stepping into one of many puddles that still lay on the side of the street. Partially jumping over one of these mini-lakes he stumbled and nearly went down, only saved by quick action from Lou, who grabbed his arm at the last second. As he regained his balance Sanderson heard a small chuckle to his left, near a lane that separated the restaurant from the next building. He looked at the dark area and could make out a man sitting there, leaning against the wall. Instead of walking directly into the restaurant he approached the man in the dark.

"So you think that was funny? Would it have made your day to see me fall on my ass?" he said as he got closer to the man.

"No sir, I was not laughing at you sir," said the man, obvious to Sanderson that this was one of Seattle's homeless. "I merely found it amazing how fast your driver there was able to get around the car and save you from getting soaked. That was all, sir. I didn't mean to insult you in any way."

Sanderson could make out the man better now that he was closer, and he could certainly smell him, or at least he smelled something that was unpleasant, and by the look of this man's clothing he was sure it was a human smell. The man wore an overcoat that was probably a businessman's at some time during the last ten years, but was now only just able to hold itself together. The man's hair stood straight up and his face showed no sign of a razor for a long time.

Sanderson looked at his watch and then up at the restaurant entrance, where he could see people sitting at window-side tables, hoisting crystal glasses filled with expensive wine. He decided to move along, and took one last look at the homeless man.

"Next time, keep your comments to yourself, or you could make things worse." He turned without another look at the dirty man, and entered the restaurant.

The door hadn't even closed behind him when Sanderson heard his name shouted out from at least two different directions. The restaurant was full to capacity and, as he entered, many people looked up from their tables to watch his entrance. He played the room like an athlete, shaking hands with men wearing expensive suits, letting his lips gently touch the cheeks of women who seemed to be in a competition as to who could show the most cleavage without spilling out. He waved and pointed, shouting out first names as if these were his best friends. In truth, he knew only a handful, but magically made it seem like he was delighted to see them all.

He finally approached a table where a well-known local celebrity, and a powerful Seattle politician were seated, sliding into a chair across from them.

"It is good to see you Deets," said the celebrity. "I was wondering if you were going to make it."

"I had a little business to finish up, and that damn construction on Mercer is a mess," he said, while looking directly at the politician, who nodded but made no comment. "Let's order, I'm starving."

The meal lasted well into the evening, and by the time the last course (and several bottles of the best wine) was consumed, all at Sanderson's table were feeling no pain. It was with disappointment that he finally forced himself away from the table and exited the restaurant, to be met by Lou at the side of his vehicle. While he was leaning forward to get into the car he happened to glance towards the lane where he had seen the homeless man a few hours before. To his surprise the disgusting man was still sitting there and appeared to be sound asleep. Instead of getting into the vehicle Sanderson straightened up and once again approached the prone man. He reached behind him, took out his wallet, pulled out a bill, and was about to place it on the man, when his movements startled the sleeping man, who yelled out, and jumped up as if prodded with a hot iron.

"Jesus! Shit man! What the fuck ya doin'?" he yelled as he skipped around Sanderson.

Sanderson, still feeling the effects of too much wine said, "you almost scared the shit out of me, you dirty old scumbag! I was just tryin' to give you a few bucks so you could, you know, maybe grab a hot meal or something. But if you don't want it that's fine too, I really don't give a shit now."

"No, no, I'll take it. I'm sorry 'bout that but you scared the shit outa me too." And he reached out for the money in Sanderson's hand.

Sanderson handed him the bill and turned to walk back to his vehicle. He was almost there when he again turned around and faced the ragged man. "Do I know you from somewhere?"

CHAPTER SIXTEEN

AT 5AM exactly, the horn sounded, and Su, startled as she was by the loud screeching, was also surprised at how well she had slept. She quickly tidied up her area, and for the next hour she followed the others as they went through the motions of relieving themselves in the tiny bathroom (Su had never before used an indoor bathroom), sprinkling water on their faces from a rusty tap and equally rust stained sink, and then finally flowing through the meal line. Here Su was again given a plate, real this time, and a knife and fork, still plastic. She stepped through the line-up and received her food, a blend of what looked like mashed eggs and a piece of toast with a tiny patch of butter melting on it. She took her place at a table with several other girls from her group and was soon joined by Lucy, who seemed quite lively and ready to meet the day.

Lucy started to talk almost immediately and in between mouthfuls she said, "Girls, today you will be expected to learn several things. Do not worry if it is difficult at first, but you must try to learn quickly as you will be expected to keep up. Mrs. Chow will be watching your progress, and I too will be judged on how you do. The machines are not difficult to learn if you pay attention when I am teaching you. You must also learn the language they speak in this country. It is called English, and will seem very awkward at first. It is also important if you ever hope to one day pay your debt and be free in America.

Su listened carefully, and, as she had already told herself, was determined to learn as much as possible in as short a period of time as she could. She knew this would be the only way for her to someday gain her freedom and begin her search for Ling.

The thought of her little sister pulled her concentration away from Lucy and it was only the stare from another girl that brought her back. Although Lucy was still talking about fitting in and working hard, Su could not help but return the stare of the other person. It was the same girl that had given her hateful looks from the work table when she had first arrived. The girl's stare was so intense Su felt that it peered into her very soul. She thought, do I know this person, or did I do something to offend her? She wanted to shout out to her but did not want to attract attention, so she simply returned the look, not allowing her eyes to leave the other girl's. Eventually the other girl made a flicking gesture with her fingers, shook her head, and looked away. Su knew there would be trouble but hoped she was wrong, and thought again, what did I do to anger a total stranger?

Su and the others finished their meager meal and were escorted, by a still animated Lucy, downstairs to the work area. Lucy's table was closest to the stairs and she placed each of the girls at the same table, four to a side facing each other, with Su situated beside Lucy. In front of them they each faced a strange looking machine, but Lucy calmed their fears by slowly going through what the machine was to do, and how they were to work with it.

It didn't take long for the girls to learn their tasks and, although thoughts of escape, and a reunion with her little sister were never far from her mind, Su managed to settle into a daily routine, awakening to the horn at five AM six days a week, moving slowly through the habits of cleaning up in their sparse washroom, receiving their meal, and eating at the same table with the same group of girls.

Su had no difficulty learning her particular tasks with the machine in front of her, especially after spending nearly twelve hours each day with it. She learned how to feed the material into one end, always at the perfect angle and depth, place another smaller piece of material, which she later learned was a label, into a slot on the machine above the original material, depress a small switch which caused the machine to hum loudly for a few seconds while it fastened the two pieces together. She then had to gently pull the material out of the machine and pass it along to the next girl, whose machine did something different. Su assumed the product was complete once it finished its journey down the table.

At the end of each day they would again make their way to the dining area, eat a quick meal, usually only noodles and rice, and then thankfully collapse onto their beds, sometimes asleep before changing into their sleeping clothes.

Su was fortunate in that the mundane daily work was also broken up a little by the fact that she sat next to Lucy. Over the weeks Su learned very much from Lucy, learning to speak and understand some simple English words and phrases, and never stopped Lucy from teaching her more. She knew that one of the secrets to escape would be in knowing some of the local language and customs.

Lucy also seemed to know much about how the warehouse worked. She explained to Su that trucks brought in bales of material and left with boxes of clothing, mostly cheap t-shirts and sweaters, which she had worked on since arriving. But Lucy also knew a bit about the management of the place. Although Lucy was responsible for a small group of girls, they were all under the rule of Mrs. Chow who, thankfully, had not had any interaction with Su other than stopping by her table and watching her work, occasionally making sure the labels were being attached properly. Mrs. Chow reported to Mr. Sanderson, whom Su remembered from the ship and her arrival at the warehouse. She had only seen him a few times since that arrival and only then at a distance. Every time he visited he left with three or four of the girls, who were never seen again. Lucy only said that they were taken to work at a different location. On more than one occasion the man had been accompanied by the same man that had taken Jing-Wei. When he was there he made a point of walking along the tables, watching the girls work. Su felt he was only pretending to inspect the work, but was more interested in the workers. Su could not stop the fear that washed over her, especially when he stood near, and seemed to watch her every move.

On one of his visits Su found herself under closer scrutiny from this man, as well as Mr. Sanderson. Despite her fear that she would be one of those taken from the factory, her anger at being used by these men overcame her fear for a moment, and she looked up from her machine as the men stared at her. She allowed her eyes to meet theirs in turn before slowly dropping them back to her work. In the men's eyes she saw only cruelty and not even a measure of caring for the individuals that were slaving at their work. She was disheartened to know that her freedom had to be somehow obtained through them. They also held the answer to where her sister was. Su had to find a way to get to them, but how?

Her thoughts on that day were quickly brought back to reality as Lucy punched her softly on the shoulder. "Do your work Su! These men are the owners of this business. It is not your place to even look at them."

Then she whispered, "Su, please be careful. These men will kill without even thinking, or worse. They will take you to their houses and you will have to do terrible things. You must not draw their attention."

"I understand," said Su. She returned to her work without another word. Her mind, though, would not be quieted so easily.

The routine was broken on the seventh day of each week. On this day it was expected that the girls would clean their own personal space, do their laundry, and simply rest. There was nothing else to do anyway although there was a small deck off the dining area which was used by the girls to get some fresh air. Not much could be seen from the deck as it faced another building's blank concrete walls, but it offered a sampling of the sounds of a busy harbor. They could hear many different sounding fog horns and, of course, the non-stop squawking of the gulls. Every once in a while a solitary, wet looking, gull would fly close, even landing on their deck for a moment, before soaring off.

It was now deep into the fall, so often times the steadily falling rain prevented the girls from staying out on the deck. Su found that she didn't mind the rain and, in fact, often felt re-energized when looking up as the drops fell towards her.

It was on one of those rainy rest days that Su found herself on the deck, enjoying the light drizzle that fell over her, when Lucy approached her, a serious look on her face. "Do not look over your shoulder but I fear that Mei is watching us and wants to cause trouble," she said.

It was only natural for Su to look anyway, and sure enough, there standing in a group of other girls, was Mei, the same one that had stared at her from the work table. Although in a group, Mei's attention seemed to be only for Su, and the look was not comforting. When she noticed Su returning her look she broke away from the group and walked briskly towards her.

Before Su could say anything, a huge arm circled Lucy's shoulders.

"Well now," she spoke in heavily accented English. "What are you two girls whispering about over here? You two are always mumbling to each other and its starting to piss me off!"

Su looked up at the larger woman, "Why would you want to know what we talk about? Are you afraid that we are talking about you?"

"Well, were you?" The woman scowled.

"Why would we waste our time talking about you?" responded Su, drawing a chuckle from several of the other young women, who were now watching intently, anticipating trouble, anything to break up the monotony of their days.

"So you think you're some kind of wiseass, do you? Wiseasses piss me off even more." said Mei.

Su, although still intimidated by this woman, could not stop herself, "Our conversation is none of your business, and, as I said before, we wouldn't waste it talking about you."
Mei pushed Lucy aside, where she stumbled and fell to the deck.

The larger woman walked to within inches of Su. "If you want trouble with me then I will be glad to give it to you."

Su was surprised to find her fear was not building but was being replaced by anger. She was trapped in a foreign land, being treated as a slave to men who had also taken her sister away from her, and she could not hold back. She lashed out, put both of her hands on Mei's shoulder, and pushed her away.

"If you think I want trouble with you then you are wrong. It is you that must decide if you want trouble with me!"

Mei, who had been caught by surprise and had not expected the smaller woman's action, barely managed not to fall beside Lucy, who was still lying on the deck and looking up at the other two. Mei was furious at being bested in front of a growing group of women on the deck.

"You have messed with the wrong person, you little whore! I see you watching when the men come. Maybe I should speak to them and tell them you are interested in them. Maybe it is time for them to take you to work in their houses, keeping their dicks clean too! That would be good for you!"

Su did not understand what the other woman meant but had calmed down and did not want to make this worse. "Just stay out of our business. We are not talking about you or any of the other women. I do not wish to make trouble for anyone, even you."

"Even me?" The woman shouted. "What do you mean by that? You think I am different, do you?"

Su was now completely calm and said, "Never mind Mei. Let this go."

Mei grabbed Su, and, snaring her shirt in her fist, pulled the smaller woman to her, spitting as she yelled, "I'll teach you respect, you little bitch!" She raised her arm, and was about to punch Su, when a voice rang out.

"What is happening here?" hollered Mrs. Chow who, having noticed the gathering of women on the deck, and the raised voices, had approached quickly.

"Su and Mei looked at the angry old woman and Su spoke, "Nothing Mrs. Chow. We had a little disagreement. It is nothing."

"Then get back inside, all of you!"

Mei reluctantly let go of Su's shirt, but before walking away, turned and spoke softly, "You want trouble with me? You will have it!"

Su watched Mei walk away and was surprised that several of the other women stayed behind and helped Lucy to her feet. They cast admiring glances at Su. It was obvious that Mei had, at some time, bullied most of them too, and they were glad to see someone stand up to her, but also fearful for what was to come.

The days and weeks passed and their routine continued without change. The weather grew damper and colder so their short respites on the deck were limited to only a few minutes here and there. They made garments of all sizes and shapes, all day long. Every week or so the men would arrive and quietly take a few of the girls away, to where no one knew. They ate and slept at the same times each day with the only 'break' in their lives being their 'day off', and even those were becoming less and less restful.

It was on one of those boring, rainy, days off, that Su, having just finished rinsing out her meager laundry, heard a commotion from behind her. She turned to see what was happening, but had only made it part way around when something hit her from behind, sending her sprawling into her basket of laundry and the wall beyond it. She was able to deflect part of the collision by reflectively putting her arms up in front of her, but not without the wall causing damage to both. Her forehead still made hard contact with the wall and her vision blurred. A second later there was an enormous weight on her and she felt, rather than saw, Mei leap upon her from behind.

"I'll teach you to be a wiseass, you little bitch!" Mei screamed as she tried to pummel Su into the floor.

Although still dazed, Su managed to deflect most of the blows aimed at her head but some of them got through, splitting her lip and seeming to crush her nose. Su saw her own blood splatter into the air and on to the other woman, who was now only inches away. Su realized she was in deep trouble.

Suddenly the blows stopped but Su could not move. Her hands had been pinned by the weight of the other woman who was now grinning wildly. "Who's the wise one now, little girl?"

Su managed to free her right arm and, in desperation, took a full swing at her opponent. The blow caught the other woman by surprise as Su's fist landed squarely on her left temple, causing her to tumble to the side, finally freeing Su to take a much needed breath.

Mei was quick to recover from Su's surprise punch, and again launched herself at the smaller woman. Su, still reeling from the first attack, and barely with any breath in her, had no chance. Mei once again landed on top of her and, laughing out loud. She punched Su in the face, droplets of blood splashing both women and the floor around them.

Su knew she was quickly losing consciousness and tried to raise her hands in defense, but it was no use. Mei's weight was too much to overcome.

"I'll teach you who to respect. Maybe the men won't want you so much if you are blind and ugly. Then we'll see how much of a smartass you will be."

Su was on the verge of completely passing out, and her final sight was as if in slow motion. Mei sitting on top of her, grinning like a mad person, and in her hand, a pair of scissors, blades separated, coming directly at Su's face. She closed her eyes.

CHAPTER SEVENTEEN

"DO I know you from somewhere?" The good looking, slightly drunk man asked for a second time.

The grizzled man in the stained, once grey trench coat, gathered up his few belongings and started to shuffle away, but then suddenly stopped, turned around as if hearing the question for the first time.

"Of course you know me. Which golf course do you belong to? You've probably seen me playing there, or maybe in the lounge after my under-par round. Oh no, wait! I know! Do you have your own plane? Of course you do. That's where you know me from. I've got my plane parked in the hangar beside yours! Jesus Christ!" he chuckled, and shaking his head, slowly walked away, not giving the other man another look.

"Crazy old bugger," laughed Deets Sanderson as he joined his two very large shadows at the SUV.

The old man continued his uncertain shuffle down the street and when the SUV passed him he did not even look up. Instead he rounded the corner and walked a block or two until he came upon a roadside dumpster, the kind used by neighboring small businesses. He took off his coat, balled it up and threw it into the dumpster, where it joined the day's other refuse.

Won't need that again, thought Jonas, as he continued up the street, but at a much faster pace. A few minutes later he arrived at an old yellow Buick, a cab wannabe, and jumped in. He rested his head against the cracked headrest, closed his eyes, and let out a sigh. When he opened his eyes a moment later he saw himself in the rear view mirror, shook his head, and then began removing the bushy eyebrows, wrinkled pieces of faux skin, and even a large 'growth' from his nose. Bradley had done a great job at the back of his costume store. Jonas was confident that Sanderson had no idea who he had been talking too, although there was a moment there at the end when it appeared that he might be wise, but luckily that turned out to be the booze talking. He was also sure that Sanderson would not recognize him when he saw him again, this time without the aid of the homeless guise. And see him again he would.

Jonas put the car in drive and drove the twenty minutes to his 'dummy' apartment, parking it in the underground stall, and visiting the actual apartment only long enough to strip down from his 'street' clothes, grab a quick shower to wash off the cat urine he had conveniently used from a neighbor's litter box (that had somehow penetrated through to his pants). He replaced them with a fresh jogging suit, and quietly left the building through the fire exit door and jogged, using the golf course as a short cut, to his real, and much more comfortable, home.

During the run he went over what he had learned while dressed as the smelly homeless man. He had heard that Sanderson went to that particular restaurant often, and the welcome he got there proved that correct. He also learned that his two bodyguards did not enter the restaurant with him, instead parking down the street, waiting for him in the vehicle. Neither of the two left the vehicle but kept a close eye on the entrance to the restaurant. Jonas saw this as an opportunity, and a plan was starting to form. He was still running possibilities through his head when he arrived at the front of his building.

"Well, hi there neighbor!" Tracy was sitting on the entrance steps common to both their condos. He had been so deep in his thoughts that he had not noticed her, and the sound of her voice startled him.

"Oh, Tracy, Hi, I didn't see you there. I think you scared the-you- know-what out of me," he laughed.

"Sorry Jonas. Next time I'll sneak up on you instead of sitting here in the middle of the stairs," she said, sounding serious but obvious to Jonas that she was teasing him, and rather enjoying it too.

"Very funny," he said. "I was just surprised to see you out here so late."

"It's only ten thirty and I often like to sit out here and listen to the distant sounds. You know, it can be quite a mix here. We can still hear the traffic in the distance, but the golf course behind us has its own set of sounds. I swear I heard a coyote the other night, although I'll be damned if I know how it could get here through the streets. And I'm sure I also heard an owl. I guess that's more possible. I mostly sit out back and hope for those nature sounds, but tonight I wanted this." She held her arms wide to indicate the surrounding houses. "Go figure."

Jonas stood at the bottom of the steps, looking at her. "I've heard a few noises from the golf course too, but don't really know what they were. Maybe phantoms in the night," he laughed again.

She laughed along with him and scooted over on the steps. "Would you care to join me? I have a pretty decent wine open but don't ask me what kind or year. I only sip the stuff and wouldn't know one from the other."

"That would be great but would you mind if I quickly run inside and clean up a bit. Even I can't stand being near me right now and don't want to scare off a pretty lady so soon."

"Well, that is certainly gallant of you kind sir! You go freshen up and I'll go grab the bottle and a couple of glasses."

Jonas found himself smiling and bouncing up the short stairs into his apartment which, as usual, Muriel had in immaculate condition. Even though it was his place he was almost afraid to move anything, so he went directly to the shower. A few moments later, freshly cleaned and dressed in a light T-shirt and jeans, he found Tracy back in the same spot on the stairs, this time holding on to two wine glasses, already half full of the red liquid.

He sat beside her, took a sip and spoke, "umm, this is pretty nice. I would say a Bourgeoisie 1977 if I am correct."

Tracy looked at him as if suitable impressed. "Wow, I didn't see that coming. I didn't see you as a wine expert at all," she said.

Jonas laughed out loud, "I'm not. I'm just pulling your leg! I haven't the slightest clue what this is but I do know it tastes good."

Tracy's laughter joined his, "Oh, so you can be a bit of a shit eh? That's good because I'm told I can be as well. We'll have to see who is worse."

"Yes we will," replied Jonas. "But what do you do besides sitting out here staring at the sky and dreaming about mysterious animals?"

Tracy was wearing a knit sweater that appeared to be a couple of sizes too big for her, and as she tugged the collar up closer to her neck she answered. "I own and run a small advertising and marketing firm downtown. I used to have a partner but she decided she couldn't take the stress and bailed on me a couple of years ago."

"Is the business that stressful? The few times I've seen you I didn't notice any signs of stress." Jonas said.

"I guess I hide it well. Owning a business these days, especially the type I'm in, is a struggle. It wasn't always so. Up until two thousand eight it was gung-ho, full speed ahead. We could barely keep up with the business." She turned and looked at the beautiful building behind them. "Thus the nice digs here.

We were making great money, had a solid list of steady clients, and, as I said, were just barely keeping up, happily so, I admit. But then, that nasty thing called the recession hit in late oh-eight and it has been a struggle ever since. My partner couldn't handle it and signed over everything to me at a price I could afford. I am surviving okay, but it takes a lot of work. I guess that is why I love sitting out here at night, although I usually sit out back and stare at the golf course. I like to imagine I am in a cabin way out in the woods, with nobody within miles of me. Strange isn't it?" she stared up into the sky.

"I don't find it strange at all. I think everyone has to find a place that is safe for them, even if only for a few minutes at a time." He said, also looking up at the stars.

"Where is your safe place, Jonas?" She asked.

"I'm not sure I have one just yet. I have been away for a long time and I guess I'm still searching for something, or someplace. I'll find it one day."

Tracy looked at him and said, "I hope you do. In the meantime I think I'd better be heading off to bed. I've got a serious meeting with one of my few remaining big clients tomorrow morning and I'd better be sharp. Can't have the neighbor dude keeping me up past my bedtime, now can I?"

Jonas watched her finish her wine and make her way up the stairs to her doorway. Just before she opened her door she looked back at him. "We will have to do this again sometime." She said with a smile and a slight twinkle in her eye. "I'm really glad we're neighbors."

"That goes for me too. I think we are going to get along just fine. And next time I'll bring the wine."

"You're on mister!" she said before disappearing in to her home.

Jonas watched the door close behind her and decided to sit on the steps for a few more minutes. He found himself replaying every word of their conversation, maybe enjoying it even more the second time around.

It was quiet tonight, with the usual Seattle evening chill starting to set in, and Jonas found his thoughts meandering. He looked behind him at the lovely apartment building that his Grampa, with the help of Harold, had set him up in, and he remembered the letter. He thought of his sister who should still be enjoying life, finishing school, starting a career, getting married, and having a family. All of those things had been robbed from her and Jonas's resolve did not weaken. He would find those men responsible and he had no doubt that he would be strong enough to make up for what Chrissy had lost. With that thought he slowly climbed up the stairs and to his apartment, where he changed, and fell into a deep sleep.

The next morning Jonas called Brent Jameson, who agreed to set up another meeting with Bradley and AC for later that day.

After making that call Jonas took his time getting the rest of his day started. Muriel, of course, had a full breakfast ready of sliced ham, hash browns and eggs, prepared before he knew it. As he had come to expect, the meal, although simple, was perfect and Muriel seemed to glow after receiving his compliments.

"My God, Muriel", he exclaimed, "Why aren't you married? Your cooking is second to none. And look at this place! You've got everything exactly where it is supposed to be and spotless! I would have to work hard just to mess it up," he laughed. "And I never even know you're around, you're so quiet!"

Muriel smiled. "Well, Jonas, I actually was married once, a long time ago, but the poor man took ill and never recovered. He's been gone a long time now and I'm quite content with the way I live my life. Looking after this place is so easy and you're practically never here, so I do have it quite soft, if I might say so. Besides, your neighbor, Tracy, wants me to help her around her place too so I think that will help fill in some of my time."

"That's great!" said Jonas. "Although I don't think she is around much either. She told me she is at her office most of the time."

"Yes, that is what she told me too," replied Muriel. "She also told me about your little rendezvous outside last night."

"It was hardly a rendezvous Muriel," Jonas said with a chuckle, "Just a neighborly chat on the steps."

"So the wine glasses were a figment of my imagination? Funny how there was one in your sink and one in hers this morning? Hummm, I wonder," Muriel said, a hint on mischief in her voice.

"You're no one to talk, my good lady. I've seen you and Harold makin' eyes at each other. Don't think I don't notice," said Jonas, now struggling to contain his laughter.

"Oh, go on with you!" responded Muriel, now clearly flustered.

A few minutes later, Jonas, dressed in a t-shirt and jeans, jumped in his gleaming BMW and headed for Bradley's warehouse, where they had agreed to meet.

When he pulled into the parking lot in front of Bradley's he noticed that 'his team' (as he now called them) had arrived before him. Grabbing three large and loaded pizzas he had picked up on the way, he entered the building, still feeling like he was in an old western and entering a saloon. He wondered what the Wild West would think about these pizzas.

"Hey man, I could smell those before you hit the steps!" shouted AC. He too was dressed in t-shirt and jeans. The front of his shirt read 'READ THE BACK BEFORE PEELING' with the back side reading, 'WHAT'S TAKING YOU SO LONG!'

"Those do smell mighty fine," added Brent. "I didn't know I was hungry until you brought those in."

"Same goes for me," added Bradley, as he relieved Jonas of the pizza boxes.

After making most of the pizzas disappear, the four men moved from the lunch table to more comfortable, face to face deep seated couches. The room was made up of four walls completely covered with shelving, those which were full to capacity with neatly labeled (cowboy outfits, fake beards, swords, fairy outfits etc.) costume boxes.

"Relax gentlemen" said Bradley, after flopping down at the end of one of the couches. "Jonas, I assume you called this meeting, so where are we?"

Jonas dropped himself on the opposite end of the same couch.

"I think I have a plan, but wanted you guys to tear it apart, and then help me stick it back together," Jonas said.

Jonas spent the good part of the next hour explaining what he wanted to do. When he was finished Brent was the first to speak.

"That all sounds pretty solid Jonas, but I see one big problem with your plan."

"Go ahead Brent, I knew there were parts that might not fit right so anything you say will be appreciated," said Jonas.

"Well, that's just it. You need help. Your plan needs a couple more guys, because what we have here," he made a circular motion with his hand, "is a cripple, me, a computer whiz, and a businessman," Brent said, pointing at AC and Bradley in turn. "I think you need some muscle to pull this off. If you're okay with it, I might know of a few guys that would like nothing more than to help take out these scumbags."

Jonas was reluctant when he replied. "I don't want a hit squad, Brent. I'm not going on a killing spree. I'm only after the people responsible for Chrissy's death. The rest of them will get theirs from somebody else. Are you guys okay with that?"

"That's fine Jonas" said Brent. "That is the way I see it too. In order for your plan to work some of these guys will have to be minimized. I agree that we don't have to kill a bunch of people to get to the head honchos, but they will have to have some pain inflicted upon them," said Brent. "Bradley can help at his end and AC will set us up with communications, and I'll make sure I get a couple of guys I trust to help with the heavy lifting. Does that work for you guys?" asked Brent, looking at the others.

Jonas looked at each man in turn and then spoke. "Alright gentlemen, I need two things. I need something strong enough to knock down a horse, and it has to be fast acting. I also need somewhere out of the way where noise will not be a problem. My soon to be new best buddy, Deets, will be answering some questions, and I don't want to disturb the neighborhood.

"Guys," said Jonas, "this is where it gets serious. I intend to find all of the men responsible for my sister's brutal death, starting with Sanderson. I will not tread lightly, and when I find the rest of these animals, I will do what is necessary, without question. If you are on board with that I need to know. If you are not please say so now, and I will certainly understand, and will shake your hand goodbye."

He looked at the other three men in the room, all of which looked right back at him. "I'm in," said Brent.

"Me too," echoed AC.

"Well guys," said Bradley, "at the risk of sounding like a movie cliché, I say let's kick some ass!"

Jonas smiled, but thought, this could get bad. We will have blood on our hands!

CHAPTER EIGHTEEN

SU was too dazed to see exactly what happened, but she saw something, maybe a shoe, connect with the side of Mei's face, sending the woman sprawling to the side, and the scissors flying even further. She felt an enormous weight lift from her, and she struggled to take in air.

Through barely open and puffy eyes she felt, rather than saw, other women lifting her off the floor, and carrying her into the building. Even though she could now breathe she was having trouble remaining conscious, and when the women laid her down on her bed she gave in to the light-headedness and closed her eyes.

When she woke she was alone in the big room. She could hear the sound of the machines below so knew where she was. She raised herself from the bed and was immediately hit by a blinding pain in her head. Shaking it off as best she could she managed to get to a sitting position and held her head steady until the throbbing thankfully subsided.

Using the bed to steady herself she managed to stand, and when that didn't feel too bad, she started to make her way to the top of the stairs with more of a shuffle than actual steps. She was about to start the long descent to the work area when someone approached from the bottom, and, two steps at a time, bound up towards her.

"What are you doing up?" came Lucy's cry in English. "You should not be up yet! We do not need you downstairs until at least tomorrow so let us get you back to bed."

Su allowed Lucy to turn her around and lead her back to her bed. Once there, and again laying down, but on propped up pillows, she spoke. "What happened, Lucy?" she asked. "I remember Mei pushing me and something about scissors, but that is all."

"Mei attacked you on the deck, and yes, she tried to hurt you with scissors but before she could Mr. Sanderson kicked her hard and she fell off," said Lucy.

"Where is Mei now?"

"Mr. Sanderson kicked her very hard. I do not know her condition, but the men with Mr. Sanderson carried her to their vehicle and they drove away. Mr. Sanderson was very angry. I do not think we will see Mei again."

Su looked around the empty room. "I should be downstairs working. Mr. Sanderson will be angry enough at me without me being down there. I don't want him to take me away too," she said.

"No, you are to rest today." Lucy responded. "We have someone else at your station. You will work tomorrow. I must go now. Sleep now, and I will see you later."

Lucy walked to the stairs, turned and looked back at Su for a second, and then was gone.

Su slept soundly past dinner and through the night, not even hearing the other women when they returned from their shift. When she awoke it was early morning, and almost time to start the work day. Her headache was gone. She was able to get out of bed and make her way to the bathroom, which she needed badly.

After cleaning up she joined the first of the women in line for their breakfast, and discovered that she was famished.

The woman dispensing the rationed food must have noticed her condition, or had heard what had happened, because she dished out extra food, and an extra slice of toast to Su's plate, adding, "we have all heard of your fight with that bully Mei, and are happy that you stood up to her."

Su wanted to say that she had hardly stood up to Mei but instead whispered a quiet thank you, and joined the other women at the eating tables.

Throughout the meager, but to Su, wonderful meal, several women from her work crew passed by with comments.

"Thank you for getting rid of Mei," said one.

"You stood up to that terrible woman, so I thank you," said another.

"Mei was a bully to all of us. You were very strong to not back down from her," said yet another.

Su wanted to tell them that she had not actually done anything and, in fact, had almost been killed or hurt badly. Only Sanderson's arrival had saved her. But she said nothing, allowing the women around her to keep their thoughts and maybe feel a little better about their situation this morning.

Over the next weeks Su worked regularly with the other women but noticed that their attitude towards her had changed. They seemed to look up to her and often sought her out in the evening for advice, or just to talk. They all knew that learning the English language could be helpful if they were ever to leave, so they also used this time to learn from each other. Su found that she was a fast learner and, although the language sounded very strange to her, after much practice she now had a passable grasp on its use, so much so that she and Lucy now only used English when speaking to each other, sometimes laughing together when one of them used an incorrect word, and the true meaning was finally figured out. They became close friends.

One day, while Su and Lucy were working side by side, a commotion broke out from the big main entrance doors.

The doors, which were always locked, were being opened and everyone stopped what they were doing and watched closely.

Mrs. Chow was seen rushing towards the doors while yelling back at the women, "Keep working! This is no business of yours!"

Soon the big doors were fully opened and Mr. Sanderson, and the other man that usually accompanied him, entered. Su remembered his name as Gant, or something close to that.

The men were followed by six girls dressed in ragged clothes of all colors. They looked around fearfully, and were followed by two armed guards. Su remembered that feeling and her heart went out to the lost souls that simply stood there quietly.

The two businessmen and Mrs. Chow entered the small office near the foot of the stairs. After a few minutes Mrs. Chow came out and waved at Lucy. "Lucy, you are to come in here now," she bellowed.

Lucy turned to Su in panic. "What did I do?" she exclaimed.

"You did nothing wrong," said Su, pointing to the girls hovering at the door, "I think it something to do with the new girls."

Lucy nodded and quickly made her way to the office.

Through the window Su could see the men speaking to both Mrs. Chow and Lucy and after a few minutes Lucy returned to their work table.

"Su, I have been told that I will be moving this crew to other tables and the new girls will be trained here," she said.

"But how are they to be trained if we are all over there?" asked Su, pointing at the empty tables across the room.

"You will not be moving with us, Su. You will be staying at your table and will be responsible for the training of the new girls." Lucy replied.

"Me? I have not been here long enough. I don't know how to train," Su said.

"Su, you have a way with all of the women," said Lucy. "Since Mei was taken away they have all looked to you. You are the strong one and these girls will be very lucky to train with you. Now you must go and get your new students. It is better this way. It will keep you here, and the men will not want to take you to work in the houses."

So Su did just that, strangely going through all the same motions that she herself had gone through only months ago. She showed the girls their sleeping quarters and then, in the morning, ate her breakfast with them and later showed them to their work stations, and started the process of teaching them their individual tasks.

It did not take long for Su to find herself as a natural leader and she very much enjoyed the feeling. Not only did she now have her own crew but the women throughout the entire building, including Lucy, now looked to her. Even Mrs. Chow, albeit very reluctantly, saw that the other women worked better, with less complaints, when Su was there.

One day, the familiar commotion from the big front doors revealed only Mr. Gant. The usually always present Sanderson was not with him, nor were there any new girls. Gant looked disturbed as he quickly made his way to the office, calling for Mrs. Chow and now Su, as a floor leader, to join him.

Su and Mrs. Chow stood in front of the small battered wooden desk behind which sat Gant, who looked up, staring at them before speaking. "There have been some changes to the organization, and will be changes here as well," he said.

"Where is Mr. Sanderson, and is he aware of these changes?" asked Mrs. Chow.

"Mr. Sanderson is not your concern. You will take your instructions directly from me. I need you to leave here with me today."

"But Mr. Gant, I have been here a long time. I have worked hard for you."

"You will still be working for me but I need you elsewhere. I have heard that Su here has developed into a bit of a leader. She will take over from you here. Gather your things. We will be leaving immediately, and Su," he looked directly up at here, "I shall expect you to lead these women, and to increase productivity in a very short time, or your stay with us will not be quite so comfortable."

Su was still catching her breath from this series of announcements when Gant abruptly got up from the desk and left the room, stopping only to say to Mrs. Chow, "I'll give you a few minutes to get your things and give instructions to Su, but I am in a hurry so don't waste any time."

Mrs. Chow hurried out of the small office, followed closely by Su, through the large work room, showing Su what was expected of her and where to locate the things she would need, such as keys and supplies. She then threw all of her belongings into a large bag and left, without another word.

Su looked around her in disbelief. All of the women had now stopped working and were looking at her. She gave them a smile and then said, "Let's get back to work ladies!"

CHAPTER NINETEEN

JONAS sat at the restaurant's bar, slowly sipping a drink. His 'new" mustache and bushier sideburns and eyebrows were hard to get used to but, thanks to Bradley, the itching was minimal. The scar, also masterfully created by Bradley, ran from his left eye down to the cheekbone, and added greatly to the disguise. His suit fit perfectly and easily concealed the handgun tucked in a holster under his arm.

He wore Ray-Ban glasses like a lot of other men in the room. His hair length helped conceal the small hearing device planted in his right ear. He was startled at the clarity of AC's voice and several times had to stop himself from carrying on an out-loud conversation with him. He again reminded himself that he was new to this type of situation and had to be extremely careful.

AC had used his skills to hack into Sanderson's emails and noted that he intended to dine here tonight. Jonas had a laugh when AC explained what he had done to obtain the information.

"You see Jonas," said a fired up AC. "It really is a science. The definition of a hacker is simply "'a clever programmer who breaks into a computer system'," but hackers are eventually caught. What I've done is set a data trap to get Sanderson's password. Once I had that, I set up a data worm, which basically steals his information without him knowing it. I guess you could still call it hacking but this way is with stealth."

Jonas again shook his head at AC's explanation, but whatever the hell he did, it had worked, as here he sat, like a hawk, circling in the wind, in search of prey. He hoped the rest of his plan went as smoothly.

Shortly after ordering another drink the atmosphere in the room seemed to change. Jonas felt, rather than saw, Dieter 'Deets' Sanderson make his appearance in the crowded restaurant. Jonas watched as people almost tripped over themselves in order to be in the general vicinity of the man.

Sanderson, as he had done the last time Jonas had watched him in the building, made the rounds. He patted backs, shook hands, gave high-fives, and kissed a few cheeks. Jonas noted that the cheeks he kissed were usually accompanied by a low neck line, sometimes very low, so as to offer a generous amount of cleavage for him to peruse.

Jonas had to admire the way the man seemed to control the room, not by anything he was doing, but just by being present. His trademark bow tie and the loosely wild hair seemed to charm everyone that came in contact with him.

Sanderson eventually settled at a table with the same people he had sat with on his previous visit. Jonas had spotted them when he came in, and was able to grab a spot at the bar as close to them as the layout would allow.

That table was loud, so listening in to their conversation was easy, albeit quite boring. The women were making an effort to listen to every word spoken, despite the fact it was mostly about golf or the Seahawks. They seemed to be happy just to be at the same table. The men were a different story. They competed to be the loudest, have the best story or jokes, but mostly to get the attention of the star guest.

Sanderson took it all in stride. After all, he was used to it, and felt it was well deserved. He was a self-made man. He had started small, using his good looks and big vocabulary to work his way into the right crowd. Even in his late teens he had associated with, by choice, the future leaders of the community. A few political types yes, but the young men he had started out with would grow into the hardened men who now controlled the waterfront, oversaw the Northwest's lucrative drug trade, and human trafficking, which supplied both cheap labor and a very profitable prostitution ring. Life was good for Deets Sanderson and he reveled in its enjoyment.

Jonas found he was almost mesmerized by Sanderson's interaction with the surrounding group and, in fact, caught himself staring at the man who was his target.

For a brief moment Sanderson looked up from the buxom blonde that was practically in his lap, and met Jonas's eyes. For the briefest of seconds something passed between them but only Jonas knew what it meant. Sanderson's eyes blinked and then turned to resume looking at the blonde's breasts, which had all but escaped from the plunging design of her dress.

Jonas swung around on the bar stool, fighting a growing restlessness in his stomach. He was so close to the man that had murdered his sister and forever changed the lives of those attached to her. Instead of giving in to the queasiness in his gut his resolve seemed to build. This evil man, sitting oh so close, was the opening act of the play, with the curtain falling only after all of those responsible had paid.

As the evening progressed Jonas had made idle chatter with a few people, turning aside obvious advances from a few more, even women clearly there with their husbands.

"Who cares," they said, as their partners were somewhere else in the room doing the same thing. Jonas was repulsed by the whole scene but fought the impulse to walk away. Sanderson was still close and getting quite drunk. It wouldn't be long now.

Outside, and down the block, sat Sanderson's huge black SUV. Inside, the two thugs, Cam and Lou, occupied themselves with stories from their past. Mostly bullshit stories, to be sure, but both men knew that and accepted them anyway. Anything to pass the time while watching their boss having a good time.

"Look at those fucking people," said Cam. "They're all filthy rich, can do anything they want, go anywhere they want, and they just sit in a stupid fucking bar, getting shit-faced trying to impress Deets. I don't get it!"

Lou ran his hand over his bald head, "Yeah, fuck if I know either," he said.

Lou had an annoying habit of leaning sideways every once in a while and letting out a line of farts, which he did now.

"Jesus Christ!" Cam cried, waving his hands around in the air. "What the fuck did ya eat? That fucking stinks, man! It's gonna take a week to get that stink outa the seats. Did you shit yourself this time?"

Lou acknowledged that this one really did stink but he was laughing too hard to speak. Then he noticed a man pushing a wheelchair, with a woman in it, down the road towards their parked vehicle. They seemed to be coming straight at them, albeit in slow motion.

Lou leaned forward. "What the fuck?"

Cam watched the approaching people. "I think the guy pushing the chair is pissed. He can't stay straight."

Sure enough, the man behind the wheelchair seemed to be having a lot of trouble steering the thing, and its passenger also seemed to be having trouble sitting up straight. The reason became obvious when the street light reflected off a large bottle that the woman passed up to the man behind her.

"Will you look at that, for Christ's sake?" laughed Cam. "I don't think I've ever seen anything like that before, have you?"

Lou responded, also laughing and shaking his head, "They're both fucking hammered! I wonder if they could be pulled over for wheel-chairing while impaired."

They both exploded with laughter.

"What the fuck are they doin' now?" asked Cam. The weaving man and his wheelchair bound passenger started up again, heading straight towards the SUV's front bumper.

"Are you shittin' me? They're gonna fucking run right into us." Cam yelled.

And sure enough, the couple kept on coming, and as predicted, ran straight into the front of the big truck. The man stumbled and almost fell over, but the chair and its occupant suffered a worse fate, completely falling over sideways, with the woman dumped to the pavement.

"Give me a fucking break!" Lou said. "They have the whole road and run right in to the middle of us. I can't believe this!" he repeated.

Both men exited the vehicle, no longer laughing, but pissed and worried that these two drunks had put a dent in the boss's truck. They approached the front of the truck where the wheelchair lay on its side, one wheel still spinning slowly, beside which lay a woman who looked dead, but was probably just passed out. The man that had been pushing the chair was still standing but bent over in a crouch, mumbling something but laughing to himself too.

"What the fuck are you doing man?" shouted Lou, who was now very pissed at the stupidity of these people. "You had the whole fuckin' road to work with, and you still couldn't miss a truck this fucking big? What the fuck is the matter with you?"

The man looked up and mumbled some more.

"What did you say? I can't hear a fucking word you're sayin'," asked Cam. He looked at the woman still lying motionless on the pavement, and said to his partner, "You'd better take a look at the old woman. At least put her back in the chair. Shit! Next thing you know they'll be suing us for hitting *them!*"

Lou approached the prone woman and was about to grab her arm to lift her when she suddenly looked up and moved at the same time. Lou quickly pulled his arm back, but not before feeling a sharp pain in the palm of his hand.

"What the fuck!" She fucking bit me or something!" he yelled, almost instantly feeling faint. He had trouble forming the words.

Cam was looking at his partner and did not see the other man's movement until it was too late. He felt a sting in this leg and looked down quick enough to see the man pull back a tiny needle.

"Son of a bitch! What the fuck......was......that? He tried to say.

Both men staggered, but with amazing quickness the man and woman, not drunk at all, were on their feet and joined by two other men, who had been hiding near the back of the truck. It took all four of them to quickly load the oversized bodyguards back into the truck. They were situated upright with their heads against their respective windows. For added touch, the 'woman' turned on the radio, and with a chuckle, found a religious talk show, and turned it up.

"We didn't kill them, did we?" asked a nervous, but energized Bradley.

The 'woman', Brent, answered, "No, no, don't worry, they'll be out for a while, and sicker than a dog for a day or two, but that's about it."

He turned to the two men who had appeared from nowhere and said, "Thank guys, I owe you."

"Let us know if we can help again. These slugs deserve worse than this so if you need us, we're there!" said the taller of the two as they left, once again fading into the darkness from whence they came.

Bradley watched them leave. "Who were those guys?" he asked.

"Just a couple of good cops trying to do what's right," Brent replied. "C'mon, let's go before the restaurant starts to empty out. We need to get the van and be ready."

They again resumed their roles as wheelchair bound woman, being pushed down the road by her man. This time though, if anyone had been watching, they would have noticed that the chair was moving faster down the road. A lot faster.

Inside the restaurant, people were now standing, reaching for their coats and fumbling with wallets and credit cards in order to settle up with the eager staff.

Sanderson's table looked to be going nowhere soon. Jonas was again wondering if this was a good plan. He didn't want to be one of the last people here and was giving serious thought to aborting the evening when Sanderson finally stood up.

"Well, kids, it's time for me to head out. I have an early day tomorrow, or at least I think I do," Sanderson said, which led to more laughter.

"By the way, Rupert," he said, looking at one of the men at the table. "What the fuck kinda name is Rupert anyway?" Before the other man could answer he continued, "Never mind. It's okay Rupert. As long as you let me stare at your wife's nipples I don't give a shit what your name is," he said, slightly wobbling where he stood.

The group laughed again and all looked at the women of Sanderson's attention and, sure enough, her breasts were so exposed that one of her nipples had indeed escaped and was in full view. She turned a dark red in the face while quickly tucking her breast back into the dress, but then joined in the laughter.

Sanderson threw some bills on the table, bid them goodbye, and made his way toward the door. Once there he stopped, pulled a cell phone from his pocket, and dialed a number. He watched the front door, obviously waiting for his ride.

Jonas settled his bill, and joined Sanderson at the door.

"Do you need a lift, my friend?" Jonas asked.

"No, but thanks, my guys are just across the street. Don't know what the fuck is taking them though," Sanderson replied.

Sanderson quickly lost patience and started down the outside steps to the sidewalk, not noticing that he was being followed closely behind. He reached the sidewalk and, seeing his vehicle still parked down the road, started waving.

"C'mon boys, what the fuck you waitin' for?" he yelled.

Jonas looked over at the SUV and saw a white panel van parked beside it. To all appearances the two men in the SUV could have just nodded off, bored with the radio sermon that could be heard coming from inside the vehicle.

Sanderson seemed unsure what to do and was now having difficulty standing up straight.

Jonas approached him. "Is that your truck over there?" he asked.

"Yeah, that's it. Man, I drank way too much tonight. I'm fucked up," Sanderson managed to say.

"C'mon, I'll help you over to your truck. I think your driver is asleep or something," Jonas said.

"Christ, there are two of them in the damn truck. How can both of them be asleep, dumb bastards! Maybe I'll fire 'em both!"

He turned to Jonas, "Thanks man, I'm afraid I'm a bit shit-faced. I don't wanna fall down in the middle of the fuckin' street," he said, breaking out in laughter.

Jonas laughed along with him as he led him across to the SUV. Sanderson didn't notice the nearby van's lights come on. It begin backing out of the parking stall as they stumbled towards it.

When the men neared the SUV Sanderson's brain finally started to realize that something was wrong. "What the fuck gives?" he said, looking at the two men slouched against the windows of the truck. But he was a little too drunk, and a little too slow to react when the white van arrived beside him. The side panel opened, and he was pushed inside, followed by Jonas, who quickly closed the van's door.

Once inside Sanderson tried to put up a fight but was easily held down until he felt a sting on his arm. It was followed by a warm sensation that quickly spread through his body, followed by blackness.

Jonas looked back at the restaurant entrance but they had been lucky. No one had come out and no one was there to see the van pull away.

The van had only driven a few blocks when Jonas spoke to the driver, "Okay, Brent, pull over here. Your work is done for the night."

Brent pulled the van over to the curb and turned in his seat to address Jonas who was still sitting beside the prone Sanderson.

"Are you sure about this, Jonas?" he asked. This is where it gets real sticky. After this you can't go back."

"I know. I've thought a lot about it. Christ! It's just about all I think about but I've got to do this. For Chrissy and for Gramps, it's something that needs to get done and I'm ready to do it. Sanderson here is the key to the rest of the group. Before the night is done he'll tell me who else was involved. Now, get out of here and I'll call you tomorrow. You've done enough."

"Alright Jonas, just be goddamn careful. Once this is done they will be looking for you."

"I know. I'll do my best and we'll see what happens."

Brent left the van without another word, and walked away. Jonas slid in behind the wheel, started it up, and drove out of the neighborhood, his passenger slumped unconscious on the van's back floor.

He did not have to drive far as the old warehouse soon appeared before him. He exited the van before a high metal gate, made sure there was no one around, and then removed the padlock that he had placed there himself only a few days ago. He pushed the gate open enough to get the van through and once there relocked the gate and drove around the back of the big old building. There was still a light stench of fish hanging over the place from years of use as a collection house for a fleet of fishing vessels. These vessels now used much more convenient and modern facilities elsewhere. AC had found out about these old abandoned buildings through the internet, and Jonas had spent some time scouting this one out before making the decision to use it for his purposes.

He pulled the van close to a much used metal door and, once that and the van's door were open, he dragged Sanderson's limp body into the warehouse. He set the man on a chair against the wall at the far end of a large open area and returned to the van for a sports bag with the equipment he had brought with him. He secured Sanderson to the chair using zap-straps on his arms and legs so that there would be very little movement allowed. Once that was finished Jonas moved the van further into the shadows and re-entered the building. He grabbed another chair and settled in to wait for Sanderson to awaken. It wouldn't be long. It wasn't yet one AM so he still had plenty of time to do what he had to do.

It wasn't long when Sanderson's head, which had been hanging down over his chest, started moving side to side. Then, as he opened his eyes, he was able to lift his head slowly and look around. His eyes opened wider when he realized where he was and what his situation was. His head was the only part of his body he could move and his look turned to one of panic, followed surprisingly quickly by one of anger.

"What the fuck!" he yelled, noticing another person in the room, who simply stared at him.

"Who the fuck're you? What the fuck's going on?" he again yelled.

Jonas finally rose from his chair and approached Sanderson.

"Good morning Mr. Sanderson. Or should I call you Deets?"

"Do I know you?"

"I guess you could say that you do," Jonas answered. "We golf at the same golf course. Oh, and wait, we keep our airplanes in the same hangers too. And tonight we almost had a drink together but you were too busy trying to cop a feel, and didn't see me."

"What the fuck are you talking about?" Sanderson asked, but then realization started to work its way through the liquor to his brain. "Wait a minute, the homeless guy outside the restaurant. Now I know where I've seen you."

Jonas bent over so his face was close to Sanderson's. "You knew me before that Sanderson, and this morning we are going to talk about that," he said, looking directly into the man's eyes.

"I'm not talking to you about anything. Besides, I don't have clue what you're talking about," said Sanderson.

"Okay, I'll help refresh your memory," said Jonas. "Forget about the homeless guy, and yes, that was me. And forget that I sat about ten feet away from you all night in the restaurant. No, Deets, I want to talk about a night a few years ago, a night that ended in a dark alley."

Jonas raised his voice, and continued, "A night where you and your scumbag buddies raped and murdered an innocent young woman, and left her in a fucking garbage bin like rubbish! That's what we are going to talk about!"

Sanderson looked around and not seeing an easy way out turned back to Jonas. "Look, I don't know what you're talking about. I was never in an alley and sure never hurt a girl."

Jonas, now calm again, spoke with a reasonable voice. "Let's see what you remember Deets! Maybe I can help you remember."

Jonas walked to the other chair and pulled his HK45 from the bag sitting on the floor beside it. He preferred the Glock Brent had also gotten for him, but the HK was what he needed tonight.

He allowed Sanderson to see him screw a sound suppressor onto the barrel of the gun as he approached.

"What the fuck are you gonna do with that?' Sanderson yelled. "Jesus man, do you know how much shit you are already in?" he asked, his voice rising.

"Deets, I don't give a rat's ass about how much shit I'm in. I am going to ask a few questions and you are going to answer them."

"I'm not answering shit. But you are close to being a dead man," Sanderson spat at Jonas.

"Not as close as you Sanderson. Now let's just see where this is going to go and how tough you really are. As they say all the time on TV, we can do this the easy way, or we can do it the hard way, it's your choice."

"Fuck you" said Sanderson.

Jonas walked back over to Sanderson, placed the extended barrel up against the top of Sanderson's left knee and pulled the trigger. The gun made a 'pffft' sound and the soft-nosed bullet made a small entry hole right above Sanderson's knee cap. It did not, however, make a small hole when it exited. In fact, it crashed into the floor taking with it a good part of Sanderson's knee, ligaments, cartilage and muscle, which also splattered on the floor, blending in with the million other stains already there.

Sanderson screamed, causing a terrible echo throughout the old isolated building. "Jesus, oh Jesus, that fucking hurts! You son of a bitch! You are fucking dead!" he cried while shaking his head frantically from side to side.

Jonas walked to the side of the moaning man, and was momentarily overtaken by nausea in his stomach. He had never deliberately hurt another person in his life, and regardless how much he felt this was justified, and how much he hated this man, it still laid a heavy weight on him. He kept hearing Chrissy's last screams and the thought that he couldn't do anything to save her. When Sanderson's wail was down to a whimper Jonas took a deep breath and asked, "Do you follow baseball, Deets?"

"What the fuck are you talking about? Are you insane? Oh, Christ, this hurts! You blew my fucking knee off! You gotta stop this shit!"

"I asked if you follow baseball." Jonas asked again.

"Yeah, yeah, I do. What's that got to do with anything?"

"Well, the knee was strike one. I'll ask another question and if you fuck up the answer it will be strike two, and you'll never walk again. Now, who was with you in the alley when you murdered my sister?"

"Your sister, I don't know what you're.................!

Jonas moved the gun to his right knee.

Sanderson's eyes opened wide and he screamed, "Wait, Wait, I have to think about it. It was a long time ago!"

Jonas pulled the gun back and smiled. "Okay, I'll give you a minute to think of something, but if I don't like what I hear, you lose your other knee."

Sanderson rolled his head and tears ran down his cheeks, blending with the snot that ran from his nose and settled on his bow tie, which hung from his neck.

"Oh, oh, I remember one night a bunch of us guys were out drinking. I remember running in to a girl I used to know, tall, blonde, and really cute? She didn't want any part of us. That must have been the night eh?" He looked hopefully up at Jonas.

Jonas stared back at him. "Just keep talking. I want to know who else was with you that night."

"Fuck man, my knee is on fire! How the hell can I remember who was there? I was out most nights back then, with a lot of different guys."

Jonas approached again, the gun inching towards Sanderson's right leg. "It wasn't every night that you raped and murdered a pretty girl now was it? You've got ten seconds to give me names!"

"Fuck you man! I don't know who was there! Oh, no, please!"

Jonas shot Sanderson's right knee, the bullet taking off most of the knee cap and nearly severing the leg entirely.

Sanderson screamed, and lost all color in his face. He pushed the chair back against the wall, and his head hit the concrete hard. He was about to pass out. Jonas had only seconds. He leaned in close to the crying and weakened man.

"Tell me Deets! Give me a name and I'll get help for you. The pain will stop!" Jonas shouted.

Sanderson's head tilted to one side, and he looked up at Jonas and whispered. Jonas put his head closer to Sanderson's.

"What did you say Deets? Say it again and your pain goes away."

"Gant," whispered Sanderson. "It was Gant and Westgate, and some other guy, German guy. I was scared shitless of them," he said, as his head flopped to the side.

Jonas again bent over and looked into Sanderson's eyes and whispered, "you deserve a lot worse, you son of a bitch, but I promised to take away your pain."

He put the mussel of the gun against Sanderson's chest, and pulled the trigger.

CHAPTER TWENTY

"YOU guys don't look so fucking good!" said Gant, looking across his desk at the two thugs, who resembled whipped dogs rather than the tough guys they were supposed to be. The two men had awakened from their drug induced sleep, one still supported by the SUV's door, the other making it to the pavement before being violently ill. It had taken the men some time to empty their stomachs and calm themselves down enough to phone for help. Unfortunately for them, their boss was nowhere to be found and the help that arrived was not the kind they wanted. It led to their current situation, sitting across from Allan Gant, trying not to sound like fools and without upchucking on the big boss's desk.

"How did you guys manage to fuck this up so badly?" Gant slammed his hand down on the desk.

"Look at you two! You're found pissin' in each other's pants while you fuck up the one thing, the only thing, you have to do! To protect Sanderson," yelled Gant.

Cam swallowed more bile and mustered up the courage to reply.

"They took us by total surprise boss." said Cam, trying hard to make eye contact with Gant. "We were just sitting there waiting for Mr. Sanderson and this old guy is pushin' a lady in a wheelchair, and they ran right into the fuckin' front of our truck. It was almost funny boss. They walked right into us and then the chair tips over, and the lady falls out, and the guy's about to have a fucking heart attack. We had no choice. We had to get outa the truck. They were right in front of us. Anyway, when we got out they stabbed us with something and that's all I can remember."

Gant fired back. "How the fuck did you end up back in the truck, and don't tell me some little old lady carried you gently, like a fucking baby, and laid you down in the front seat so you could catch a nap!"

Lou spoke this time. "We don't know boss. Whatever they stabbed us with just knocked us out. They had to have help putting us back in the truck though."

Gant starred at the two men across from him.

'Where the fuck is Deets?' he thought. 'Who would take him out?' It's been pretty well trouble free for a long time, almost since they started, and Deets, while being the weakest partner, had been responsible for getting Krause and Westgate involved. Gant remembered when he and Sanderson first started. They had been just out of college. Two young men, kids really, that wanted to do what every other young person wanted to do, conquer the world. They had a different approach to that goal than most people though. They did not want to waste time doing things in a conventional way. They had started small, buying and selling small amounts of grass. This was so easy that it wasn't long when the amounts were no longer small, and grass wasn't the only drug on their menu. Their operation started to branch out and they no longer did the direct street work as they established a network of like-minded men to handle that end of the business.

One day Gant had been approached by a drunken buddy about a party he was trying to set up. He only had one problem. He needed girls that would not only want to attend the party, as most young girls liked to do, but girls that were guaranteed to put out for his invited friends. The girls this guy hung out with were also part of the college crowd and would not be comfortable attending that type of party. He wanted hookers and that was what he had approached Gant about.

Gant and Sanderson had used contacts made through their drug business and had found enough hookers to supply the party. It was such a success, and the college boys didn't shy away from the cost, that they decided to add this service to their growing business.

As good as their local contacts were however, they soon ran into the age old problem of supply and demand. The parties were so successful that the requests soon outnumbered how many girls they could supply. Sanderson solved that problem when he heard about a guy named Westgate who was rumored to have access to women when needed. Sanderson had no qualms about where the women came from as long as they performed the duties they were ordered to perform, and kept his clients happy.

Gant remembered their first meeting with Westgate who, although very friendly on the outside, did not do a good job of hiding a very tough inside. It was as if Westgate took over their whole operation. He agreed to supply the women needed for that side of the business but insisted that he be involved in their drug operation. He was very convincing and both he and Sanderson had realized at that meeting that they were, in fact, small time businessmen, and that Westgate could help take them to the next level. From that meeting on they agreed that Gant and Sanderson would run the drug and party side of the business while Westgate, and a fellow named Krause, who was not at that initial meeting, would provide the unlimited supply of young girls as needed. The fact that these young girls were smuggled into the country did not bother the men at all. They had a business to run, after all.

They had celebrated their new partnership that evening with a night on the town. They were joined by the fourth member of the partnership, Lamar Krause, a strict sounding foreigner with a deep tan who was a man of few words. They had all gotten quite drunk and Gant could still only remember bits and pieces of the evening. The drinking, the women, the occasional scuffle with jealous boyfriends of the women they showed attention too, and, at the end of the evening the episode with the guy and his hot girlfriend. Deets had known her, he thought, but it didn't seem to matter. Westgate and Krause were out of control that night, and it did not end well for the young man and his girl.

Gant sat back and continued to stare at the two men, but his mind was still elsewhere. 'If Deets was indeed kidnapped what did it mean? Was someone wanting in on their business? Did Westgate get greedy and take him out? Or was it someone else?'

The business had prospered and expanded. They had the drugs, of course, and the parties were still making them a fortune, especially now that they had set up a few *houses* that could host the young, overly horny, and loaded, young men. Gant has also been pleasantly surprised that Sanderson had taken the girls not suitable for the houses, and set up a cheap clothing assembly warehouse. The girls actually made a small wage to work there and the profit margin was huge. So, overall, things were running smooth, until now. He leaned forward in his chair and looked at the two giants that faced him. "I don't give a shit what you have to do. You fuckers had better take an aspirin or something, and get out there and find him! Now get the fuck out of here!"

The two men looked at each other, then rose shakily from their chairs and walked out the door.

Gant again sat back. 'They had better find Deets before Westgate gets wind of it. We're fucked if that happens.'

CHAPTER TWENTY-ONE

OVER the weeks Su got used to being the one in charge. At first she was too shocked and astonished to make any difference to their working conditions. Every day she dutifully reported to a work station, albeit a different one from when she had first arrived. She would assume the duties of that station, but was frequently interrupted by the other girls. Their questions were about every aspect of their own jobs and Su was at first overwhelmed with it all. How could she answer all of their questions when she didn't even have the answers for herself? It was one afternoon, after an unusual amount of questions from the girls, that she was visited by Lucy.

"Su, you must learn to change. Gant has put you in charge now. You are the new Mrs. Chow and must act like it." she said. "The girls, even the older ones, are frightened and are looking to you to be strong for them. They need someone to lead them, and even if you do not like it, you must do it, for them, and for yourself. If you do not I am afraid that they will take you away to work in one of their other places."

Su shook her head. "What do I know about this place? There is so much here that I do not know or understand and I cannot answer all of their questions. They should have another leader."

"You are the one Mr. Gant has given the task too, so you do not have a choice," said Lucy. "You are strong but do not yet know it. You must try harder because Gant will not be tolerant."

Su realized that what she was hearing was true. She did not have a choice. She could not hide, and, whether or not she liked it, she had to try.

She immediately assigned another girl to take over her work station and began walking around the large work area, visiting each girl in turn, and learning how each station worked. It did not take her long to get a good grasp of the details of each station and before long the girls' questions became fewer and farther between. Those questions and problems that did come her way were now easier to answer.

Until one day an older woman, who, it was rumored, had worked there since childhood, approached Su and asked in a quiet voice.

"Why is the food so awful? They expect us to work hard without some nutrition and energy! Can they not make something different once in a while, perhaps something with some real meat that these women need badly?"

It was a good question, and one that Su had even asked herself a time or two. "I cannot answer your question right now but I will see if there is something I can do," Su responded.

A few days later Su left the work floor and visited the eating area. She walked past the many long tables, their chairs standing deserted before them, and entered the kitchen. There she found several older women of mixed nationalities. Some were moving pots and pans every which way. Some seemed to be standing guard in front of stoves, and yet others were busy chopping up vegetables, which made up a huge portion of their diet, after rice. Despite the rather bland fare that made up their meals the combination of smells in the kitchen was very pleasant, and seemed to strengthen Su's resolve.

"Who is in charge here?" Su asked the woman nearest to her.

The woman pointed to the far end of the kitchen to a small Japanese woman seated at a beaten old table.

As Su approached, the woman looked up and bellowed, "Who are you, and what are you doing back here? You cannot come back here!"

Su spoke back to her, trying her best to sound stern and forceful, "I am the floor leader! You must talk to me with respect!"

"I do not know who you are, and besides, you are not allowed back here. Only those that work the kitchens are allowed back here so you must leave." She yelled back at Su.

Su found herself getting angry. She was used to fear and anguish, and much sadness and frustration, but she had not allowed herself to feel anger... until now. She had to admit that it felt good. Maybe Lucy was right, it was time to take charge. "As floor leader I am allowed to go anywhere I want," she said, hoping it was true.

The old woman seemed to back down a step and asked, "What do you want? We are very busy making a delicious meal for your girls."

"You call our meals delicious?" Su fired back. "We are fed the same thing every day! Rice and vegetables! There is never any meat or sauce, never anything different!"

"We feed your girls what we are supposed to. Mr. Sanderson does not allow us to purchase much meat," she said.

Su looked around the kitchen and returned to the old woman.

"Mr. Sanderson is no longer in charge. Mr. Gant is the boss now, and he put me in charge of this building. My first order for you is to have a decent portion of meat at least three days a week. And you will make a sauce for it too. Not the runny crap you put on the rice, but a real sauce. Use the leftover meat and bones to cook it." She ordered.

The old woman looked at Su. Was that a look of newfound respect? Su hoped so, and before the woman could speak, Su said, "Mr. Gant will be advised of this new direction. He will be disappointed if it is not followed."

Su hoped she could convince Gant as easily as she convinced this old woman, and herself.

Later that week, following their usual long tedious day, the first women in the food lineup were surprised when their usual helping of rice was covered by thick gravy, filled with chunks of what appeared to be the white meat of chicken. The first few women looked around to see if they were somehow in the wrong spot. The other women, now noticing what was going on, and more importantly, what was on the first plates, also stopped to look around the room and then settled on the head cook, who merely smiled and pointed to the big room's entranceway.

"Do not look at me like that," she said. "This was her doing, Lord help us when the boss finds out."

As a group the women turned to see who the cook was pointing at and saw that it was Su, who stood in the entranceway to the large eating area.

Su found her cheeks turning red as she was now the center of attention.

"Eat up girls! To work hard you need energy and strength and this food will help you get that. The boss will expect you to work harder for it. Now, enough gawking, eat!" She said with a nervous smile. It felt good to do something nice for these women.

It was a meal like none of the women had experienced in a very long time, and for some, ever. The line was humming with conversation, and something that had been void in the building, laughter.

Su stood for a while at the back of the room, just watching the women interact and eat their meal. Outside she was satisfied that she had done something good for these deserving people but inside her stomach wrestled with what she had done. She hoped she knew what she was doing.

Over the next few weeks her theory was proven correct. Serving a better meal at least a few times a week improved everyone's attitude and energy levels. Even the cooks were now seen laughing and chattering with the women, and somehow, once in a while, managed to conjure up a small helping of fruitcake or pie for them. Production in the work area increased dramatically as the women, being better fed, and in a better frame of mind, could now sleep better and had more energy during the day.

At first Gant had argued with Su about the unnecessary increase in costs but even he noticed that production had increased, and the profits had also increased above the small cost of the extra food. He acknowledged that Su had been responsible for the changes, and he started watching her more and more, to the point where Su was becoming very uncomfortable in his presence.

It was on one of Gant's visits, that he called Su into the little office at the bottom of the stairs, formerly used by Mrs. Chow, and so little used by Su. Su preferred to do her paperwork at a vacant work station where she felt more comfortable, more a part of the rest of them.

When she arrive at the office's doorway Gant waved her in, and told her to take a chair. Su's hairs on the back of her neck stood up. Something was wrong.

"You've been doing a pretty good job here Su." Gant said, his eyes traveling the length of her body.

"Thank you, boss. We are all working hard here." She replied, not making eye contact.

"I just have one little problem Su," he said. "All of the changes you made were made immediately after Mr. Sanderson was gone. Why is that Su?"

"I was not in charge when Mr. Sanderson was here." She replied. "It was you that put me in this position."

Gant nodded. "That is true, but I can't help but wonder about the timing of all of this."

"I do not know anything about the timing and I do not know anything about Mr. Sanderson." She said, looking directly at the man.

"I am hearing a different story Su. I am hearing you women here may have had something to do with Mr. Sanderson's disappearance."

"That is impossible boss. How could we have anything to do with that? We are never allowed to leave this building, and you say Mr. Sanderson has disappeared? I did not know that until now."

Gant continued to stare at her. "We shall see Su, we shall see. I certainly hope you are not involved."

He got up from his chair and walked around the desk, getting close to the back of Su's chair. His hand touched her shoulder and then her hair, which he caressed softly. Then he abruptly grabbed a handful of her hair, and roughly pulled her head towards him so she was bent back over the top of the chair. She was forced to look straight up at him, smelling his stale breath and seeing the menace in his face.

"I have plans for you Su, and I hope you are not involved in this. If I find out differently, it will not be good for you. We have other places that we could put you to work, much more unpleasant than here. I do not want that for you. I want to look after you, but cannot do that if you are causing trouble," he said. He gave her head a strong pull before letting go, and quickly walked out of the room.

CHAPTER TWENTY-TWO

"WE'VE found a body" said the Latino detective, as he passed Farrell's desk.

"Way to go Amigo, have fun with it!" said Farrell, barely looking up from the pile of files on his desk. It really didn't matter how hard or how fast you worked, the cases just kept coming, threatening to drown anyone near. The last thing he needed right then was another one, especially with a body. He hoped Delano would just keep going, but, of course, he did not.

"This one will be of interest to you," said Delano, now standing right beside Farrell.

Farrell reluctantly looked up and immediately wished he hadn't.

"Why would it be special to me my little fucked up Latino buddy?" he asked.

"Because we think the body is Deets Sanderson." He replied.

This definitely got Farrell's attention and he sat back quickly in his chair. "Okay, what ya got, Delano?"

"Found a body tied to a chair in an old fish factory down off Lander on Harbor Island. Whoever did this could care less about ID. I guess he thought the rats would take the body before we did. Anyway, some guy waiting for his dog to take a shit beside a door to the building smelled something worse than his dog's stuff and had a quick look inside. He saw a guy tied to a chair and called 911. The wallet was still on him. Still had his credit cards and DL, even had a couple of hundred bucks so no way was it a robbery." said Delano.

"Who's at the scene?" Farrell asked.

"That's the thing Rick. This guy just phoned it in so there's really nobody out there 'cept a couple of squad cars."

"Get them to close if off for me, okay? I'm leavin' in a minute."

A few minutes later Farrell found himself in his trusty department-issue Chevy. He'd had exclusive use of this particular car for a year now and was comfortable with it. No high performance looking Camaro's or Mustang's on the force in Seattle, but that was okay. The Chevy wasn't glamorous but it had lots of guts and hadn't let him down yet.

As he arrived at the bottom of Lander he had no problem determining in which old warehouse the body had been found as a cruiser with its lights blinking partially blocked the gated entrance. It was once probably a booming parking lot which looked like it serviced several different buildings during the busy fishing years. Modernization had moved those businesses to a different location, many processing their product right on their boats, so this lot was now home only to cracked pavement, stubborn weeds filtering their way through each crack, and, of course, seagulls which still used the lot as a major landing area. The place was made even bleaker with the constant falling drizzle.

As he drove past the cruiser, he rolled down his passenger window and yelled out to the young uniform sitting inside his vehicle, trying to stay out of the rain. "Make sure no one touches that lock or the gate posts!"

As he pulled away he watched in his rear view mirror as the officer got out of his vehicle and, with a roll of yellow police tape, walked towards the gate.

It didn't seem that long ago that he had been a raw rook, thought Farrell. Putting in his time, and even walking a beat in a rougher downtown, when Pike's Market was the tourist's, 'place to be' during the day, but not during the night. Farrell couldn't say he enjoyed that duty but he had to admit that without it he wouldn't have been able to establish such a strong network of snitches. Those same shady individuals had helped him establish a solve record second to none in the department, not to mention indirectly setting up more 'meaningful' contacts throughout the city.

Yes, he could have accepted the promotions when offered but chose instead to stop at the level he was currently at, lead homicide investigator. He had more than enough money through wise decisions and investments, and had the freedom at this level to do what he had to do with minimal supervision or pressure from the powers above. That would probably change considerably with this case. Sanderson was a very influential person in this city and had numerous 'friends' in high places. Pressure would be applied to find out what happened, and who had made them happen, quickly.

Farrell pulled his car up to one of many old abandoned warehouses, this one clearly marked by the presence of numerous squad cars, and the forensic van, which had beat him to the scene. As he got out of the car he noticed the ever present squawking of the gulls. Why the hell did they still hang around places like this? Was there enough fish odor saturated into the old walls to keep them interested? Surely they hadn't had a meal here in a long time, or maybe they were sensitive to the smells of death.

He noticed that smell as soon as he moved past an officer at the door, and entered the large old building. Like most of the surrounding buildings this one had been used by fishing companies to sort and store their catch. Maybe the gulls had it right, as Farrell could still detect the faint odor of dead fish.

The building hadn't been used in a long time and the interior showed it. Cracks had developed in some of the walls and the constant dampness of the area had no problem seeping through, leaving huge wet stains on just about every wall. The ceiling was high and offered birds a place to call their own without bother. The sound of water dripping never stopped. At the far end of the building there was a separate room which looked like it had been, at one time, closed off from the rest of the place. It was still closed off by a huge double latching door, but it had seen better days, and was just barely attached to the hinges on one side. It looked like it had been partially removed, probably when larger equipment had to be taken out when the place had shut down. Judging by the thickness of the door, and the latches, this room must have been a giant freezer.

As Farrell entered he first saw several men and women, all wearing white smocks and gloves and rubber boots. They reminded him of ants on a hill, scurrying every which way, examining every part of the room with tiny brushes and taking samples, placing them in little vials, carefully labeling them. It was all about the evidence these days, thought Farrell. Screw up the evidence and you were fucked.

Almost exactly in the middle of this group against one wall was a chair occupied by what used to be Dieter 'Deets' Sanderson.

His face showed no visible signs of abuse thus he was easily recognizable. The rest of the body was a different picture.

Farrell approached a man he recognized, Chief Coroner, Mike Hablock.

"Fill me in Mike." He said.

The man, who had been closely examining the corpse, stood up and looked at Farrell. "Hey Rick. I've done a prelim but haven't moved the body too much. It is pretty easy to see what happened to it," he said.

"Give me the quick version Mike."

"Okay. First, cause of death was a close order bullet through the middle of his heart. It was very close as you can see the powder burns all around the wound. Whoever did this was probably only a few inches away from him. He was probably looking right into his eyes when he put the gun against his chest. Pretty fucking cold, if you ask me. The other wounds, although not the cause of death, were made to cause pain. He took a shot to each of his knees, issued from the top-down. Also from very close range. This man was tortured before he died. All of the wounds happened within a short period of time so I can't tell you in what order they came, but it is pretty sure to say the heart shot came last."

"Like he got whatever information he wanted then ended it quickly," said Farrell.

"Probably a good summation," replied the Coroner.

Farrell studied Sanderson's body. Although his head hung to the right side, both legs, and whatever was left of his knees, were pointed back at the entrance door. Farrell walked slowly back and forth in front of the body, looking at it from all angles, and at the room from all directions, finally arriving back in front of the body. He looked up at the ceiling, the walls, and then leaned over to examine the floor. After a few minutes of slowly pacing a small quadrant of the floor in front of the body, Farrell looked up and said. "Where is the other chair?"

Hablock looked at him. "What other chair?" he asked.

Farrell waved him over and pointed to a spot on the floor. "Look closely," he said. "The whole floor is pretty grimy and dusty. It's probably only seen rats and birds for years. Because it's close to airtight in here, with the door mostly closed, I'm betting even the rats and birds have mostly stayed out. If you look over at Sanderson's chair there are scuff marks on the floor right under each chair leg. There's not enough dust or grime in here to see footprints, but you can see marks where his chair moved. He was probably screaming and bucking around like crazy. I know I would be if somebody had me tied up and was blowing off my legs.

"Okay, I see the marks on the floor where his chair must have slid around a bit when he was squirming, and he has a pretty good lump on the back of his head where I assume he cracked it against the wall. What's your point Rick?" asked Hablock.

Farrell again pointed to the floor about eight feet in front of where the body was situated. "See here," he indicated a particular spot. "Same type of scuff mark. And there's another one. I see four of them. Our killer sat in another chair facing Sanderson, probably talking to him. There's another chair here somewhere. We find it, maybe we get prints or something."

It didn't take that long. One of the white smocked officers found a chair in the far corner of the warehouse. Well, it wasn't exactly a chair, but rather pieces of one. The officer was looking closely at a pile of old lumber and plywood when he noticed what could have been a spindle or something. The officer's dad had spent his retirement years tinkering in his garage where he built gazebos and park benches for fun. The spindle caught his attention because it was similar to the ones his dad put on the benches.

He called for assistance and, with the help of other officers, they were able to pull apart the lumber pile, and find enough pieces to account for a chair similar to the one upon which the body now occupied.

Farrell was impressed with the officer's discovery, and after acknowledging him, turned to Hablock. "I'm bettin' you find something on those pieces. Get me something Mike, a print, or a hair, something!" he said.

He left the building, and the crew to their work, walked to his car, started up and drove away. He noticed that there was now a wide circle of crime scene tape around the entrance gate and posts.

"We're gonna find you, you bastard, and when we do......."

CHAPTER TWENTY-THREE

"*I* need everything you can find on a Gant and Westgate," said Jonas. "And there's another guy, probably German, but I don't have a name."

It had been an emotional few days for Jonas. He fought between being glad that he had enacted at least a small measure of revenge for Chrissy's murder. But he also fought with the sickening feeling in his stomach when he thought about what he had done. Who was he now? What was he now? Was he a cold-blooded killer, a vigilante? Or just some guy who had taken steps now, to make up for ones he didn't take before to protect her.

Jonas spent hours walking, and talking to himself. Sure, these men were animals, but did that then say it was okay to be one too? Arguments on both sides were strong but he kept coming back to Chrissy's screams. No one deserved to be treated like someone else's garbage, used, and then just thrown aside with the regular trash. No matter how much he was sickened by his act, he was convinced that it was something he had to do. He had to track these evil men down and make sure they could not do what they had done the Chrissy, to anyone else. Again, he said, "Let's uncover every rock these scumbags can hide under."

Arthur 'A.C.' Chapman looked from Jonas to the others in the room, his 6 feet 5 inches not fitting with the thin, wiry, be-speckled man he was. Of course this was foreign to him, even though he had heard many horror stories from his ex-cop father, who used to think his son could not hear him when he spoke about his day to his wife in the kitchen. It was those very stories that led him to a very different route. He too wanted to solve crimes however, despite his size he wanted to do so from in front of a computer screen. For that reason he knew he would do his best now to help this young man track down the men he was hunting for.

For Bradley Howes it was a completely different story. Being only five feet ten inches was enough to make sure he qualified for bullying throughout his early years of school. Being black didn't help either. Add being gay, and the trifecta was in place to make most of his childhood days miserable. Only through very hard work, and long hours, was he able to establish himself, and his business, to the point where it was a bit easier to forget the past. But he had had his share of problems getting there, and had to fight back when he could, sometimes crossing over lines that he never thought he would have the courage too. But he had crossed the line a few times and was lucky enough that Brent Jameson was the one on the other side. Without Brent intercepting a young, and sometimes bitter and out of control young man, Brad would never have eventually found himself back in control of his own destiny. For this he felt he owed a large debt to Brent. He knew that the thugs Jonas was tracking were the same men that had done severe harm to Brent, so he was fully on board with being a part of this shadowy team.

Brent watched Brad and AC turn their thoughts around in their heads but, knew that these two good people would no doubt help him and Jonas with their task.

As if on cue. "I think we have a lot of work to do so, why don't we get at it!" said Brad.

"I agree" said AC. "Digging up dirt on these guys isn't all that difficult Jonas. These guys aren't exactly low profile, at least Gant and Westgate aren't. And maybe it will lead us to a German connection. Gant and Westgate seem to be into everything, real estate, golf courses for sure. Shit man, I think they own Boeing or something. This could actually be fun."

Jonas allowed himself a quick smile and then said. "Let's just see what you can dig up and maybe there is a way I can get at these guys. I'm thinkin' bank records, addresses of property they own, cars, and especially anything illegal you might get a hint of."

"So, tell me again how you got these names? Sanderson just volunteered them?" asked AC.

"Look guys," replied Jonas. "You don't want too many details, alright? I'm in this to right a wrong, and these guys are some real assholes, and one of them, one Deets Sanderson, is no longer a part of their slimy little gang."

"No problem Jonas, I just think we need to know in case some crap starts to hit the fan," said AC.

"Guys, I guess it's going too pretty quick, so if you are still in this you have to lay low, big time. Everything you do from here on in has to be off the radar," said Jonas.
Brent joined the conversation after watching all three men closely.

"Look, Jonas, whatever Sanderson got, he deserved. The same goes for the other guys. So fellas, let's see what we can get on Gant and Westgate, and maybe we'll also flush out the other one."

"Thanks guys. I know I said this was going to get dirty and, to be honest, I wasn't sure I could do it. But I'm all in now and don't intend to turn back. Let me know what you find," said Jonas, as he walked out the door.

Jonas walked to his car, sat in the luxuriously handcrafted leather seats, and closed his eyes. He thought of his sister, so full of life, and so deserving of better, deserving of a life surrounded by loved ones. A loving husband, a career, a few kids, (she always did love kids), and a nice family home in the burbs. You could have made me an uncle many times. He felt a tear in his eye and dabbed it away. Remember when we were little? Everybody was playing dress up or something, pretending to be a nurse or an astronaut. Not you. You had those chubby rubber babies all tucked in to their own little crib. I can remember you singing to them. You weren't that good a singer but the little ones never minded.

But she was not just his sister. She was his best friend, his buddy. Their grandpa was wonderful to them, but it was still mainly just the two of them, doing everything together, inseparable. He was the quiet one, not great looking through school, and overweight. She was the beauty to his beast, but she treated him like no one else. She always told him that one day he would find a woman that loved him and she would be the pain in the ass sister that always had too much to say. They would laugh about that. And he chuckled briefly now, his head resting back on the seat.

Chrissy, Chrissy, Chrissy, why couldn't things have been different? You should have lived a long and happy life. And grampa! How it must have hurt for the last years of your life, your little special angel gone. And it was up to me to protect her, and I failed.

Jonas opened his eyes and sat forward in his seat, the leather making its familiar crunching sound as he did. "Well, grampa, I know it's too late, but this is going to get done, or I will die trying. You both deserve that!" He said out loud. He starting the car and put it in gear.

A short time later Jonas pulled into the front lot of his condo building, hit the auto garage opener, and was about to drive under the building, when something caught the corner of his eye. He stopped, reversed the car, and there, sitting on their shared steps, was Tracy.

She gave him a little wave.

He backed the car up until he was directly in front of the steps, put the vehicle in park, and pulled himself out until he was leaning over the top of the car, looking at her. Man, she's stunning, he thought.

"Hey you," he said, "what are you doin' just sitting out here? It's only three o'clock. Shouldn't you be at the office?"

"Ha!" she replied. "When you're the boss............not to mention the only employee, you can take whatever time off you choose."

Jonas had an idea. "Well, if you're off for the afternoon can I talk you into an early dinner, or call it a late lunch if you want?" he grinned.

"That's the best offer I've had in a while and I'd love to. Let me grab a sweater."

A few minutes later she was seated beside him and he drove.

"Where too, fair lady?" he asked.

"If you don't mind a bit of a drive I know a nice place up the freeway a bit. Just past Lynnwood. I'd love to show it to you."

"Sounds good to me"

They drove north on the I-5 all the while making small talk.

Jonas couldn't help looking over at her whenever he could. He liked the way her eyes twinkled when she laughed, especially when she was looking right at him. He felt stirrings he hadn't felt in a long time, if ever. Taking this ride was the perfect therapy for him at that moment. It allowed him to forget the last couple of days and, if only for a short time, lose himself with this beautiful woman.

"Oh! Oh! Here it is coming up!" she almost screamed at him, laughing at the same time. "Take that turn off," she said, waving her hands in the air and pointing.

Off to the right they approached an older looking building. It seemed to be surrounded by old farm equipment, mainly rusty old tractors.

"Where are you taking me Tracy? I'm getting a 'deliverance' kind of feeling here," he laughed.

He drove down a long driveway completely bordered by old relic tractors. These appeared to be of every make and size that ever existed in the farm-tractor- world, and it seemed like John Deere dominated the line.

He pulled into a parking lot which was surprisingly almost full.

"I guess we're not the only guests," he said.

"Nope, this is a popular place. It's actually one of my clients, but they really don't have to advertise anymore. It's mostly for tourism brochures. The locals all know about it and keep it pretty busy. My dad used to bring me out here. The menu is pure meat and potatoes, which is him to a tee. No fancy fillet this, or mignot that, here. Just throw a steak on his plate and he is happy."

When they entered they found an open spot close to the back of the restaurant, which held about twenty tables, mostly full. The décor was like the outside, leaning heavily towards old-style farmhouse, with many shelves on the walls filled with old milk jugs, collectible dishes from many years past, and of course, pictures of pastures and horse-drawn wagons, and rugged-looking workers.

Once seated, Jonas sat back and looked at Tracy. "So, tell me about your parents. That is if you don't mind?"

"No, I don't mind, although there's not much to tell. My mom passed away when I was little, some rare form of Leukemia. I remember bits and pieces, but I was only five, so I can't recall much. My dad raised his little girl all by himself. He was an army mechanic so it wasn't easy. We moved around a lot, and he got really sick right after my mom died, and it was like, you know, why fight it when he had lost the love of his life, and all that. But I guess somewhere inside he realized he had a little girl that he couldn't leave behind, and one day he just started to get better. Eventually he was well enough to get back to work. He left the army and got a job out here with Boeing and he's still there, although he's about to retire sometime next year, I think. There, now that I've thoroughly bored you with my past it's time you do the same for me."

Jonas, although uncomfortable, decided he could share a bit.

"Well, we do have something in common. My mother also passed away when I was a kid, but it was my grampa who raised my sister and me. It seems that my dad couldn't handle having two kids around and no wife to help out, so he took off. I don't know where he went but he never came back. My sister and I became really close, and my grampa was the best! Anyway, as a kid, I played a lot of football, but I was always the chubby one, and I think I only made the team because it was tough for opposing players to get around me."

Jonas looked down at the table. "My sister was killed a few years ago and, I have to admit, that changed my life, probably forever. You would have loved her. She was my best friend. She and I could talk about anything and everything. I miss her a lot."

Jonas lifted his head and noticed that Tracy was nodding so Jonas asked, "Why do I have the feeling you already know some of this?"

Tracy looked at him. "Muriel told me you had been through a traumatic experience involving your sister but she didn't say more. Don't get mad at her, okay? We were just making conversation and I think it slipped out. She clammed up right away."

"Good old Muriel, always looking after me," he said.

"She didn't mean to talk about secrets. I think it was just her way of maybe warning me that I wouldn't be able to get too close, and all that. You can tell she cares a lot about you."

"Yes, she does, and I'd be lost without her. One day, I'll tell you all about my sister, and what happened. But for now, let's eat and enjoy the day. I'm starving and I'm enjoying your company."

Tracy flipped her hair away from the side of her face, which Jonas noticed was a habit of hers. A habit he was fascinated with.

"I really like being with you too, and you really are going to love the food here!" she said.

And so he did! He went with Tracy's recommendation of T-bone steak, served medium, with a generous portion of garlic mashed potatoes, with a corn and broccoli mix covered by a white sauce. Tracy had the same. After their meal, which, of course, was followed by home-made apple pie topped with vanilla swirl ice cream, they found themselves back in Jonas's BMW, and on the way back in to the city, both too stuffed to talk for a while.

Eventually they again filled the car with back and forth chitchat, and both could feel a connection building between them. Each of them felt that they might be on to something here, but were not willing to say anything out loud, perhaps fearful that the other did not feel the same thing happening. That fear was increased though, when, at one point, they locked eyes, before laughing and turning away. Jonas had felt it too. It was a good feeling.

Jonas pulled up to the front of their building and stopped near the step to let her out. She stepped out of the car, but, before closing the door, leaned back in and kissed Jonas on the cheek.

"Thanks for a wonderful first date. I had a blast and hope we can do it again," she said, with that same twinkle in her eye.

"I had a great time too, and you can bet we will be doing this again. Soon I hope," he said.

"That's great!" Tracy said, sounding and acting a bit like a teenager and obviously enjoying herself.

She bolted up the stairs without another word, leaving Jonas sitting there in his idling car, wondering if a bolt of lightning had just struck him.

CHAPTER TWENTY-FOUR

*"**BUT** Su, I cannot get this to go through as it is supposed to,"* said the young girl named Jay, whose English was one of the best in the factory, but whose talents to run a machine lagged far behind.

"Look, I'll show you again, this time more slowly. You will get it, do not worry," said Su, trying to be patient.

Su took the material and, looking at Jay, showed her where the fold should be. She then held it up for the younger girl to see. They both nodded. Su, using her right hand, put the folded corner into the sewing machine; hit a button on the side with her left hand, and the fold was permanently sewed into the fabric.

"Now you try again Jay," said Su, handing her the next piece of material in the pile beside her.

The young girl smiled nervously, but this time was able to successfully fold the material in the right place, and feed it into the machine. Following Su's example the end product was very close to perfect. Triumph radiated from Jay as she looked up adoringly at Su.

Su gave Jay's shoulder a light tap and was about to move on to the next world-threatening problem, when the front doors opened and in marched Mr. Gant and the usual rifle-carrying guard. Su's first thought was that the guard, and others like him, must actually live right outside the doors to this place. They were always there when the doors opened, thus the reason that no one had tried to escape. Not that there was anywhere for them to go.

Gant called out to Su and Lucy to meet him in the office.

"Immediately!" he called out.

Su caught Lucy's eyes from across the room, and both shared a look of panic.

What could he want with us? Su thought, remembering the last time one of the bosses called a meeting. That one was with Su and Mrs. Chow, who had been taken away, and had not returned.

It could not be poor production. Despite a slightly higher cost for the new food, which now included meat three times a week, Su had the women working hard, and, in fact, production had increased considerably, more than making up for the extra costs. So it couldn't be that.

So it was that Su was at a loss when she and Lucy entered the small office to see Gant sitting on the corner of the battered old desk.

He looked at Su. "I asked you before what you knew of Mr. Sanderson's disappearance and you said you knew nothing! Yet, he has been murdered and his body was found in a building not very far from this one. Do you still deny knowing anything about this Su?" he shouted.

"Boss, I have no knowledge about Mr. Sanderson at all. I am not lying to you!" she cried.

Gant was pretty sure these women had no knowledge of Deet's killing, but it didn't hurt to have something to hold over them. And his informants did report Deet's body being found near here, in an old fish warehouse very similar to this one and within easy walking distance.

"Su, I will admit that you have done a good job here but I do not trust you. I think the other women see you as one with some power, and their leader. This I cannot have!" he said.

For the first time he looked at Lucy. "Lucy, from now on you will be in charge. Everything will remain the same as it is only with you as the head girl. Su, you will be coming with me."

"But boss" cried Su, "I have done nothing wrong. I work hard and make sure the women work hard too! As you say, production is higher too! Why do you take me away?"

"It is not up to you to decide where you go. It is up to me, and only me! Do you not want to pay off your debt and start a new life?"

"Yes, of course I do, but I was working hard for that here!"

"Never mind, it is decided. Go and pack up your things. You are coming with me. Now go, and be quick!"

Su, in shock, went to her little area and gathered up her meager belongings. The work process had stopped when she walked past, and all eyes were on her when she came back down the stairs carrying her things. She walked towards the door but had to stop several times to receive a hug, or a quick kiss on the cheek, from many of the women, some of which she had considered enemies not that long ago. She hardly noticed them, and soon found herself in the back seat of a big black vehicle, the guard driving, and Gant in the passenger seat beside him.

They drove for a time, crossing over a bridge, and through areas of many large warehouses similar in size to the fabric factory Su had been taken from. All of this Su saw with wide-eyed amazement. At home they thought it odd to see more than one truck a week, and that was to pick up their produce for the market when their father could not take it himself. But here there were many trucks, and cars, all traveling at high speeds. Her thoughts drifted to her father, so hard and so cruel, and of her mother. She knew her mother would miss her two girls but Su hoped her life was a little bit better with them gone. They were no longer a burden, so hopefully this eased the fights between her parents. She thought too of little Ling, and wondered how she was. I'll find you one day little sister, she said to herself.

Her thoughts were interrupted by a sudden honking noise from the biggest truck Su had ever seen. Their vehicle had joined many others on a road wide enough to hold more than a dozen vehicles side by side. Su could only look out the side window with amazement. How do these people drive their vehicles so fast without killing themselves, or each other? They were travelling so fast and swerving in and out, and side to side. Even their big vehicle moved at a great pace and changed places from left to right and then back again. Su watched a vehicle as they flew past and saw the driver, a man, raise his had in some kind of wave, but with one finger sticking oddly upward. Su just watched as they left that car behind. What a strange place.

It wasn't long when they turned off the busy highway and onto a much quieter road. Su still saw many buildings, but they were much smaller than the warehouse, and here and there houses were mixed in with them. After winding down a long road with both sides taken up by large old houses they turned into one that seemed larger than those surrounding it, and was either newer, or much better maintained.

The men got out of the vehicle. Gant walked towards the house while the guard opened the back door and motioned Su to get out.

She walked on a paved pathway to a large wooden door, constantly being prodded from behind by the guard. The door was partially open and Gant was already inside, calling out to someone. By the time Su make it up to the door it was fully open and there, to her surprise, stood Mrs. Chow, who greeted her coldly, although Su detected a very slight twitching at the corner of the older lady's mouth, which could have been a smile.

"Come with me girl!" she said to Su, while moving off down the hallway.

Su followed her down the long carpeted hallway. She passed an opening to a large room and at a quick glance it seemed to be full of fancy large padded chairs and couches. She could not see much though as Mrs. Chow hurried her along. They came to a stairwell and started up.

Mrs. Chow spoke, "Su, although it is nice to see a familiar face it is not nice that you are here. I must keep my distance from you and we certainly cannot appear to be friendly. Do you understand?"

"I think I understand, but what is this place?" Su asked.

"It is a place where men, mostly white, come to be pleasured by women. They pay big dollars for this."

"But why was I brought here, I do not know anything about men?"

"You are not going to be pleasuring many men like the other girls. Mr. Gant has asked that you stay here for his pleasure only. It is good that you will not be used by other men but if you do not please Mr. Gant, it will go very bad for you."

"But what do I have to do?" Su asked.

"You will be taught when the time is right. For now you should keep quiet and cause no trouble," said the woman.

They reached the top of the stairs and were going along a hallway when, almost immediately after Mrs. Chow's words, a door opened and out stepped Mei.

"What is this little bitch doing here?" Mei yelled.
Before Mrs. Chow could reply a man's voice came from the stairs.

"She is my guest Mei, and will be treated as such!" Gant yelled out, as he reached the top of the stairs and faced the women.

"But boss. She is a trouble maker. No good will come of her being here! Let me take care of this problem right away for you," she said.

"I said, she is my guest! You don't have to like it but that's the way it is. Are you going to be a problem for me Mei?"

Mei stared daggers at Su and said, "No sir. It will not be a problem."

Mei stared at Su when she walked by with Gant and Mrs. Chow.

As Su came close to her she whispered. "You're dead, you little bitch!" and walked away.

Su tried not to think of Mei, but knew in the back of her mind she would have to face her again, but for now she was too busy looking around. Although the house looked older from the outside, it looked much newer inside. She had never seen lighting so bright and beautiful, and of many different colors, some actually moving. On the walls were many paintings, the subject of which was primarily naked people in various entanglements. Su tried to avert her eyes but the paintings were everywhere. The flooring was plush carpet which Su had only seen a small amount of in the office at the warehouse, and that was tattered and torn in places, and certainly nothing like this. She had seen carpet similar to this at a market she had visited when she was girl, but it too had been a small piece. This carpet was everywhere.

They came to a doorway at the end of the hall. "This will be your room," said Mrs. Chow. "Mr. Gant says you are to be the only one in this room and no one is to enter without permission. Do you understand?"

Su did not understand at all but was smart enough not to say so.

"Yes, Mrs. Chow. No one is to visit my room without permission. I understand." She said, hoping she sounded convincing.

The door was opened and Su entered her new living quarters. It was very much like the rest of the house, nicely colored, paintings on the wall, and the same thick carpeting throughout. There was a double bed set against one wall on top of which lay several pillows. Sur turned to Mrs. Chow, who spoke before she could.

"Yes, it is a beautiful room. It was used to entertain special clients, but Mr. Gant has ordered that this be yours, and so it shall be. I will come by later to tell you the house rules. For now you are not to leave the room except to use the bathroom which is the door right beside yours." Mrs. Chow turned and walked out of the room, leaving her alone with Gant, who had been watching the women, but not saying a word.

He approached her from behind, and, as she still stared at the luxurious room, he allowed his fingers to softly caress her long hair.

She turned at his touch, afraid to back away but could not force herself to just stand still. "What is it that you want from me?" she asked.

Gant had a gleam in his eye but also seemed to be nervous when he spoke. "I want everything from you Su. If you behave yourself here it will be much better than living in the factory. Life could be very good for you here."

Su stood back a step. "I only wish to pay off my debt and be free. That is all!" she said.

Gant also stepped back, grabbed the door and made to leave, but turned back to Su. "You will do as you're told, and whatever I order you to do! If you do as I tell you, and do not make trouble for me, you will one day gain your freedom. If you don't, my little Su, your life will have a bad ending!"
He walked out, closing the door softly behind him.

CHAPTER TWENTY-FIVE

*"**GOOD** call on the extra chair Rick. I doubt the guys would have looked through that pile of lumber, at least for a while"* said Delano. He had stopped in front of Farrell's desk.

"Yeah, well, we got lucky that the young cop noticed something, and had the brains to dig," Farrell said. "Any prints on it?"

"There's not much, maybe a partial but I don't think it's enough.

Interestingly though, forensics did turn up some hair."

"That's interesting. Maybe the guy sheds."

"No, nothing so easy, they say this stuff isn't real. Its fake, you know, like a fake mustache or a wig."

Farrell shook his head. "Great, like there's only about a million places he can get that shit. Don't you have any good news?"

"We may have something on a car. Some guy letting his dog take a dump thinks he saw a car around there that night, but he was pretty far away. It might have been a cab."

"This must be dog shit central. Wasn't it a guy walking his dog that found the body?"

"Yeah, but it was a different guy. Probably a different dog, so different dog shit too," Delano laughed.

Farrell slapped his hand hard on the top of his desk.

"That's it! Case fucking solved! This guy goes to the restaurant and hangs out with Sanderson. People saw him leaving with a guy but of course everyone was blitzed and too busy looking at all the tits in the room, so they didn't really look closely at the guy. They don't remember what the fuck he looked like or anything else about him. Anyway, they finish their night and, this guy, fake mustache itchin' like a bitch, hails a fucking cab and gets the driver to take him to this old warehouse. Just park here and wait will ya, he says to the cabby. I just have to take this guy in here for a while, strap him to a chair, blow his fucking legs off, chat for a minute or two, and then put a bullet through his heart. Then the guy comes out, got a little blood there on your wig sir, says the cabby, where too? How am I doin' here so far Delano?"

"That's just great, wonderful! I think you nailed it. Want me to file the case-solved report, or do you want to?" asked Delano.

Farrell got serious again. "Look, obviously it wasn't a cab but maybe it looked like one. You said the dog guy was a long way away, right? So maybe it was a big yellow piece of shit that looked, from a distance mind you, like a regular yellow cab."

"Yeah, he was at least a couple of hundred yards away, maybe more. And he only looked because his dog was dropping a major turd, and he had time to look around."

"Okay, I'm thinkin' no way this guy uses his own wheels so he needs something common and easy to blend in. Something people see every day and think nothing of. What better than a yellow fucking cab? Let's see if there have been any recent sales of big yellow Buicks or Chevy's. Maybe Fords and Dodges too. I think they use them as cabs too."

"I'll get the guys on it right away," said Delano, making his way over to his own desk.

Before Delano got too far Farrell yelled at him. "While you're on the phone get Sanderson's two bodyguard goofs in here."

Two hours later Cam and Lou again found themselves seated in front of an angry person's desk. This time it was Farrell's.

After listening to their story Farrell said, "Okay guys, let me get this straight. You guys are sittin' in your SUV, behaving yourselves, and watching your boss have a good time. Then some little old man, pushing an equally little old lady in a wheelchair, come along, and crash into the front of your truck. You guys get out of the truck, and these two senior citizens stick you with some kind of needle, that knocks you both out. How am I doin' so far?"

"That's right. Pretty well exactly like it happened," said Cam.

Farrell continued. "And then these two old farts somehow find the fountain of youth, or Viagra, or some fucking thing, because they somehow manage to carry both of you two very big guys back into the truck. What do you guys weigh?"

"About three sixty," said Cam

"About the same," followed Lou.

"Okay, so these old geezers manage to carry around seven hundred and twenty pounds of dead-weight humans, pick them up from the ground, and place them neat as a pin back in their seats. Don't you guys see why I'm having a difficult time buyin' this?" asked Farrell.

Cam leaned forward in his chair. "I know it sounds fucking impossible. It does to us too so we've been thinking......"

"Oh, you've been thinkin'," interrupted Farrell. "Well, I'm glad to see you two aren't just pretty fucking faces. What have you been thinking so hard about?"

"Well, you're right about us being too big for old fuckers to move, let alone lift. So we were thinking that these two had help hidden away somewhere, or maybe they weren't really that old. You know, like maybe they were wearing disguises or somethin'."

"Okay guys, who are you working for now that your boss is gone and you're probably getting the blame, right?" asked Farrell.

"Yeah, you're right about that. There are powers out there that are some pissed." said Lou.

Now Farrell leaned forward in his chair. "Care to tell me who?"

"You know we can't do that. Let's just say Deets was a businessman, and businessmen have partners. I guess we work for them now. Are you about done with us? We've co-operated and told you everything we know."

"Yeah, you can go. But, listen up boys! This is a police matter. I don't need two giant thugs out there hunting people down. Do you guys get that?" asked Farrell.

"We got it," they both said at the same time, as they rose from their chairs and left the office, lumbering their way past desks and cubicles, almost making the building shake with their combined weight. All eyes watched their passage.

Before Farrell could leave the interview room Delano stepped in.

"So, was that a lovely couple or what? I kinda like the strong quiet one in the back," he said, shaking his head.

"I think it's time to start a story board" said Farrell, walking over to the far wall which was primarily a white board writing surface.

He dug Sanderson's picture out of his file and taped it up high on the left side of the board, about a foot from the ceiling. With a marker he printed 'SANDERSON' under the picture. He then taped a photo of the two bodyguards below Sanderson's and printed their names below each. He stood back and stared at the photos and the blank expanse of the wall to the right of them. He went to the desk and rummaged in a drawer until he came out with a large sheet of blank white paper. He approached the wall and hung this paper on the far right, an equal distance from the ceiling and about six feet over from Sanderson's. Under this paper he printed 'KILLER'. Under this he put two smaller pieces of blank paper under which he wrote, 'LITTLE OLD LADY/WHEELCHAIR' and 'LITTLE OLD MAN'. Below those he put up two more small pieces of blank paper and printed 'HELP?'.

He stood back and had a long look at the entire board. He then walked up to the board, and, with a colored marker, drew a line from the bland KILLER paper to the center, and wrote YELLOW VEHICLE/LIKE CAB in a circle.

He had a lot more details he could have put on the board, like probable weapon type, bullets used etc., but he didn't want to clutter up the wall just yet. Those details could be added later. He just wanted the bare basics staring at him for now.

He stood beside Delano and both looked up at the wall.

"So, Sanderson goes out for his usual good time, lots of food, booze, and tits. His thugs drop him off and park just up the street, supposedly keeping an eye on him. Two people, dressed like geezers come along, pull the big trick with the two bozos in the truck and, I think, at least a couple other guys are hiding, probably right behind the SUV, to help lift them back in to the thing. Set them up nicely, like they were sleeping. Our guy comes out of the restaurant with, or right behind, Sanderson, pops him on the back of the head and helps him into a vehicle. I know the dog walker saw a yellow car at the warehouse site but I'm bettin' he saw that a different time, maybe when the guy was scopin' the place out earlier. Sanderson's a fairly big guy so I doubt they used the yellow car to haul him out there from the restaurant. I'm guessin' a van of some type, easy to get him in and out of. There's only about a million vans in this city too." He paused.

"Anyway, he takes an unconscious Sanderson to the old fish warehouse, sets him up nicely in a chair, grabs a chair for himself and sits down, waiting for Sanderson to return form lullabyeland. When he does finally wake up, he sees this guy sittin' there, holding a gun. The guy starts askin' questions right away. I'm thinkin' he didn't get the answer he wanted to the first one, so the guy calmly walks over, and puts a hole through Sanderson's knee. Don't know which one was first, but it doesn't matter. The guy then goes back to his chair and waits for Sanderson to stop screamin'. And it must have hurt like hell so he was definitely screamin'. When the screamin' stops I'm bettin' Sanderson starts calling this guy every name he could think of. Somewhere Sanderson fucks up. He either doesn't give the guy the answers he wanted or he called him one too many nasty names. Doesn't matter, because the guy gets a bit pissed and again walks over, and POW! This time he blows off half of his other leg. This time Sanderson jerks so hard his head hits the wall behind him, hard. The guy then sits back down, and again waits for Sanderson to stop screamin' and bucking around in the chair. This time good old Sanderson is a changed man. Whatever this guy wants he can have. Just ask and he'll answer. Just don't hurt him anymore. I'm thinkin' our shooter now gets more serious with his questions. The first ones were done almost on purpose so Sanderson would be forced to lie and then get his knees popped. The shooter needed to show Sanderson that he was serious. So now he gets down to business, the real reason he was there in the first place. What he really wants to know. When he finally gets the answers he wants he walks over to Sanderson, and probably whispers some sweet goodbye in his ear, and while he is doing that he puts the gun against his chest and finishes him."

Delano had been listening closely. "Fuck, Rick, that's pretty cold. This guy is bad news."

"Yeah, I agree," said Farrell. "Once he got the info he wanted he had to eliminate Sanderson as a witness because I don't think he was wearing a mask or a hood. Otherwise we probably wouldn't have found the fake hair."

"Jesus!" said Delano, slowly shaking his head.

"Yeah, it leaves a ton of unanswered questions of our own. Firstly, who the fuck is this guy, and why Sanderson? What did he know that this guy needed? And the biggest fucking question is simply......who's next?"

Delano looked over at Farrell. "You think there will be more?"

"Oh yeah!" answered Farrell. "This might only be the first and Sanderson might have helped him out."

"Do you think he's going after Sanderson's crowd?"

"That would be my bet. This isn't just one guy. I count at least four in on it now, and there might be more."

Farrell walked up to the wall and tapped the blank KILLER paper hanging menacingly on it. "Delano, this whole thing is personal. Otherwise, why shoot the guy's legs off. He wanted to cause a lot of pain. This is payback for something. And I don't think he's anywhere near done!"

CHAPTER TWENTY-SIX

ALTHOUGH the meeting was being held in the same Saloon-styled building, owned by Bradley, there was a distinctly different mood throughout when Jonas walked through the double swinging doors. Gone was the casual 'lounge on the couch with your buddies' attitude. Instead, Jonas found the couches and ottomans had been pushed aside to be replaced by a large table, upon which were two laptop computers, a printer, and reams of paper, in several different stacks spread around the table.

AC was situated at one end of the table with the two laptops facing him, side by side. He seemed intent on studying the screens of each, his head swiveling from one to the other, while his fingers busily clicked away at the keyboard in front of him, seemingly unaware that there were other people in the room.

At the opposite end sat Brad, who was looking through documents that were being fed to him by the laser printer in front of him. Jameson was at the counter on the far wall, throwing sandwiches together.

Neither of the men seemed to notice Jonas as he entered, and all were slightly startled when he called out. "Hey guys, what do we have so far?"

"Well, we've got lots of stuff on Gant and it's leading us towards Westgate too, although he's buried deeper. I'm still digging on him as we speak," said AC, looking up only briefly from his computers.

"Okay, let's see what you've got so far on Gant," said Jonas.

Brad waved a stack of papers at him. "We've printed out most of it for you to look at. He's been around or near Seattle most of his life."

"Give me the short version now and I'll go through all of this stuff later."

"Well, as I said, he's been around here pretty much his whole life," continued Brad. "His father hit it big back east and moved out here when Gant was just a kid. Typical rich kid, lots of toys, nice cars, couple of houses, fast friends. I get the feeling he didn't get along with his dad much. Can't find a reference to a mother, although with Gant and his dad being high-rollers, if there was a mom, she was probably way in the background and not seen much. Anyway, he might not have liked his dad much, but it didn't stop him from enjoying his money. It didn't just provide the toys, but also the parties, drugs, and of course, the girls. Interestingly enough he seemed only to be seen with oriental women, beautiful, well-built to be sure, but always oriental. I can't find any names, but these women always seemed to remain silent, never stealing the limelight from Gant. All of the searches we've done, and any articles with photos we can find always show him with an oriental woman, but not always the same one. It seems like he spends time with one and then, all of a sudden, he appears with a different one on his arm.

There are lots of rumors out there that he, Sanderson, and Westgate, are into human trafficking and prostitution. I'm betting the oriental girls are a product of that."

"Have you tracked any of this down to specifics?" asked Jonas.

It was AC's turn. "It seems their prostitution does not involve simple street hookers. They are concentrating their women in houses only. These houses, and those women, must only cater to specific people known to Gant and the gang, because I can't find any signs of advertising anywhere, legit or underground, on the web. We've looked through lots of ads and shit, but it is the usual massage or dating crap you see every day. I've tracked them as far as I can, but they're dead ends."

Jonas sat down in a chair at the table. "So we are basically nowhere then."

"No, I wouldn't say that," said AC, a slight smile on his face.

"Go on." Said Jonas.

"We've had a close look at Sanderson's credit card statements."

"You can get access to those?" asked Jonas.

AC was now definitely smiling. "Oh, hell yes, we can! Don't ask me how, okay? Just suffice it to say that with a few clicks here, and a few clicks there, most of which are illegal as hell, and, presto! I have financial records on one Dieter 'Deets' Sanderson."

"Anybody hungry?" yelled Jameson, approaching the table carrying a huge tray filled with sandwiches in one hand, a jug of some type of juice in the other.

"I'm starved" said Brad.

"Me too," echoed AC, finally looking up from his work.

"Jesus guys! You're gonna leave me hangin' while you eat?" said Jonas.

Jameson had put the sandwiches and juice on the table and stepped towards Jonas. "C'mon Jonas, lighten up. These guys have been at this for hours. Grab a chair and take a few minutes to let them catch their breath, and get something in their stomachs."

Jonas realized he had been pushing it. "Yeah, you're right Brent. Sorry guys. I guess some of this is getting to me. Go ahead and eat. Take your time, and you can fill me in more when you're done."

"Hell man, I can eat and talk at the same time," said AC through a mouthful. "What we found is several high end purchases through his American Express card. They were for renos to a place over by Kinnear Park. It's not a neighborhood he would live in, so I think we may have found one of their 'houses'."

"Give me the address and I'll check it out later," said Jonas.

AC wrote the address down on a slip of paper and handed it to Jonas. "I've Google-earthed the place. I think you'd be safer at the back. It looks like there is an alley running behind it that might allow you to get fairly close without being seen. No way can you just park in front. Either way you will have to be careful."

"I'll just do a quick drive by and maybe walk the alley but that's all unless Gant is there. Then all bets are off. Now, what have we got on Westgate?"

Bradley reached over his food and grabbed a handful of papers.

"Alex Westgate," he read, "A self-made multi-millionaire several times over through buying and selling real estate. Everything I've got here looks legit. It is interesting though, because he's made a lot of money through transactions involving city hall. Not directly, but when I trace the transactions back quite a few of the properties were once city-owned. If I was a betting man, and I'm not, but if I was, I'd say he's got some pretty good contacts high up in political circles. A lot of these things need special permits and permissions, and he always seems to get them. So, if not illegal, they are at best of the shady variety. But I've just started on him, so maybe I'll know more once I've spent more time on him. It also seems he has several residences, both here and around the country. He spends a lot of time in L.A., but I'm thinking Seattle is still his home base. I'll get more for you on that too."

"Great work guys!" said Jonas. "Maybe I'll leave you to this stuff and take a drive over to Kinnear Park, see what I can see."

Jameson stood up from the table, wiping his mouth with a paper towel. "Just watch your back. Let us know what you're doin', preferably before you do it, okay? AC set you up with that fancy new cell phone for a reason. Make sure you use it if you need too."

Jonas patted his jeans pocket which contained the new cell phone Jameson was speaking about. AC had set it up for him and shown him the basic operations so he felt he was good to go. "I'll be sure to do that," he said, as he rose from the table and left the room.

It had turned out to be one of those sunny Seattle days that made you forget how many rainy ones you had to go through just to get to one of these. Not a cloud tainted the blue as far as the eye could see, and only a light comfortable breeze moved the trees pleasantly. It was fast approaching late afternoon and it was promising to be a nice evening. Jonas thought of Tracy and wondered if an evening walk was in order.

Kinnear Park snuck up on him while he was thinking ahead to the evening and he almost missed his planned turn. Looking quickly at the address scribbled on the paper he made a quick right hand turn. It wasn't a bad neighborhood, just not one that sees too many sprawling family houses or big yards. The bright afternoon sun shone on mostly asphalt and old roof shingles. The mix between commercial buildings and houses was about even, with the houses competing for the same 'used' status as their commercial cousins.

It wasn't hard to pick out the subject of his search as it stood out from its neighbors, mainly because the neighboring buildings had been demolished sometime in the past and had not been replaced.

The house was old but had been recently renovated, which jived with Sanderson's American Express card spending history. It was a three-storey, with a covered porch that ran completely across the front and wrapped around one side. In the short time it took Jonas to cruise past he could see that most of the rooms had lights on. Perhaps he would get a better look from the back, as advised by his crew. He drove down another block, turned right and parked where he could see the lane that followed all of the properties. He could walk to the back of the house from here.

He locked the car and took a quick look around. Nothing seemed to be active in the immediate area so he set off down the alley. Unfortunately all of the properties, even the vacant lots, had high wooden fences bordering the back, so perhaps the view wasn't going to be as good as Jonas had hoped.

He walked slowly down the alley, sticking close to the high fence, on the alert for a dog, or somebody else walking. He encountered nothing, and finally made it to the back of the house he wanted. He stopped, and stood up against the fence. After again looking around for anything else moving, and satisfying himself that he was alone, he looked over the fence, his height allowing about a six inch clearance.

There were several large and fully leafed trees lining the inside of the yard's fence, making it difficult for Jonas to see directly to the house. Inching his way along the fence, he finally found a spot where the branches from side by side trees did not completely meet, allowing him a view of the back of the house.

Once again, as in the front of the house, most of the windows were well lit up. Jonas could see the shadowed movement of several people inside, appearing to be mostly women. He glanced at his watch. It was probably way too early for much business so these people were probably all getting the place ready for the night's entertainment. When the figures got close enough to the window for Jonas to get a better image, he noticed that most of them appeared to be shorter, possibly oriental. From his vantage point there also seemed to be four substantially sized 'shadows' standing in one spot, and not moving around like the others. Guards, thought Jonas, had to be.

He'd seen enough, and didn't want to push his luck by staying too long and made ready to move, when some motion caught his attention. It came from the third floor of the house where there was a small balcony of some sort. Behind this balcony was a tall window, which was curtained. The motion he detected came from those curtains moving aside and a woman coming out to lean on the balcony's railing. The woman was able to look directly down at him, and he directly up at her. They both froze where they stood, Jonas waiting to see if she gave him away to the guards inside. He was unsure of what to do, so he did the only thing that came to his mind.

He smiled, and waved. Part of him expected the woman to immediately run back inside to notify someone that there was an intruder, but he hoped that wouldn't happen, and it appeared that he was correct. The woman simply stared back at him. Perhaps she too didn't know what to do. Her face was too far away to make out fine details but he could see her long black hair falling over her shoulders. He could tell also that, like the other women in the house, she was oriental, and he wondered if she was one of the working girls, smuggled into the country on false promises. But why did she seem to be isolated on the third floor. The way the house was peaked it was obvious that the third floor contained only a small area, probably one or two rooms and maybe a bathroom. Everyone else in the house was on the first two floors.

For what felt like a long time, but in fact, was only seconds, they continued to stare at each other. Then a shadow appeared at the balcony's door behind the woman, and she made to re-enter the room. Before she did though, she hesitated, turned back to Jonas, and to his surprise, gave him a hurried wave. In his mind he saw a tiny smile too.

CHAPTER TWENTY-SEVEN

SU paced back and forth, from one side of the bedroom, around the bed, to the other, and then back the same way, over and over again. She was thinking. She hardly noticed the many nice things in the room. The dresser with a build-in recessed area to sit and apply make-up (not that Su was even remotely familiar with applying make-up, but had seen the pleasure girl's facial transformations), the lamps with their colorful shades, the thick comforter on a bed, much bigger than any she had ever seen, and easily large enough for two or more, and, of course, the thick carpeting beneath her feet. This she was familiar with as she remembered the merchants, where her parents sold their produce, who had different types of carpets on display, all made painstakingly by hand over many months. But this carpet was different. It did not have woven borders but instead covered every square inch of the floor right up to the walls. No matter where she paced she could feel its thickness, and often looked down to watch her toes sink into its plushness.

She was looking down now as she made her way to the sliding door which opened to a small balcony. A slight breeze shuffled the curtains and seemed to call to her. She slid the door to the side and stepped out to the small area, barely big enough for two people to stand side by side. There was a short railing that completely surrounded the small deck. Su was able to lean on the top of it and look at the yard below. She knew it would be difficult to get past the guards below, even though they stayed in the shadows, but up here there were no guards, as the distance to the ground was too far, with serious injury to follow if a jump were attempted. She had been out here once before, and had looked down the twenty feet or so to the ground. The yard was mostly dirt with a few patches of unattended grass. Surrounding the yard was a high wooden fence. There were several tall oak trees growing near the back of the yard, just inside the fence. They were taller than the house, and Su briefly thought she could jump to one of those and scale down to the top of the fence and then over and away, but she knew that it was simply too far. The branches, now fully leaved, were so thick that they did not allow much of a view of the house's surroundings. When the wind blew them briefly to the side she caught glimpses of other buildings, and could hear what she now recognized as vehicle noises off in the distance.

Su continued to lean on the top rail with both arms, her hands extended out towards the trees. Still deep in thought, she followed the big branches from their tips down to the trunk and to the fence, where many hung far out into the narrow roadway on the other side. She could hear voices approaching from inside the house and, although she knew she should go inside immediately, she didn't want to leave the peacefulness of the balcony.

Suddenly her eyes spotted something that did not fit with the rest of the scene. There was a slight breeze causing the branches to sway, and when one of them moved she was sure she saw something near the back fence. She watched the spot closely and, there it was again! It was a face! This time she was able to move a bit to her left and was able to get a better sightline. Yes, there was someone there looking over the fence.

She continued to watch closely as the man, yes, it was a man, peered over the fence looking at the house, his head moving from side to side, like her, trying to get a good viewing angle through the moving branches. Suddenly he looked up in her direction. She froze. She could see only his head but she could tell that he was a white man with close cropped hair. He was obviously tall as he could see over the fence. She could see that he was looking directly at her.

The voices inside the house were getting louder as they got closer to her room. Su was about to leave, when the man seemed to smile at her, and waved, a short gesture with one hand slightly above his head, but a wave nonetheless.

Su turned to re-enter her room but stopped. She looked back at the man, who still stood there, and lifter her hand and returned the wave, and almost smiled. She then completed her turn, pushed aside the curtains, and walked back into her room.

The sight of the man was instantly forgotten because of who now stood before her in the middle of her room.

"Jing-Wei!" cried Su, as she unbelievably saw her friend standing there staring at her.

"Su!" echoed Jing-Wei who almost ran the few steps between them, throwing her arms around her.

After a lengthy hug they separated, and while keeping their hands on the other's arms, they were able to have a longer look at each other.

Jing-Wei, who was quite a bit taller than Su, looked down at her friend. She saw that Su was still very pretty, but noticed right away that there now was a toughness about her that had not existed before. She still stood straight as she had always done when they were together on their journey from their homeland.

"Your hair is so shiny, and so long!" Jing-Wei said, while laughing and reaching out to lightly grasp a few strands of Su's long black hair.

"I forgot how tall you were, my friend," she said to the taller woman. As she looked her over she noticed that some of the hardness that had existed before seemed to have been replaced by something else. Jing-Wei was well kept. Her clothing was elegant and fit well but they did not suit the person Su knew her to be. Her face now wore much make-up as if to hide the real person beneath, and her eyes were framed by numerous lines that could not hide what was truly there.

Su stood back and said, "So, Jing-Wei, you must tell me where you have been and why you are here."

The expression on Jing-Wei's face changed and she moved over to the end of the bed, quickly sitting down and waving Su over to join her. "It has been a very tough time Su. I won't lie to you, but I have to be careful what I say. I am not supposed to be up here with you, but managed to get a few minutes that the others won't talk about."

"Why are you not allowed up here? Are you too a prisoner of this place, of these people?" Su asked.

"My friend, they told us we have a debt to pay and then we will be free. Have they not told you the same thing?"

"Yes, many times. I have been saving all that I can to pay my debt."

Jing-Wei looked closely at Su. "Su, there is no debt. No matter how much you save it will never be enough."

"But Jing-Wei, they have told us..........."

"It is a lie! They will keep us as long as we are useful and then cast us aside like trash. If we are lucky we will stay healthy enough to last longer, but in the end we will all end up the same."

Su stood from the bed and began pacing the floor, as she had done earlier. "But Mr. Sanderson promised us that if we worked hard we would one day be free to leave," said Su, and then, as if in afterthought, "Do you know what happened to him? Is this why you think we will not be allowed to leave?"

"No Su," replied Jing-Wei. "I do not know what happened to him, only that he is gone, and now Gant is in control, and he is much worse than Sanderson."

"How do you know this?" asked Su.

Jing-Wei sat further back on the bed, one hand going to her face to wipe away a tear that had appeared. "Su, it has been a terrible time for me since you and I were separated. I was made to do awful things just to save myself. I became Sanderson's pleasure girl, which, on one hand was good because no one else could touch me, but was also very bad because Sanderson could have me whenever, or wherever, he wanted. He likes tall oriental girls so that is why he picked me. That is why I look like this," she said, gently rubbing her hand across her made-up cheek, coming away with a red powder on her fingers.

"Jing-Wei, now that Sanderson is gone what will happen to you?"

"I do not know Su. I am afraid they will send me back to the factory or worse, will make me be a regular pleasure girl in one of these houses."

"Is that what they are planning to do with me?" asked Su.

"No, I do not think so. Gant has put you up here so no one else will touch you. I think you will be only his like I was with Sanderson."

Su stopped pacing. "I will not let him touch me!"

"You will not have a choice. He is a strong man and will have guards to help if you fight him too much. That is what happened to me." Jing-Wei said, turning away. "They tied me down and Sanderson did unspeakable things to me. He even shared me with another man, a man with a filthy beard. I could not even fight back."

Su sat beside her friend and held her close. Jing-Wei allowed herself to cry on Su's shoulder for a moment but then sat up straight. "I cannot be found here. It would not be good for either of us. I must go!"

"But Jing-Wei, we have much to talk about," said Su, an idea forming in her mind. "We must make plans to leave this place."

"Oh Su, escape is impossible. Where would you go? We are in a strange country. We know a little of the language, but that is all. They would send Mei after us and she is..............."

Su jumped up from the bed. "I saw Mei when I first arrived. I could not believe it. And she has power here?"

"Yes, Mei is in charge of any discipline needed, and she enjoys her job. If you do not do as you are told she will not go lightly on you. You look like you know of what I speak."

Su resumed her pacing while looking at Jing-Wei. "Yes, I know Mei. She tried very hard to kill me at the factory and would have succeeded except for luck being on my side. She has sworn to get even with me."

"I had better leave now, said Jing-Wei." Please try to take care of yourself, and when Gant comes for you try not to fight. It will make it easier."

Su watched Jing-Wei walk to the door.

"I will be careful Jing-Wei, but if I have to, I will kill Gant to get away. Someday I must find my sister and I will do anything to do that. Let us talk again when we can, and we can make plans to get away before anything happens."

Jing-Wei looked back before shutting the door. "I will try, my little Su, I will try. I am so glad you are well, and we will see each other again soon."

After the door closed softly, Su returned to her pacing, her mind again thinking there must be a way to escape this nightmare.

CHAPTER TWENTY-EIGHT

"**OKAY** guys, I've got a lock on this guy Westgate," said an excited AC.

It was Saturday night, not raining too hard, at least for Seattle, and Jonas, AC, Brent, and Bradley were in the old saloon, as Jonas now called it, having just finished a pizza and a few cold ones. AC, as usual, did not sit for long and had left the couches quickly after wolfing down his meal. He had been in the middle of something and had only reluctantly taken a short break, and only after the other guys threatened to physically carry him away from his work area. He had spent the last twenty minutes with his eyes locked on his monitor, and his fingers flying over the keyboard.

"I followed a bunch of info on our friend Sanderson, God please *don't* take mercy on his soul, and he, and our newer friend, one Allan Gant, have some history together. It looks to me that they got together a few years ago and have been partners in a whole lot of things ever since. I've traced some stuff through their legal holdings, and Jonas, you might be surprised to find that they own a few warehouses near where you last saw Sanderson breathing."

Jonas sat up. "Jesus, wouldn't that be something if it was one of their warehouses?"

"Nope, I've cut into the police stories and the one you used is not theirs, but damn close. On the same block of buildings, I think."

"Can you see what they use the buildings for?" asked Brent.

"No again," replied AC. "I think they are mostly abandoned. They might be worth a drive-by though."

"Good idea," said Jonas.

"Anyway," continued AC. "Whenever I search company records on Sanderson and Gant, this guy Alex Westgate shows up too. Actually, he shows up on the top of the lists most of the time."

"What does that mean?" asked Bradley.

"Well, I'm thinkin' Sanderson and Gant work under this guy Westgate. He's probably the money in the group, so I'll assume he's also the boss. I've only tapped into their legal stuff but they all show Sanderson and Gant as Directors, whereas Westgate is almost always the CEO or President of whatever enterprise they are in. They own a lot of shit and have a lot of different companies listed, but I'm still guessin' Westgate is the man."

"Okay, what have you got so far on Westgate?" asked Jonas.

"Not a whole lot yet, other than his attachment to the other two, and their companies, just some ordinary shit. I do know he owns a brand new mansion on Mercer Island overlooking Lake Washington. Maybe you should take a look at that too, while you're drivin' around."

"Agreed," said Jonas. "Tomorrow I'll do a quick drive by those warehouses and take a spin over to the island to check out his new place. I'll need the addresses AC."

"No sweat. Let me just print this stuff and you'll be good to go."

The next morning Jonas found himself seated at the breakfast nook with Muriel. As usual, she had toasted bagels and jam with fresh coffee, ready when he was. He insisted that she join him, which she did.

"So, how are things with you and Mr. Bartlett?" he asked her.

"Now Jonas, I can see the look in your eyes." Muriel blushed. "Mr. Bartlett and I are becoming quite good friends, but there is no hanky-panky going on."

Jonas decided not to tease her too much so he simply said, "Well, I'm glad you two are getting along so well. You need to have friends, and you could do a lot worse than Mr. Bartlett, that's for sure."

She smiled and said, "You're one to talk, Jonas. I don't see you with a very active social life either. I know you have to do what you have to do, and don't get me wrong because I don't want details, but you have to be careful to take care of yourself too. And that includes having friends and doing things besides this 'mission' that you are on, which I am not supposed to know about, so won't mention. You know, Jonas, there is a very nice young lady not too far from your front door that would love to be one of your friends."

Jonas, never comfortable with this topic, said, "Yeah, Muriel, I know, I know. Tracy seems like a great girl. I'm just not sure I should go there right now. I never was good around girls, and even though I've shaped up somewhat, I still feel uncomfortable when dealing with them."

"I know you've been through a lot Jonas, but you are not the same chubby, shy kid, you used to be."

Jonas looked up, but Muriel cut him off before he could speak. "I've seen the pictures of you from before the accident. Believe me, you are not the same kid you were before that. You came out of that hospital a different man. I'm just saying that you need to have a life too. At least give Tracy a call once in a while, okay?"

Jonas got up from the table. "I'll tell you what Muriel. I'll do better than that. I'll go pound on her door right now and see if she wants to go for a drive with me."

Muriel watched as he walked out the front door, and she thought she noticed a little jump in his step.

Jonas's bravado in front of Muriel quickly dissipated as soon as he closed his door behind him, and faced Tracy's across the landing. He took a deep breath and made his way to her door, hesitated for a second or two, took another deep breath, and thought 'what the hell' and knocked. He heard motion from inside the apartment and a moment later Tracy opened the door. Jonas felt like a wind had hit him full force. Tracy wore a light blue summer dress and her hair flowed over her bare shoulders. Her eyes twinkled as she looked at him.

"Well, good morning sir! You must be my new mail man, or do I owe you money?" She asked, while laughing.

"Well, ma'am, I'm neither," deadpanned Jonas, all of a sudden enjoying himself. "Ya see, ma'am, I'm about to go out drivin' and was wonderin' if'n you'd like to come along. Maybe ride shotgun with me," he continued, in his best 'John Wayne' voice.

Tracy could no longer keep a straight face and laughed out loud. "Kind sir, this little lady would certainly be happy as punch to come along with you. Just give me a minute to fetch my things and I'll be right along." She swung around and disappeared into her apartment, but her laughter was loud, and joined with Jonas's.

A few minutes later they were in Jonas's BMW and turning left on Madison, headed towards the I-5.

"Where are we going, Jonas?" Tracy asked.

"I told you that I would tell you about my sister, and I'd like to do that. But first I thought we would go to see her, if you don't mind?"

"Not at all Jonas, where is she buried?"

"It's not that far. That is one of the reasons I live in this area, to be as close as I can."

They drove down Madison, took a right on 23rd Avenue to Aloha, and then up to 15th, past the Asian Art Museum to the gates of Lakeview Cemetery. The cemetery was calm, as most are, and there were very few people visible from the car. They parked, and Jonas led Tracy down a narrow paved walkway that was only wide enough for maintenance vehicles to make their way through the grounds. They didn't have to walk far and Jonas stopped in front of two headstones, each about three feet in height.

One read 'Marisa Carterell, Beloved Mother', the second, 'Christine Carterell, wonderful sister and best friend'.

Jonas spoke with his head bowed, "I wasn't much older than her, but after my father took off I thought of myself as her bodyguard, her protector. Unfortunately I didn't do a very good job of that." He wiped a small tear that threatened to run down his cheek. "We actually didn't get along as little kids, but Mom passed away, and our father just couldn't take it and left us with our grandfather."

Tracy moved closer to Jonas and reached out to grasp his hand.

"Tell me what happened, Jonas, tell me about her."

And he did. He told her of their childhood, their early years with typical fights and arguments that most kids go through. But eventually they had become inseparable. He told her about the many things they had in common, like the music they shared, that they both hated onions, but loved chocolate. How she loved to sing and he couldn't hold a tune. How they talked endlessly of the future, of having families of their own. Family barbecues and trips they would all take together. And kids, they both wanted kids. She would name her son William, and he would name his daughter Christine. How none of that would happen now because of one night, and one time where he couldn't protect her like he should have.

He told Tracy about that night, at least all that he could remember. He told her about the hospital in Canada, Mr. Bartlett and Muriel, and his move back to Seattle with a new name and identity. He only hesitated a moment, and then he told her a small part of his wish to make up for that night in the alleyway.

She let him speak without interruption, occasionally wiping away a tear with her left hand, her right hand never leaving Jonas's. When he was finished, he pulled his eyes away from his sister's headstone, where they had been locked, and looked at Tracy.

"So there you have it. I'm not the guy you might think I am. I have a purpose and it's not a pretty one, nor a legal one, but one I feel a moral obligation too. I hope you don't mind me telling you. All I ask is that you don't tell anyone what I've told you today."

She surprised him by saying, "Jonas, I'm not sure what I would do if it were me in your place, but I would like to think I would be doing the same thing. I don't know if I could actually do it, but I think I would try."

"So you don't think of me as some crazy, revengeful, son of a bitch?"

"No, I don't. I see a great guy who lost someone who meant everything to him, a guy that has to try to set things right, or at least as right as they can be. I hope I can help you in some way."

Jonas smiled at her. "You already have, Tracy. It feels good just to be able to share this with someone." He turned back to the grave and said, "But you can't help me, Tracy. This is for me to do."

"All I'm saying, Jonas, is that I'm there if you want me to be. You can't do this on your own."

"I'm not completely alone. I have friends that are with me for their own personal reasons, so I will have help."

"Maybe I'll get to meet them sometime, but just know that I might be able to help too. I may be blonde but I can be tough too," she said, smacking him lightly on the arm.

"Okay, let's get going," said Jonas.

Before leaving he dropped Tracy's hand and leaned down towards Christine's headstone. He pulled a few vagrant weeds from the base of the stone and said, "Rest easy little sis. I love you."

When they were seated in the car Jonas looked over at her and asked, "Are you sure you want anything to do with me now?"

"Jonas, I can see in your eyes that you are a good man. I can also see that this is something you have to do, and something that has to be done, or you will never fully recover. I want to help in any way I can. And besides, I like hanging around with you, a lot."

Jonas didn't know what to say so he simply put the car in gear and said, more sharply than he intended, "Me too, let's go for a drive."

Traffic for a Sunday morning wasn't all that bad and they made pretty good time down the I-5. Of course, there was construction mid-city, which slowed them down, but, once through that, they were able to use Edgar to get on the Alaskan Hwy South. They each watched the piers and warehouses pass by as they made their way to Spokane Street and over to Harbor Island.

Jonas felt strange approaching the very same area in which he had left Sanderson, but the directions AC had given him were leading him toward it. Thankfully the building on AC's map came up before he had to revisit the dreaded one, and he breathed a silent relief.

Tracy had been holding AC's hand-drawn map, and she suddenly pointed out Jonas's window. "This is it, right here!"

There was no one else on the road so Jonas was able to simply come to a stop in the middle of his lane. The area they looked at was exclusively large warehouse-like buildings, all of which were surrounded by a high wire fence. Hanging on the fence in front of each building was a weathered wooden sign with mostly faded numbers. The number, or at least the remaining shadowed imprint of a number in front of them, matched the number AC had scrawled on his map. The building itself, like many others in a line along this road, was located about fifty yards from the road, and details were hard to make out.

"Look there!" said Tracy, pointing to the corner of the building. "I thought I saw someone walking over there."

They both watched closely until someone, a man, appeared right where she had pointed.

"It's almost like he is on guard. Maybe he's just a security guy," she said.

"You're probably right, but why have security guys out here?" asked Jonas, "Unless there's something inside worth guarding. I would love to have a look."

"Not now Jonas, we're too out in the open here. If we can see him he can see us. Let's go."

Jonas looked from the building to his passenger. "You really are riding shotgun, aren't you?"

She smiled and said, "You know what they say, in for a dollar......."

Jonas put the car in gear, "okay, let's get out of here."

"Where to now?" asked Tracy.

"There's a house I want to have a quick look at. Then maybe we can grab lunch or something."

They followed the same route back to the I-90 and quickly, by Seattle's standards anyway, made their way to Mercer Island. Just before the tunnels they turned south on West Mercer.

"We're looking for Pearl but I don't know if that's a street or avenue," said Jonas. "All I know is that it's new and there's probably a lot of construction."

A moment later they spotted a temporary wooden sign that read 'The Pearl' and an arrow pointing to the left.

"Okay, maybe it's not a street or an avenue but a friggin' neighborhood," he exclaimed, turning left and driving up a winding, newly paved road. To each side were lot number signs, and a closer inspection showed white pegs, which marked the outer extensions of each lot. "I'll bet you this will be gated eventually. You can see the concrete running all along the sides. I wouldn't mind being the realtor here."

"AC said we're looking for number nineteen. Whoa! What's this?" Jonas said, as they approached an area completely unlike the rest of the neighborhood. As the lower lots were covered in dirt and some stubby trees, this area was heavily treed and each property was surrounded by shrubbery and wire fencing. "It must have cost a small fortune to bring in this much mature growth."

They drove by a brick and stone sign with the number '19' in gold letters on it. The driveway was made of hand-laid red brick and led up to a rod-iron gate, which stood like a sentry, about ten feet tall.

"I'm going to swing around up here and park down below. I'd like to walk back up and have a closer look. You don't mind waiting a bit for that lunch do you?" he asked.

"No, you go ahead," answered Tracy. "I'm not much good in this dress anyway. But be careful and don't let anyone see you sneaking around."

Jonas pulled into the driveway of a house still under construction. "I'll only be a few minutes, oh, and by the way, you look terrific in that dress," he said, already walking away.

Tracy smiled and watched him walk back up towards number nineteen.

Jonas approached the house, but soon learned that the driveway past the gate curved sharply to the left, leaving him no view of the house. He looked around, couldn't see anyone watching, or see anyone at all for that matter, and stepped off the newly poured sidewalk and followed the shrubs to the left hoping to find a break in the greenery to at least get a glimpse of the house. He eventually discovered the corner of the property and followed the fence around. He was now moving slowly down the side of the property, constantly keeping his head on a swivel, looking for any movement. The shrubs were interlaced with some type of vine so getting a good look through was difficult, but he could now get at least a few glimpses of a massive house on the other side. He found a very small break in the branches closer to the ground, and crouched down to get a better look.

The house he saw couldn't actually be called a house at all. Mansion didn't even seem to cover it. It had to be the size of a small apartment building. From his spot he could see the entrance to the home. On each side of double giant wooden doors were two thick concrete Greek columns. There were three stories and Jonas noticed that most of the windows, on each level, were floor to ceiling, obviously to take advantage of a view of the lake.

Jonas knew he could not stay longer, and as he was about to leave he felt a presence near him. He slowly turned his head to the side and looked into a pair of eyes. Struggling to hold back a yell, he realized the eyes belonged to a small dog that stood there patiently, waiting for Jonas to notice him.

"Jesus, buddy. You scared the crap out of me," he said to the dog that was still just standing there, wagging the stump of it's tail. "Some detective I am eh, buddy?"

Jonas reached out to let the dog sniff his hand and then gently rubbed her head and scratched her ears. The dog was a female German Schnauzer, mostly grey in color, with only a stub for a tail, and big brownish whiskers at the sides of her jaw. Interestingly enough her ears remained standing at attention.

Suddenly a man's voice called out from the house. "Tanzer, hey Tanzer, where are you girl?"

The dog looked from Jonas and immediately, and very quickly, made her way through a hole under the fence in front of Jonas, before taking off towards the house.

Jonas watched her run to the house, where she disappeared around the side. He looked down at the hole the dog had obviously used many times to escape the yard, and an idea began to form in his head. He carefully made his way back to the car where Tracy sat with the passenger door open.

"See anything interest?" she asked.

"One bigger than life house, and a really nice little dog," he replied.

"Are you going back again later?"

"I don't know. When I was crawling around the shrubs I noticed infrared sensors mounted every ten feet or so. It might be tough to just drop in, but I may have a way around that. Let's go get something to eat, I'm starving."

CHAPTER TWENTY-NINE

RICK Farrell walked through the department, past Delano, who was hunched, as usual, over his desk, his face inches from his computer screen, and to his own desk where he sat down with a sigh. "What ya got Delano?" he asked.

"I don't know Rick, maybe a wild goose chase, but there was something that happened a few years back that stuck with me for some reason," answered Delano.

Delano was a short man, with jet black hair. Most people thought him to be of Latino decent but he only came by the name via a wayward father that he hadn't seen in many years. Although shorter than most in the department, he was known to be one of the toughest. He was also a 'keener' who never seemed to need sleep and had to force himself to temporarily give up a 'scent' at the end of a long day, only to be back in front of his computer early the next day continuing the hunt.

Farrell knew to trust in Delano's instincts and asked, "Yeah, what was that?"

Delano looked up from his computer and sat back in his chair. "Well, remember when that couple was attacked in the alley near Dragons?"

Farrell sat up in his chair. "Yeah, I remember it happening, but not the details."

Delano continued. "Well, that's the thing. This guy and a chick get mugged, or something, after coming out of Dragons. They find the guy in the alley, busted up bad, but the girl is gone. They didn't find her until a few days later, in a dumpster."

"Okay, I'm remembering it now, but what about it?" Farrell asked, now paying closer attention.

"It turns out they weren't a couple out on a date. They were brother and sister. Musta been just having a sibling night out, I guess."

"So, what's your point?"

"Like I said, the sister turns up dead. The brother is seriously hurt and taken to the hospital. Then he fucking disappears! I've called everyone I can think of, the hospitals, emergency and general admittance, and records, everything. He vanished. The closest I get to him is his grandfather, who looks to me, somehow got him out of the hospital and into a private facility somewhere, but that's where I lose him. He's just fucking gone after that! I can't even follow up with dear old Grampa because he's dead now too. Cancer got him."

Farrell looked at Delano, raised his hands up high and asked, "So what's all this got to do with anything?"

"I don't know Rick. Maybe nothing, but at the time a bunch of guys were reported to have been in a tussle with these two kids and our friend Deets Sanderson was somehow implicated for a while."

Now Farrell was fully attentive. "Was he charged with anything?"

"Nope, it seems the only witness was killed in a hit and run shortly afterward."

"Jesus."

"Yeah, that was what I was thinking too. But it gets weirder."

"What do you mean?"

"Well, the investigating officer, a Brent Jameson, was nearly killed in an accident too. Also a hit and run. It left him crippled up. He disabled out of the force. He's still around, I think. I've heard of him."

"Holy shit man! That would certainly screw up any investigation, wouldn't it? Main witness knocked off, and the investigator fucked up, and off the case. End of file! Man, I think I'll do some pokin' around. Give me what you got, and good work Delano. What were the kids' names?"

Delano shuffled with some papers in front of him, "William and Christine Carterell, both in their twenties."

"Thanks man, I'll take it from here. See you later," said Farrell, as he accepted a folder stuffed with papers from Delano, and left the office.

Once he was away from the busy office it was quieter and he could think more clearly. His mind took in the information from Delano and he mentally reviewed it all, checking off the names he had so far.

William Carterell: - Beat up but lives.
                       - Goes to hospital then disappears.
                       - Obviously moved by Grampa.

Christine Carterell: - Killed after attack in alley near Dragons.
                       - Body found in dumpster.

Grampa: - Gets Carterell out of hospital.
           - To private facility?

Unknown witness: - Knows who Carterells were arguing with.
                   - Killed in hit and run.

Brent Jameson: - Lead investigator in case.
               - Hurt in accident, possible hit and run.
               - Disabled-out from Force.
               - Investigation over??

The more he thought about it, and the more he ran the list of names through his mind, he kept coming up with two big questions.

Where was William Carterell?

What did Sanderson have to do with the whole thing?

He left the building, grabbed a hot dog from a street vendor, lots of onions, and went back to his office. Back at his own desk, papers in hand, he started making calls and assigning duty officers to check out some things for him. He had to get moving on this because he had a strong feeling Sanderson's death, and the way he died, could be tied to all of it, and maybe to that night in the alleyway. 'Where was this Carterell guy?' He had to find out.

Two days later Farrell sat at his desk pondering new information. His calls had been to officers to track down and trail Brent Jameson, and to the force's 'techie' department, to search Carterell's grandfather's business and personal holdings. This is where they hit the jackpot. Farrell looked at several neat stacks of paper spread out before him. It seems Grampa was a very wise financial investor and had accumulated a sizable fortune through several different entities. There didn't seem to be a conscious effort to hide, but it still took the techie's some digging to track down all the holdings presently listed in front of him. Grampa Carterell either owned outright, or was the sole shareholder in many endeavors; however one in particular caught Farrell's attention. Besides having holdings in New York, Chicago, and Oahu, Hawaii, he had owned a condo here in Seattle. This in itself was not surprising. What was interesting was that the title of the condo was, upon his death, not sold like the other assets, but instead transferred to a trust. It had apparently taken some digging, and the calling in of some favors, to find out that the trust fund was headed by a Harold Bartlett, a semi-retired lawyer in town. Bartlett now lived in a nice home on Laurel Crescent near Webster Point, so he obviously did not occupy the Carterell's condo, and on a hunch Farrell decided to see who exactly resided there.

As usual the traffic was moving at a snail's pace, and although tempted, Farrell decided not to use his lights to speed things up. He had a lot of thinking to do, so the slow pace worked to his benefit. A while later he parked his unmarked Chevy just down from the entrance to the gated condo address listed in his file. It was a beautiful building with what looked like only two side by side units in each building. On each side he could see small stretches of the golf course that ran behind the units. The condo he was interested in was on the left side of a common entry area, and by the looks of the blinds in the windows and plants visible from the street, it was certainly occupied. There were no vehicles parked out front, but that wasn't surprising. These types of condos all had underground parking. This meant he wouldn't have plates to run, so he would just have to patient and wait it out.

An hour later he was thinking of giving it up for the day, when a sleek white BMW drove through the opening gates and pulled up to the front of the building. What do we have here? He asked himself, slouching down in his seat.

A young man, probably in his mid to late twenties, jumped out of the car and walked up to the entrance of the condo. The man was tall, Farrell estimated about six two, and obviously in good shape, with slender shoulders and muscled arms. He had neatly cropped hair which reached down to the collar of a light green polo shirt. He wore designer jeans and walked with confidence. He pulled out a key and, after a second or two, unlocked and opened the main door of the building. Before the door closed Farrell watched as the man moved through the door and to the left.

"Bingo!"

Farrell shuffled through the papers on the passenger seat until he came up with a picture of William Carterell. The picture was from a college yearbook and in it, the man in question was quite chubby. Definitely not in the shape that the guy in the condo was, but there was a resemblance. 'Maybe he works out now and got himself in shape,' he thought. 'Or better yet, maybe he's been away somewhere recovering from the attack and lost all the fat that way.'

He phoned in with the Beamer's plates and when the name came back he again rifled through his papers. 'What the fuck was this guy's middle name? Here it is.'

He held up the paper. William J. Carterell.

The plates had come back in the name of Jonas Carter.

J. for Jonas, and Carterell shortened to Carter. The same Jonas Carter that now occupied the trust fund's condo.

"Well, I'll be goddamned!" he said aloud.

CHAPTER THIRTY

ALLAN Gant did not want to be here. He hated this, and he hated Alex Westgate, but there was very little, if anything, he could do about it. Like it or not, he was tied to Westgate for the foreseeable future.

Strangely enough, Alex Westgate was thinking the exact same thing. He looked at Gant with faked diplomacy, but all he really wanted to do was put a bullet between his eyes. Maybe he would do that anyway.

The two men sat in a sitting room in Westgate's sprawling Mercer Island home, just a few steps from the front door. Westgate always held his 'meetings' in this room. It was private, comfortable, and best of all, close enough to the front door that he could greet them, but not have to show them the rest of the house. Another thing he hated was house guests, unless personally invited by him, so this room allowed him to get rid of unwanted guests quickly and efficiently.

As usual Gant seemed nervous, evidenced by his constantly crossing and uncrossing his legs. Also, as usual, he was dressed in a perfectly fitting, hand tailored suit, with a tie that would cost an ordinary working man a week's wages. His expensive clothes, however, could not mask his impatience.

"I'm telling you Alex, something is going on here that we don't know about."

Westgate was an almost exact opposite of Gant. Whereas Gant's hair was always perfectly cut (every week), and his manner of dress impeccable, Westgate enjoyed a more casual look. Today he wore a thin stripped dark sports jacket and a light blue polo shirt underneath. A pair of beige khaki's and brown loafers (no socks) completed his attire. His hair, although cut short, was always messy and he sported a neatly trimmed beard that matched his hair in length. His casual, laid back look fooled many, for there were few that could be as cruel and ruthless at the drop of a hat. He stared back at Gant.

"Fill me in, Allan, and, for Christ sake sit still. You're driving me nuts!"

Gant crossed his legs one more time before getting them under control. "I've received some calls. My sources say that Deets was probably only the first on a list, and that list includes you, me, and Lamar."

"Who the hell told you that, and if it's true, why us?"

"Who told me doesn't matter. The fact that it's out there is enough. We should take steps, you know, extra security."

"You still never told me why, Allen."

"Remember the first girl we brought here, the cute blond teacher?"

"Yeah, I remember. How could I ever fucking forget that night? No matter how many times we do that it will never be as good as that night. Is this about her?"

Gant sat forward. "Remember the guy with her, the guy Lamar wacked with the steel bar?"

"Jesus, Lamar almost took his head off with that!" Westgate chuckled.

"Well, he should have taken his head off, because the fucking guy survived. At least it looks like it. That's what my guy is telling me."

Westgate sat up straight in his chair. "No shit! I woulda bet he was dead right there. Jesus, Lamar cracked a home run on him. How the fuck does anybody survive that?"

"I don't know, and I don't know if he really did, but somebody fucked up Deets real bad and I'm thinkin' we might be next."

Westgate rose from his chair causing Gant to follow. "Okay, let's tighten things up until we figure out who this guy is. Then we'll deal with him."

Westgate slapped Gant on the back of his shoulder as if nothing was wrong and said, "So, are we still on for tomorrow night? It's been a while and I'm way overdue."

Gant couldn't believe the arrogance of the man but managed a quick smile and replied, "Yeah, as a matter of fact, I've been savin' a nice piece of pretty Chinese for us. I know how much you like oriental girls and this one's perfect, completely fresh and untouched. I've kept her hidden away."

"Perfect. Set it up and let me know what time. Lamar's gotta stay on the island so it will be just you and me."

"No sweat, Alex, I'll call you tomorrow."

Westgate guided Gant out the front door and quickly closed it behind him. He checked himself in a full length mirror, messed with his hair for a second, and started up one of two sets of long spiraling staircases. His thoughts were on Sanderson's killing and whether or not Gant was right. Were they targets? It was worth looking into. Gant wasn't the only one with contacts. In the meantime he would concentrate on having Chinese tomorrow night.

CHAPTER THIRTY-ONE

SU remembered a story her mother would tell the girls when she and Ling were just little, and one they would ask for over and over. It was the story of a princess in a far-away land. She had been kidnapped by a mean old Ogre and kept in a small hut with no windows and a big lock on the thick wooden door. Every day the Ogre would pry open the door and throw a small plate of nasty tasting gruel on her little table and stomp out with only grunts. Some of the times he would simply walk up to her and push her hard. If she did not fall he would approach her again and push even harder, until she fell to the floor. This seemed to please him, so the princess made sure she fell every time on his first push, hardly needing any force to send her flying to the floor. The princess caught glimpses of trees and fields just outside but she was afraid of the Ogre and never tried to run past him to get away.

Of course, the story ended when a handsome prince on a white horse discovered the hut, and the princess inside. He dispatched the Ogre in a terrific battle, and the princess rode away with him to live happily ever after.

Well, Su had seen glimpses of the outside world but knew in order to get there she could not wait for a handsome prince to save her. She had to do it on her own.

So that is what she set out to do. Over the next few days she started taking small chances, venturing out of her room late into the night. During the days she began to pay closer attention to the actions in the hallways outside of her room. She knew she would need money if she wanted to survive once she left, and she had a pretty good idea of how the house ran its' operations, and, in particular, how Mrs. Chow kept an office.

Eventually, her 'minders', as she called them, started to leave her alone for longer periods of time, especially at night, where she found, if she was extremely careful, she could wander throughout the house's upper levels, while everyone else, including the guards, slept. On these late night trips she discovered places where small amounts of money were hidden. She took only a little each time and added to her savings. She felt badly for taking from the other girls but knew she had to do something if she was to survive this place long enough to get away.

Very late one night she decided to venture to the lower level of the house. She crept slowly down the hall, passing the rooms that she had visited briefly over the last few nights, until she reached the top of the stairs. She listened for movement both from below and from the rooms near to her. Hearing none, she took the first step down, then the second, ready to bolt back to her room at any sound, but the house remained silent. An eternity later she reached the bottom of the stairs. On the way down she worried about which way to turn when she reached the bottom. Which way was safer, and more importantly, which way would take her to the one room she was looking for?

The choice was easier than she had hoped because there was only one door to her left, and, as it was partially open, she could see that it was just a bathroom. The main hallway led to her right and she started to make her way in that direction.

She knew that all of the bedrooms were upstairs and behind the doors along this hallway was an office, the living room, or customer greeting area as they called it, a supply room, and a large kitchen and dining area. Her target was the office. She remembered how Mrs. Chow had kept her little office in the factory, and assumed she would have the same habits here.

Before reaching the office door she had to pass the living room entrance. As she was doing so she heard a sound. She froze. She heard the sound again. She inched her face around the door frame and instantly saw the sound's origin. The house guard sat in an overstuffed chair, his head tilted to his shoulder, his snores filling the room. The guard was obviously in a deep sleep so she was able to slip past the door and make her way to the office. She turned the knob and was not surprised to find it unlocked. Anyone that knew the woman knew she had a habit of leaving doors and cupboards open. Su had hoped this trend would continue, and it had.

Su entered the small office, which was sparsely furnished with a small wooden desk, a faux leather rolling chair. Behind the chair was a metal four-drawer file cabinet. She immediately went to the desk. After a quick inspection of its two drawers she found nothing of value. She turned to the file cabinet, sliding out the drawers but again found nothing worth taking. She was looking only for money. Lucy had spent many hours in the factory teaching Su how to speak English but she also talked about America and what she knew, or had heard, about its' money. Su knew the small role of bills she already had, mostly one's with a few five's and ten's, would not go far once she escaped. She knew that the 'business' transacted in the house was made up of mostly cash and hoped that Mrs. Chow, who was in charge of almost everything in the house, kept the cash somewhere in this little room. She quietly rummaged through the small desk but found nothing. She knew she could only spend another minute, at the most, in the office so decided to try again on another night and leave now before she was discovered. She had closed the door behind her when entering the office and now, before opening it again to leave, she noticed a small wooden cabinet on the floor behind it, where it would be hidden from sight. Even though she knew she had been in the room too long, she had to look in this cabinet. She grabbed hold of the handle of the top drawer and pulled, gently so as to make minimal noise. The drawer slide open to reveal a small metal box with a thin silver handle on the top. She lifted the handle and realized the box was heavy. There was a small silver clasp on the side and, to Su's surprise there was no lock on it. Thank you Mrs. Chow! She slipped the clasp and opened the box a few inches, enough to get a view of its contents. There she found a stack of American bills. Again she thanked Lucy for teaching her the value of American money. She flipped through them and could see that they were mostly twenty and fifty dollar bills. Without hesitating she carefully pulled out two fifty dollar bills and slipped them in her pocket. She dared not take more. She closed the box, redid the clasp, and slide the cabinet door closed.

The return to her room was uneventful. The guard was still blissfully asleep in his chair, and the stairs were navigated without a single squeak, and no one came out of their rooms. Inside her room she added the bills to her own, stashing the role in the hollow under a tall lamp that stood sentry in the corner.

Over the next several nights she made the same trip, and noticed that the money in the cash box changed each night. It seemed to be casually thrown into the box with the denominations not sorted together. Su hoped this meant that the money was not counted regularly so she took a little more each time, careful not to take too many of each denomination. She hoped her growing role of bills would be enough to help her once she got away from this place, and these people.

It was early one evening when Su heard a knock on her door. At first she mistook it for thunder, as it was stormy outside, and she had seen several flashes of lightning in the distance. Realizing it was someone at her door, she was automatically alert, fearful that Gant had finally come for her before she had a chance to get away. The door knob turned and the door opened slowly.

Su was relieved to hear her friend's voice. "Su, are you awake?"

"Yes, yes, please come in. I am so happy it is you!" said Su, with clear relief and happiness in her voice. She jumped up from the bed to greet her friend with a hug.

Jing-Wei closed the door slowly and carefully behind her. "I should not be here. There are visitors to the house. I am afraid they are not customers."

"What do you mean, Jing-Wei?"

"They are mean looking men and said they are waiting for Mr. Gant."

Su looked at the closed door, frightened that Gant's time had arrived, and it would open at any second with him behind it, coming for her. "I must leave this place at once," Su said, as she walked to the balcony door. She stepped outside, followed by Jing-Wei. The rain was only light but they could see flashes of lightning in the distant sky.

"But where will you go?" asked Jing-Wei

"I do not know, but anywhere will be better than here with Gant."

Jing-Wei reached in to the pocket of her sweater and pulled out a small bundle of rolled up cash. "Please take this Su. Maybe it will help a little."

"I cannot take your savings Jing-Wei, I just can't. But thank you so much."

Then Su had an idea. "Jing-Wei, why don't you come with me? We can climb down these flower trestles and run down the alleyway. That was my plan anyway. You can come too. We can help each other."

"Help each other do what?" came a voice from the inside of the room.

Su and Jing-Wei turned to see Mei stepping through the doorway to the balcony.

"We will help each other get through all that is happening. That is all we said, and it is no business of yours," said Su, as she stepped towards the other woman.

Thunder cracked in the sky overhead and the rain started to fall heavier.

"Bullshit!" yelled Mei. "You are planning something. But you are too late, little bitch! Gant is here for you. I wanted to give you something to remember me by before he takes you away." Suddenly there was a long bladed knife in her hand and she lunged toward Su.

In a flash Jing-Wei stepped between the two women and grabbed for the knife. She missed and Mei drove it deep into Jing-Wei's stomach. Both women froze where they stood, and looked down to see Mei's hand still on the handle of the knife, her hand now covered with blood that flowed from Jing-Wei's wound.

"No!" screamed Su, as she tried to grab at her friend, to turn her around, to do something. But Jing-Wei pushed Su back with her right hand and, continuing the motion, swung around to grab the side of Mei's head. Both women were off balance and, in an instant, collided with the small balcony's railing and went over.

Su screamed again and leaned over the rail. Jing-Wei and Mei had fallen awkwardly landing side by side on the grass twenty feet below. Mei was on her back and her eyes were still open but her torso was leaning to one side and her head was turned completely to the other, her open eyes never to see again. Jing-Wei lay only a foot away and did not move. Blood flowed freely from her wound, and joined with the rain in a puddle around her.

Su put her hands to her face and cried. "Jing-Wei, what have you done?" She cried some more and then, with startling realization, she knew that the time to leave was now, immediately. If what Mei had said was true, Gant might be in the house already and coming for her. They must have heard her screams and would be coming. She must hurry.

She ran back into the room, grabbed a sweater and her tiny bag of personal things that she kept ready. She ran to the lamp. Tilted it to the side and grabbed her role of cash. She stood up to turn around when something hit her hard on the side of her head. She dropped her cash as she flew into the wall. She landed hard and looked up to see a huge man in a suit standing over her. He had jet black hair pulled back into a pony tail. She could also see Gant standing behind him.

"Leave her to me, Frank. Clean up the mess on the lawn and meet me at the paint shop. Alex'll be waiting." Gant said to the man.

Gant leaned over Su and hauled her up by the hair. She screamed, but the punch from the other man had left her woozy, and she had no will to fight. Gant had a firm grip on her hair, yanked her to her feet, and pulled her with him out the door, struggling with her down the stairs.

"You should have behaved my little beauty! But now we are really going to have some fun!" he said, as he forced her out of the house, and threw her into the back of a big black vehicle.

He jumped into the driver's side, slammed the door and turned towards Su, who cowered in fear on the back seat. "We are going to visit a friend of mine. If you try to get away, if you even move, I will kill you right where you are!"
He put the vehicle in gear, and tore away from the house.

CHAPTER THIRTY-TWO

JONAS crouched amongst the shrubbery in the same place he had just days before. This time he stuck his head further through the growth, and was able to confirm his thoughts. On his earlier visit he had noticed security sensors mounted to the fence. Careful not to be seen, he could now see that the sensors were mounted to each fence post, about two feet from the ground, and about ten feet apart. He assumed they would be the same all around the perimeter of the property, their faint green light easy to see once you knew where to look. The idea was to be a visual deterrent as well as an alarm. But it also gave Jonas an opportunity. He could see that the sensors were mounted above the ground so that Westgate's dog, the friendly Tanzer, would have room to run about the yard to do what dogs do. Jonas was thinking that if someone stayed low enough to the ground they might make it to the house undetected.

The skies had opened, and it was now raining hard, so he did not look forward to the long crawl on the soaking lawn. He didn't have too though, as before he started, two vehicles came from the garage area behind the house and, slowing down only to allow the automatic gate to open, drove off quickly down the road.

Jonas waited for them to be out of sight then sprinted to his car, tonight using the cab lookalike. Staying a discreet distance back he could see the two vehicles stop at the entrance to the community. One was a large black SUV, which turned right, the other, a grey newer Cadillac, turned left.

'Which one to follow?' he thought. He chose the SUV.

It wasn't long before he had a good idea where the big vehicle was headed so he was able to keep well back, even pulling behind legitimate yellow cabs so the SUV's driver would not have a chance to see him. As expected the SUV led him back to the big old house in the middle of the industrial area. Jonas did not need to drive by, and simply parked down the same alleyway he had used before.

He pulled the hood of his coat over his head and left his car, re-tracing his steps from earlier, only this time trying to stick closer to the fence without stepping in the puddles that were now starting to form. He knew he wouldn't see anything from the front so was hoping he could at least see something through the rear windows.

The rain was falling hard now and he was able to stand under the trees at the back, somewhat protected. He could see movement on the main floor but was disappointed that most of the windows were either covered by drawn curtains or were heavily tinted.

He looked up at the room with the balcony and could see at least two figures in the shadows caused by the backlighting. Then the balcony door opened and two people came out. One of them, Jonas was certain, was the same oriental woman he had seen the other night. The other woman was much taller than the first and they seemed to be having an animated discussion.

A third person, also much larger than the first, then joined them and, judging by the startling turns from the other two, had taken them by surprise.

A loud crack of thunder!

The rain increased and now fell in sheets.

The two bigger women drew close to one another. Jonas could tell their voices were raised, but could not make out their words. It looked like the two woman came together in a struggle and then, shockingly, they both tumbled over the railing. He heard the heavy sounds of them landing hard, and the other's scream. He could see that both women on the ground were seriously hurt, and were not moving. He looked back up to the balcony.

The smaller woman stood there for a few seconds with her hands to her face. Then she ran back into the room. Jonas could see her shadow moving frantically around the room. Suddenly two more people appeared. The partially open balcony door allowed him to see that they were men. One of them became a shadow again as he stepped past the door and appeared to strike the woman, who fell to the floor. Seconds later the second man could be seen forcing the woman out of the room, while the first man came out on to the balcony and looked down at the bodies of the fallen women. He then turned sharply and re-entered the house, disappearing from Jonas's view.

Jonas knew he had to move quickly, and made his way along the fence to his car. He was able to drive around the block just in time to see the SUV's tail lights speeding away. He again kept his distance. He hoped the hard falling rain would help to disguise his vehicle. His windshield wipers were going full speed, and he was just able to keep the SUV in sight. He followed it down Olympic to Second, then left on Mercer right into a construction zone. Most of the crew was gone for the day, so the roadway was awash in yellow blinking construction lights, and white and red sawhorses.

While weaving through these Jonas saw the SUV make a sudden left off Mercer. As he drove by he saw it pulled up to a big grey brick building, its back up lights flashing briefly as the driver put the vehicle in park.

Jonas drove past the construction and found a place to pull over in front of a closed Laundromat. He reached over to the glove box and pulled out his gun, made sure it was loaded with a round in the chamber, and left the vehicle, tucking the gun into his pants at the small of his back.

There was no approaching traffic so he crossed the street and quickly walked up to the building the others had parked beside. As he got closer he heard an approaching vehicle and ducked behind a dumpster just in time to see the Cadillac pull up beside the SUV. A short stocky bearded man got out of the car and ran to the building's door. From information supplied by Jameson and AC there was no doubt in Jonas's mind that this was Alex Westgate.

Jonas stood in the rain, still looking around the corner of the building at the door where he knew both Westgate and Gant were. These were the two men he hunted, the same men who had murdered Chrissy.

He reached behind him to get his gun when he felt something against the back of his head, and then a voice speaking softly right behind him.

"I'm a police officer, do not move or I will shoot you."

*****

Once Rick Farrell knew who he was looking for things got a lot easier, and the rain tonight was making it even easier still. He followed Carter at a distance when he left his building. He almost got away when he used the side entrance to the parking garage, but luckily Farrell was parked in a spot that was just able to catch a glimpse of Carter coming up a set of steps at the side of the building. He tracked Carter across lawns, through part of the golf course, and down a few alleys. Farrell was able to guess where he was going each time, and get there quick enough to see his next move, while keeping far enough out of site. Carter was good, but not compared to a seasoned cop who had done this many times.

It wasn't long after that Farrell watched the young man enter another apartment complex, albeit this one not nearly as nice as the other. This one could have used some maintenance starting about ten years back. Its paint peeling off in places and several of the window frames were off center, as if replaced, but poorly.

"What the hell are you doing in this dump, Carter?" he asked himself.

Moments later he had his answer. A yellow sedan pulled out from the semi-underground parking lot and drove right past him. Before ducking down quickly he made out Carter behind the wheel, and he was in a hurry. Farrell quickly spun his car around and followed Carter at a distance, all the way down Madison to the I-5, then south. When he connected to the I-90 Farrell knew he was going to Mercer Island, and probably Westgate's place.

'What are you doing man?' Farrell asked out loud. 'Westgate is no one to fuck around with, especially at his own house. I think I'll just hang back a bit and see what happens.'

Because he knew where Carter was going he was able to take his time and arrived only moments behind him. On the road above Westgate's he found Carters yellow *cab*. He parked and waited. There was not much he could do right now. If Carter was stupid enough to go for Westgate here, in his own house, surrounded by security shit, well so what? He had no love for the rich scumbag. He cracked his window a little so that he wouldn't fog up in the rain, and then waited. About a half hour later he had to duck down again as Carter was running up the street towards him. Luckily the man was moving fast, and not paying attention to the cars around him, so Farrell was confident he hadn't been seen. The hard falling rain continued to help, although it was getting hard to see out the windows.

When Carter pulled out so did he, albeit a moment or so later, He made it down the hill in time to see the yellow sedan turn right. He did the same.

He followed Carter down the 90 again all the way to the Alaskan Highway where he turned north, then on to Elliott.

'Son of a bitch, he's following Gant!' he said to himself, holding the wheel tighter. 'This just keeps getting better and better.'

As predicted he followed Carter past Kinnear Park, where he turned off into an alley. Farrell pulled off into what used to be a driveway of some kind, facing away from the street so he could watch Carter's car in his rear-view mirror.

He was getting bored with the whole stake-out thing, when a loud crack of thunder shook the car, bringing his attention back up to speed. The sky opened, and it was all he could do to see anything through the rear window, which was fogging up in the heavily falling rain. He knew he couldn't just sit here with the motor running to de-fog the windows, so was about to start it up and move a bit further down the road, when he saw Carter in his side mirror, splashing through puddles to get to his car. When the yellow sedan had driven away Farrell was quick to follow.

'Something's going on,' Farrell thought, and again set off in pursuit of Carter.

He followed the sedan to West Mercer then across Queen Anne and into the heavy Mercer Street construction area. Carter slowed his car and then parked just off Mercer near some closed small businesses.

'Holy shit' thought Farrell. 'Where did this guy get his balls?' 'He's a fucking dead man now!' He parked up the street from Carter's car and then got out and began walking back, trying to look like anyone else slogging through the rain to get home after work. He saw Carter pull his hoody up over his head and wished he could do the same.

'Enough of this shit!' he said to himself, and closed the distance to Carter, his footsteps light, and covered by the heavy rainfall and intermittent distant thunder.

He watched as Carter ducked behind a dumpster as a big grey caddy pulled into the lot.

'Jesus H. Fucking Christ, that's Westgate too,' Farrell thought.

Farrell approached along the building where the younger man was peering around the corner. He watched as the man reached behind him for a gun protruding from his waist band. He quickly crept up behind the man, placed his gun against the back of his head, and said softly into his ear.

"I'm a police officer, do not move, or I will shoot you."

*****

Su remained huddled in fear across the back seat of the SUV. As the big truck rocked from side to side, all she could hear was the sound of water moving aside for the big wheels. She cried for Jing-Wei who had just given her life to save her. She cried for losing Ling. And she cried for herself. She was thousands of miles across the sea from her home, and now found herself helplessly at the mercy of these awful men. She knew very little about this strange land and wondered how it could be that there were so many terrible people in it, the worst of which was driving this vehicle. She was terrified of what awaited her once the drive was over, so she huddled into herself even more. She had to find a time to run. Where, she did not know, but there had to be a way.

To her horror the vehicle turned sharply, almost spilling her from the seat, and then stopped completely. Gant left the driver's side and opened the passenger door behind him. He reached for Su who surprised him with a kick that connected solidly with his shoulder. He stepped back and grabbed at his upper arm, and smiled at her through clenched teeth.

"You little bitch! That'll be the last time you do that!" he yelled as he climbed into the back seat towards her. She continued to kick as hard as she could and managed to land a few glancing blows, but the quarters were too close, and the man too powerful for her, Once he got close she had no room to fight. He swung at her and connected with her left ear, the second time that night, but this one had more of an effect. A blinding light shot before her eyes, and she fell limp. She barely felt him drag her out of the truck where she landed on the ground, immediately soaked by the puddled rain. Gant hauled her up by the hair and forced her to a doorway, which he opened, pushing her through. She landed hard, but managed to scramble away from him, towards a wall, her ears still ringing, and her rain drenched hair covering her face. Gant pointed a finger at her.

"Don't fucking move! We're going to have some company tonight. It's not the way I wanted it, but you fucked things up. Now I have to share, and it won't be near as much fun as I wanted. Oh, here he comes now."

Su heard car doors slamming, running footsteps, and the door she had just been thrown from, opened. The big man with the pony tail from her room entered first followed by a shorter bearded man.

"Well, well, Mr. Gant. What did you bring me tonight?" he shouted at Gant but did not move his eyes from Su, who still lay on the floor, afraid to move.

"She's ripe Alex. Just the way you like 'em. Untouched too. I've been keeping her just for you." Gant replied.

"Untouched, eh? Well I certainly like that. I like that a lot. You've done well my friend."

Su looked from one man to the other. She looked around at the building she was in. She saw empty papers and cups lying about on the floor. There were puddles everywhere and droplets were falling from the ceiling in many places, so it was obvious that the building was old and in disrepair, and had not been used in any functional way for a long time. Su could see nothing of use to her, and no way out.

She looked at the men and knew that she was about to die. These men were not going to be easy with her, so she had to fight. She had to find a way to summon her strength and fight until she was free, or could fight no more. She hoped it would end quickly. She had a snarl on her face and drew her hands up like claws, all the while backing towards a corner of the building.

The bearded man, who she now knew as Alex, laughed at Gant.

"She looks like a caged animal. I like that! This is going to be so much fun!"

*****

Jonas turned around slowly and found himself staring into the barrel of a handgun. It was held by a man of equal size to himself, and there was a police badge hanging from the man's pocket. Jonas sighed in relief. "Officer, there's a girl in there that's been kidnapped and about to be hurt badly. We have to get in there!" he said, frantically.

The cop did not lower the gun and said, "What are you talking about? All I see is a guy poking around an old building that he shouldn't be, and you're packin' too, aren't you?"

"Yes I am, but we need to get in there now. These guys killed my sister, and who knows how many others, and are about to do it again."

"Okay, first you have to calm down, and give me your weapon, carefully and slowly. Take it out with your left hand, ring finger only, and drop it between us."

Jonas did so, and when his gun was on the ground, the cop motioned for him to back up. He took a few steps backward and the cop stooped to pick up the gun, which he tucked into his own belt.

"Now, turn around and let's go see what's going on," he said.

Jonas turned but didn't move. "We can't just walk in there!" he said.

"I think we can. I don't think anything is going on, but let's take a quick looksee anyway."

Jonas walked, with the cop's gun still raised and pointing at him, past a large metal vehicle door to a man door right beside. He hesitated.

"Go on, open the door," said the cop. If you're telling the truth we'll save the girl. If not, you're up shit creek."

Jonas turned the knob and pushed the door open. He felt the cop's gun press a little harder into his back, and the two of them entered the old building.

Jonas saw the girl huddled in the corner and three men standing facing her. It was Gant, Westgate, and a large pony-tailed man. They all swung around to see who had entered.

"What the fuck is this?" shouted Westgate.

The cop gave Jonas a push towards the man. "This, Mr. Westgate, is the fucker that killed Deets!" said the cop.

Jonas swung around to look at the man holding the gun behind him, who was now smiling at him.

"What did you think Carter? That I would give you your gun back, and the two of us would come crashing in here to save the girl?" he laughed.

"You're a dirty cop!" said Jonas, moving towards the man. But he never got close, as something hit him in the back forcing him to his knees. The man with the ponytail had dropped him with a high kick to the middle of his back. He now followed it up with a solid boot to Jonas's mid-section. Jonas saw it coming, but was only partially able to block it. He rolled to the side, gasping for air. He looked up just in time to see the boot coming towards his face. He turned his head just before it arrived and took the blow on his jaw, instantly tasting his own blood. He lay there, nearly unconscious, and all he could see was the girl, on the floor near him. He spat out a wad of blood. She stared back at him.

"This is getting way too messy," said Gant. "Jesus Farrell, why'd you bring him here? If Lamar hears about this we're all dead."

Farrell looked over at Gant. "Lamar's in Hawaii, for Christ's sake, so he won't know what's going on, and besides, I didn't bring him, Gant. He's been following you guys all over town. It took a while, but I finally got enough info to piece it together. You guys fucked up his sister and left him for dead. Well, he didn't die, and he came back to even things up. I suggest you deal with him right fucking now!"

"Who else at the precinct knows about this stuff?" asked Gant.

"Only Delano, my partner, and he don't know enough to connect the dots. Make this guy disappear, and I can do the same with the file."

Westgate stepped forward, pointing at Farrell, and said, "Look, I'm taking the girl and getting out of here. You and Gant take care of this piece of shit right now!"

Jonas managed to shake his head to partially clear the cobwebs long enough to see Westgate looking down at him.

"You were supposed to die a long time ago, shithead. You're probably lucky it's Gant and Farrell, and not Lamar. If he was here he would have great fun taking you apart one piece at a time. But we don't have time to fuck around."

He signaled for the pony-tailed man to grab the girl and follow him. The man walked over to the fallen girl and smiled. Suddenly his hand shot out, catching her under the chin and sending her flying back against the wall. He grabbed her by the hair and easily lifted her to her feet. She had blood running from her nose and mouth. He forced her through the door, which slammed after them.

Jonas spat out more blood and sat up. Although his mind was still reeling he had heard most of what Westgate had said. 'Who was this Lamar?' he wondered.

"You guys fucked up big time, ya know?" he said through clenched teeth.

Gant and Farrell looked at him, and Farrell said, "What are you talking about?"

"I said: you guys fucked up. Do you think I would be doing this all on my own?"

"Just shut the fuck up, Carter. I've been following you around all fucking day and I know you're in this by yourself."

They could all hear the crunch of tires on the broken pavement just outside the door, but this engine was revved up much too high to be parking.

"What the fuck?" shouted Gant as the garage door shattered, followed by a white van, its grill demolishing the door easily. The van did not slow down and made its way directly at them.

Jonas crab walked backward as soon as he heard the loud engine and had managed to get himself into the corner of the large room.

Farrell had been standing beside one of the two foot square cement pillars that supported the building, and was caught between it and the van's front end. To his credit he got off a shot, which struck the van just above the windshield, and then he was nearly cut in half as the van took him hard into the pillar. Farrell only lived long enough to vomit up his own blood, and lay his head on the smashed hood, his hand still holding the gun.

Gant ran for a door at the end of the building but had to run past the sitting Jonas, who simply stuck out his arm and caught the running man across both legs, causing him to fly through the air straight into the wall. Before he could gather himself up, Jonas was on him. Still spitting blood and teeth, but for the moment feeling no pain, he pinned Gant's arms with his legs and looked down into the man's eyes. He saw only fear, and rightfully so.

Jonas brought his fist down hard in the middle of Gant's face, breaking the man's nose and probably his upper jaw. Gant screamed, and struggled to get out from under the younger man. But Jonas was in a rage, and Gant stood no chance.

Jonas hit him one more time, this time screaming back, "This is for my sister, you fuck! You piece of shit!"

He hit him again, and again, crying out his sister's name each time, until Gant was unrecognizable. Surprisingly he was still breathing. Jonas raised himself from the unconscious man and shuffled over to the van, stopping only when his stomach lurched, and he puked a long stream. When he recovered he made his way to the van to see Jameson still sitting there. The man looked up at Jonas and said, "We about done here Jonas?"

"Yeah, it appears so. Are you okay?"

Yeah, I'm okay, just knocked my head a bit. Sure fucked him up though. Good thing you called when you did," he said, looking at Farrell's body stuck between the cement pillar and the van's grill.

"Jesus, man, you did a job alright.

Jameson started to pull himself out of the van, "You know, I always wondered why I didn't get anywhere with the file, and after I left, nothing happened. This fucker got what he deserved. Too bad they'll make him a hero."

"What do you mean a hero? He was a bad cop, Brent."

"They aren't going to know that. Pretty soon the cops will be crawling all over this place. I'm wearing gloves, and the van is clean, so they won't get anything. I'll have to screw around a little with Gant to make it look a little different, but then I'm outa here. They'll think he and Gant killed each other, and he'll look like the good guy taking down a bad guy. But who gives a shit."

Jonas walked over to Gant and saw that, although he was still breathing, they were shallow breaths, and not spaced evenly. The man had only moments of life left in him. Together they moved him into the driver's side of the van. When he was propped up there, Jonas retrieved his own gun, which lay on the cement floor beside what was left of Farrell. Surprisingly Farrell's gun was still in his hand. Jameson manipulated the gun so it was facing Gant and fired off one shot which hit Gant in the eye, sending blood and brain matter into the back of the van.

"It looks like these two had a short gun battle, and both lost," said Jameson.

"Wish we could nail Farrell for his part in all of this."

"Do you know where they are taking the girl?" asked Jameson.

"Yeah, I'm pretty sure they'll be going to Westgate's. That must have been where they took my sister too. I've got to make sure this doesn't happen again," said Jonas, as he looked around the building before leaving. "I don't want you coming along on this, Brent. It's something I have to do."

Jameson looked at Jonas and nodded. "Yeah, I know. Just make sure you're careful. He's bound to have more than just Ponytail there looking after him. I'll clean up here and get myself home. You just look after yourself."

"Thanks Brent. I think I have a way to get past his goons and get directly to him. Thanks again man. We'll talk later."

*****

Su once again endured a ride while prone on the back seat of a vehicle, this time a much smaller one from the SUV. The bearded man sat in the passenger seat while the big man with the slick ponytail drove.

It was a longer drive than before and, despite her pain, she was able to think. She had no doubt what these men had planned for her. She had to find a way to be alone with the man called Westgate, and maybe then she would have a chance, albeit a slim one. She wondered what had happened back at the building after they had left. Surely the young man stood no chance against two armed men. She was pretty sure that the young man was the same one that she had seen from her balcony, the one that had smiled at her over the back fence. She hoped he somehow survived and she would see him again. For the time being her own survival must be the priority and she would have to wait for her chance.

The car slowed, turned sharply, went a short distance, then stopped. Su braced herself but the car started forward again. She raised her head and was able to see tall trees close to each side of the car. They slowed again and drove beside a huge house, even bigger than the one she had just shared with all the 'pleasure girls'. This one was all white and even higher than her balcony. That thought reminded her of Jing-Wei. She lay back down, fighting off the tears.

The car entered the building, and after shutting down, both men got out. Ponytail opened the back door and motioned for Su to get out. This time she thought it better not to fight. She had no chance against this big man anyhow. She needed to be alone with his boss.

Ponytail led her into the house where her eyes opened wide with what she saw. They were in an entryway in front of two grand staircases, leading upwards in identical half circles. The railing looked hand carved, like something Su would sometimes see on a smaller scale crafted in the markets in her homeland. They stood on a solid shiny floor of some type of polished rock, and the stairs themselves were covered in a plush carpet of white. Both stairways and the entrance were guarded over by a car-sized chandelier, made with hundreds of sparkling pieces. Su had learned enough to suspect these were not glass.

"Take her to the guest suite and make sure everything is locked up tight. Then make sure Ronny knows what happened tonight. I doubt we'll have any more surprises but be sharp. Cam too, I don't want to be disturbed," ordered Westgate.

Ponytail, led her roughly by the arm through a door at the side of the entranceway, and down a long hallway. She passed only one open doorway and got a brief view of a pool table, similar to the one at the pleasure house. She was swept past this room to another door which Frank opened, pushing her in. He told her to sit on the bed and not move, which she obeyed. He checked the one window which she could see did not open, as it had bars imbedded in the glass that continued into the wall frame on each side. He went quickly through the rest of the room, including a small bathroom, which was entered through a door near the corner of the bedroom. Satisfied that she had no way out, he stood in front of her.

"Mr. Westgate doesn't mind if you kick and fight. You can even scream if you like because no one will hear you. He likes his girls clean so I suggest you use the bathroom to wash the blood off your face. Maybe even put on some perfume. He likes that. There are dresses in the closet. Choose one and be ready for him. Believe me little girl, it will go easier on you if you listen to me. If you don't he will lose it with you quickly, and he will hurt you bad." His speech finished, he turned and left the room, locking the door behind him.

*****

Jonas drove as fast as he could without being pulled over. There was no way he would be able to explain the blood still on his face, and soaked into the top of his shirt and hoody. Even the hard falling rain did nothing to clean him up. He knew exactly where he was going, and made it there without incident. Parking in almost the same spot as before, he grabbed his gun, still sticky with Farrell's blood, an extra clip from the glove box, and the sound suppressor. He slowly and carefully attached the suppressor to his weapon while making his way along the shrubs, crouching low as he went. He arrived at the same spot the dog had met him before, and peered through the leaves. He saw no one but knew they were there. Not necessarily expecting company though, as Westgate was probably confident that Gant and Farrell had eliminated him, but on guard nonetheless. Jonas paused. He was about to kill again, this time men who had not been directly involved in Chrissy's murder. He felt a wave of nausea go through him and remembered Sanderson, and now Gant. He had taken their lives as they had taken Chrissy's. He fought off the sickness that threatened to take him over, and knew he had to finish this tonight if he could, for Chrissy's sake, and maybe for his own as well. There was also the other girl to think about now. Her fate would surely match Chrissy's if he quit now. He knew there was no going back, so he gathered himself together with a shake. These were bad men, doing very bad things to people, and they had to be stopped. They deserved their fate, and with that thought, he lowered himself to the small opening in the fence, previously used by the dog, and eased himself through.

Knees and elbows, knees and elbows, he kept a steady crawl and was surprised how quickly he was able to cover the distance to the house. Equally surprising was the fact that he did not encounter any patrolling guards, although he guessed the pouring rain kept them inside more than usual. He now found himself at a corner of the house, beside a well-tended flower bed. He shook off the water from his head and arms and stole a quick glance around the corner just in time to see a large man coming towards him from the opposite end of the house. Jonas recognized him immediately as one of the two thugs who were with Sanderson. He was now obviously demoted to yard duty for Westgate. Jonas pushed himself back amongst the flowers and hoped it was enough. He would find out in seconds.

The man knew that by sticking close to the house he would not set off the sensors, because he was hugging the wall and walking carefully. He was too busy watching the surrounding yard, so he didn't see Jonas hidden in the flower bed.

Pfffft! sounded Jonas's gun. The big man fell, and didn't move. Luckily he fell right where he stood, so the sensors were not alerted. Jonas rose, dragged the man's body as far as he could into the flowers, and set off along the same side of the house, following the dead man's path to keep the sensors quiet.

He passed several windows and ducked under each. Only one had lights on, and he was able to snatch a quick look to see a games room featuring a giant billiards table front and center. He made a mental note of the room's location and continued on, finally coming to what appeared to be the main back entrance. A wooden deck ran the entire length of the back side of the house, which made it difficult for him to get a look in one of the windows. He would have to chance it.

*****

Su sat on the edge of the bed for a few minutes trying to think. What could she do? She was tempted to remain blood stained, torn, and dirty. Maybe that would turn Westgate away, but no, she decided ponytail was right. It would be worse for her if Westgate was disappointed in her appearance. Maybe distraction would work. She had seen how some of the pleasure girls had dressed, deliberately showing off more skin than necessary in order to tempt the men. This is what she would do too. She went into the bathroom and completely disrobed, looking at herself in a full length mirror. Where most men would see much beauty, she only saw a young girl with dirt in her hair and cuts on her face and shoulders. She knew men found her attractive, however she did not care. She wanted no part of men, for all of her life they had treated her with cruelty and abuse, starting with her own father. She would reserve no part of her body or soul for a man. In the meantime she had to put those thoughts aside, and make herself a distraction for Westgate. She shuddered at the thought, and almost vomited, but managed to gain control. She ran the water as hot as she could stand, and climbed into the tub, scrubbing herself from head to toe with a course cloth that hung there for her. She found some sweet smelling shampoo and thoroughly washed her long straight black hair, making it glisten. When her bath was finished she walked naked to the closet, and inspected the clothes hanging there. After pulling out two or three dresses of different colors, she came across a pure white one that looked to be about her size. She slipped it over her head and stood back to look in the closet door's mirror. The material was shear and she could easily make out her ample breasts through it, with the nipples very evident. She blushed with shame and was about to take the dress off, when she stopped. There was only one way to survive this night and she knew that involved getting to Westgate. She had to make him believe he had won, and she would be an easy conquest. Then maybe she would have a chance. She looked at herself again and smoothed out her hair, which hung over her shoulders, somewhat covering her upper body. Luckily the dress was thicker on the bottom half so there was no need to cover up there. She sat on the bed and waited for the knock that was surely coming.

*****

Jonas climbed through the railing and up to the deck, carefully moving around the furniture there. Duck-walking below two windows where it was dark inside, he made it to a larger one that was backlit. Constantly looking around to make sure he was unobserved, he raised himself, and stole a glance through the window, seeing no one. It was a large kitchen so he guessed the other window was to a formal dining area. It came as no surprise to him that there were no staff on at this time, as Westgate had probably sent them all home so that his evening's entertainment would not be interrupted. 'Oh, but it will be interrupted, Mr. Westgate, big time!' he thought.

There was a huge sliding door from the kitchen to the deck and a smaller man-door beside it. He tried the knob on the smaller door, and it turned. Taking a deep breath, he stepped inside, almost stepping in a pet's water dish. Jonas froze. This was no time for the family dog to investigate. Luckily the dog did not come bounding around the corner, and he was left alone. He crossed the kitchen and came to a hallway. He could hear voices from a room near the end of the hall.

*****

The knock on her door finally came, the door knob turned, and Ponytail entered her room. He looked at her and smiled. "My, my, little girl, you clean up so very well. Mr. Westgate will be very pleased with you," he said, his eyes not leaving her partially exposed breasts.

'Good', she thought, 'if he was distracted like this, so might Westgate.' The big man stood to the side, and motioned for Su to accompany him into the hall. Su walked with him down the hall, her bare feet feeling the plush carpet below, until the man stopped her by putting his hand on her shoulder. She froze at his touch. He let his hand linger there and then lowered it towards her breasts. She stood back from him. "Do not touch me, you pig!" she spat at him. He laughed, and with both hands flung her hair from her chest back over her shoulders. She now felt fully exposed, and fought the fear and shame that was rising in her throat. She wanted to run but knew she couldn't. She was trapped.

"Mr. Westgate will want to see you at your very best when you enter," said Frank, putting his hand on her shoulder, and directing her into the room with the giant pool table in the center. Before she took her first step he leaned in close to her and whispered, "When the old man is finished and satisfied, you and I will spend some time together. You will be crying out for joy."

"I would rather die than be with you!" she said, again spitting out the words.

"That could happen too, little girl" he smiled, roughly pushing her into the room.

*****

Jonas had watched this entire exchange but could do nothing without catching the girl in the middle, so he bided his time. He waited until she had entered the room. Ponytail closed the door behind her, and strolled down the hallway in the opposite direction. He thought quickly. He could break into the room, take out Westgate, and grab the girl, but that would leave Ponytail, and anyone else on guard tonight to be dealt with, all the while trying to protect the girl. He didn't like those odds. No, that wouldn't work. He had to deal with Ponytail first, then Westgate. He figured that Westgate would be suitably busy for the next while, so it would be safe to go after his bodyguard.

*****

Su reluctantly stepped into the room. Westgate was in the middle of a pool shot, but stopped instantly when he saw her. "Oh, sweet Jesus, look at you!" he said, walking over to her, still carrying the pool cue.

Su remained standing still, but could feel his eyes searching every part of her. She fought the strong urge to run, but knew that would be suicide. He stood in front of her and raised his hand to her breast, stroking her softly. She stood back, failing to disguise her look of disgust. "Girl, you will do as you are told and it will go a lot easier for you, believe me. I can be a gentle soul if you just relax and enjoy yourself," he said.

Su walked defiantly passed him to the massive table and turned around. "And why would I believe anything you have to say?" she asked.

"Because this is my house, and in it you will do as I say. It was my money that brought you to this country. You owe me, and must repay. And repay you will."

Su felt her temper rise to the surface. "I know about this supposed debt I have to you, for the wonderful trip and hospitality that you have provided to me, and the other women, the same women that you now keep in slavery. I know the debt will never be allowed to be repaid. So I choose not to follow your *orders*, because, whether or not you believe it Mr. Westgate, you do not own me."

He moved with surprising speed, hitting her on the side of her leg with the pool cue. The pain was like a hot poker touching her skin, and she went down hard, and cried out.

"It is not up to you whether or not you like my orders, little girl! You will simply do as I say or you will be in a lot of pain," he yelled at her, leaning forward close enough that she could smell his bad breath and body odor.

*****

Jonas found Ponytail as he was about to go outside. "Hey!" Jonas called out. "Did you miss me?" The man turned where he stood, and his eyes opened wide with surprise. With one motion he reached for his gun, and tried to jump through the door. He achieved neither as Jonas shot him in the neck.

*****

Su managed to get to her feet, although her wounded leg would hardly support her. She used the table to pull herself up and leaned heavily upon it. Westgate stood right in front of her. "Lower you dress," he growled, his eyes again roving over her body.

Su did not move. Let him do whatever he wanted, but she would never help him.

He slapped her hard enough to cut her cheek, and she almost fell. "I said, lower your dress!" he yelled again, spittle flying from his foul mouth.

Su remained standing defiantly before him, a look of hatred on her face. He reached over and yanked down her dress, which fell to her waist. He stood back, staring at her nakedness, licking his lips. She didn't expect to be hit again, so he caught her off guard when he quickly swung the pool cue, catching her on the side of the head, splitting her ear, spinning her, and sending her sprawling face down against the table. He placed one hand on her back, effectively pinning her to the table. With his other hand he tore at her dress, ripping it down her body like it was a wet paper towel.

Su screamed, and he laughed, pushing his free hand over her exposed back and down over the cheeks of her buttocks, making his way between her legs. Su screamed again, and struggled, but the combination of the blows she had taken, and the strength of the man, proved too much for her. She could not break his hold. She felt his disgusting breath on her neck, and his hands behind her, between her legs, touching her roughly, where she had never been touched before. She could feel his hardness, and it was if he was having trouble breathing, when suddenly the door crashed open, and, to her and Westgate's surprise, it wasn't Ponytail standing there.

*****

Jonas ran down the hall, but now wasn't sure which door opened to the pool room where Westgate had the girl. Then he heard another scream and knew where he had to go. He crashed through the door, splitting the frame around it, knocking it off one of its hinges. "Get away from her!" he yelled at Westgate, who had the girl pinned face down against the pool table.

"Well now, look who is still around to cause me trouble," he said, moving away from the girl. "I take it Mr. Gant and our favorite policeman will not be joining us."

"No, they won't, but you will be joining them soon enough."

Westgate smiled, "I don't think so. Mr. Carter is it? I don't think so."

Jonas should have suspected something by the man's cockiness but when he did, it was too late. A sudden pain hit him in the side, throwing him to the floor. As he fell he looked back and saw Ponytail, covered in blood, kneeling in the doorway, barely able to stand, his gun falling to the floor. Jonas landed hard but was able to get his gun up and fire off two shots, one hitting the wall high, the other catching Ponytail in the chest. The big man crumbled to the floor.

At the same time Westgate had reached a small table, and grabbed a small caliber handgun from a drawer. He brought it up to aim at Jonas, who lay a few feet from him.

Su had jumped up from the table and swung her hand at Westgate. Jonas watched as the gun fell from the man's hand. His eyes rolled as she hit him again, and again. The man was out on his feet, but still she kept swinging at him. His legs finally got the message his brain was delivering, and he collapsed. Su's scream was primeval, as she jumped on to the man's back, pummeling him.

Jonas saw a white cue ball in her hand and now knew why the man went down so hard. He looked down at the bullet wound in his side, which was bleeding freely, and he felt he was about to pass out. Before he did he saw the young woman cry out and fall to the side, crying uncontrollably.

He came too moments later, and tried to get up. His side was on fire, but at least he didn't think he was bleeding any harder. A pair of hands touched his arm, and he felt the woman trying to help him stand. She had dressed again and was leaning over him.

"We must leave quickly," she said.

"Yes," he replied weakly. "Do you have somewhere to go?"

She lowered her head. "I must search for my sister. She and I were separated by these men in Hawaii, and I am sure she is being held by a man named Lamar."

At the sound of that name Jonas perked up.

"I too am searching for this man. Do you know him?" he asked.

"I do not know him, but I know what he looks like, and saw him take my sister," she answered.

He grimaced at the pain in his side, but with her help he was able to regain his feet. The two of them stumbled over to Westgate's fallen form. The man's eyes were open but fogged over. The side of his head was caved in. Jonas spent only a few seconds looking down at him.

"This man was a killer, like the others, and like this Lamar. Help me out of here, and we can hunt him down together," he said, as the woman shifted herself closer to him so he was able to put his arm over her shoulders. They stumbled together down the hall, toward the front door.

"My name is Jonas," he said.

"I am called Su," she said, a small smile on her face as she looked up at him. He leaned heavily against her.

As they approached the front door they were met by the dog Jonas knew as 'Tanzer,' her small stump of a tail vibrating from side to side. "Let's take her with us," he said.

Su leaned over and scooped up the dog, and they walked out the door, to the sounds of sirens in the distance.

The End

Coming soon:

PARADISE DARK

Jonas and Su travel to the tropical paradise of Hawaii in search of Su's sister, Ling, and to hunt down their common enemy. What they do not know, is that this ruthless man is not their only enemy, nor is he the most dangerous.

Printed in the United States
By Bookmasters